M

I looked at Mrs Fitzallan over the rim of my glass. At the lush red lips and the shadowed valley of her cleavage framed by the vee of her blouse. I considered her too-short skirt and the creamy, butter-soft gleam of her half-exposed thighs. I was stiff already.

Just the same, what about my promise to Diana?

'Well?' she whispered.

I hesitated.

'I'll double your fee,' she said.

I reached for her. We needed the money . . .

Male Order

Aaron Amory

Delta

First published in 1998 by
HEADLINE BOOK PUBLISHING

A HEADLINE DELTA paperback

10 9 8 7 6 5 4 3 2 1

ISBN 0 7472 5838 4

Typeset by Avon Dataset Ltd, Bidford-on-Avon, Warks

Printed and bound in Great Britain by
Mackays of Chatham plc, Chatham, Kent

HEADLINE BOOK PUBLISHING
A division of Hodder Headline PLC
338 Euston Road
London NW1 3BH

Male Order

Prologue

The End of a Desk Job

Sally was crouched down in the kneehole of my office desk when Irwin came in with the bad news.

Irwin was my immediate boss – and hers too for that matter – but although he was only a couple of yards from my swivel chair, he couldn't see that his secretary was squatting between my heels with her red-nailed fingers buried deep within my open fly. This was because, mercifully, the far side of the kneehole was blanked off with a panel of the same African mahogany as the rest of the desk. Anyone snugged into that space between the two banks of desk drawers was invisible to all comers . . . unless all comers were standing immediately behind one or the other of my shoulders. Since it bugs me to have people breathing down my neck, this is not a habit I encourage. Especially when the tag of my zip is at its lowest extremity. Especially when the operator tagging along is the blonde and succulent Sally Beaton.

'I'm sorry, Tom, but it's final,' Irwin said, lobbing an envelope with my name typed on it among the papers strewing the desk top. 'I just left the meeting. The bloody directors were unanimous: as of today, you're O-U-T, out. They want your desk cleared by this evening.'

'Cleared?' I echoed, nudging Sally's plump thigh with my right heel. 'What about notice? I have a contract, damn it. And severance pay – the old golden handshake?'

He shook his head. 'No way, old lad. You're in breach of. So nobody's shaking.'

'Christ!' I said. 'You don't mean they really—?'

'That moonlighting job you took on for the other agency,' Irwin explained. 'Somebody sang. We've lost the James account. They called this morning to say they didn't

3

appreciate their account executive writing clever-clever copy for a rival product. Since the after-lunch brandies, you've been bad news on the top floor.'

'They can't prove it,' I said angrily. 'I worked from home; I used no facilities here.'

'They don't have to prove it,' he reminded me. 'They sign the cheques. Rogers fires as fast as he hires. You must have known that when you stepped out of line and wrote yourself out of a living wage.'

'If the wage they paid here was generous enough, I wouldn't have had to take another fucking job!' I retorted. 'I like to live reasonably well, for Christ's sake.'

'Don't we all?' Irwin wasn't as sympathetic as I would have wished. Maybe he'd like to have engineered a second job for himself. 'Anyway, from tomorrow morning I'm afraid it'll be your own hand that's doing the signing five times a week.'

'What did you say?'

He stared at me. I had jumped, starting upright in my chair as he spoke. Sally's hands, which had been cruising between shirt-tails and briefs in search of my non-office equipment, had finally zeroed in on the hardened proof of her expertise. She had stealthily extracted my cock from its nest during our conversation, subsequently fingering out the balls above the zipper tag. It was the imprint of the red nails, followed by a graze of teeth against the hot, distended skin, which had provoked my sudden, unexpected jerk.

'Something stung you?' Irwin enquired. 'I said you'd be signing on at the Job Centre tomorrow. And the day after. You'll find all the necessary paperwork in that envelope.'

He paused. The tip of my cock was engulfed in a scalding cavern of flesh. I felt the muscled swirl of a tongue quivering around the super-sensitive skin below the rigid head. The nerves behind my knees were trembling.

I caught my breath. Sally was a sexy little bitch. Nothing turned her on so much as the knowledge that there was a third party, present but unaware, while she was sucking or being sucked, fucking or just wanking in her secret way. Her speciality was to jerk me off while I was on the phone

4

– particularly if I was speaking to my wife.

'I put in a word,' Irwin said, glancing at the envelope. 'Amongst all the pay-slip crap and the PAYE details and the official dismissal notice, you'll find there's an ex-gratia payment – a cheque for a month's salary. Which I think is pretty generous. In the circumstances.'

'Big deal,' I said, picking up the envelope. 'But thanks just the same, Irwin.'

'Don't mention it,' he said.

Hot lips closed firmly over the throbbing shaft of my tool as Irwin nodded and turned to leave the office. Sally's skilled mouth was already sliding wetly up and down the stiffened shaft of my cock by the time the door swung shut behind him. I drew a deep breath.

The phone rang.

I brought one hand back from under the desk and picked up the receiver.

The head of the art department was telling me – a shade gleefully, I thought – that the advertising director of the James company had already turned down my campaign for their product before the account was withdrawn and I was fired. 'Too bloody risqué, old boy,' he said. 'I told you you'd overstep the mark one day and go a shade too far.'

'Thanks for the inside story,' I said bitterly, slamming down the phone.

Somehow, this was the final blow – Sally was fondling my balls, the mouth tantalizingly, agonizingly, excruciatingly milking my inflamed staff – for the account had been my special baby, a campaign I'd been particularly pleased with. Proud of, if you like.

The James firm made twin-cylinder motorcycle engines. In the ads they were popularized by sexy, leather-clad twin sisters who were in fact a successful rock duo in the record business. Bearing in mind the name of the company, the scintillating copy minted by yours truly married the twin-spark engine, technical details of the bike's gearing, and the tag line of author Henry James's most famous short story in the punning campaign slogan: *The fact that there are two sisters makes it an extra screw of the turn!*

5

So much for literary account executives! In any case, the joke wasn't original: I'd pinched it from a line in – of all things – an erotic novel entitled *Hard At It!*

I squirmed in the swivel chair, swaying my hips a little from side to side, belaying the shaft of my aching cock from one corner to the other of Sally's practised mouth. The sucking clasp of her lips seemed to be drawing every nerve in my body flaming down to my crotch.

Sod the people on the top fucking floor. Sod the fucking art director, their miserable cheque and humiliating chuck-you-out letter. Sod the bleeding board of James and Company P-L-fucking-C! I grinned. It was on this floor, beneath this desk, that the only genuine fucking in this whole tacky advertising agency took place . . .

With anyone as expert as Sally, however, genuine though it might be, it never took long!

One of her hands had relinquished my scrotum now and was busily skimming the sensitive skin of as much of my penis as remained outside of her gorging mouth. Hoarse nasal breathing echoed within the confined space of the kneehole. My own breath was accelerating, deepening. I heard the stealthy susurrus of nylon on nylon, the subtle creaks of a heaving body. My balls were hanging free, cool in the disturbed air of the office. Maybe she was using the freed hand for a subdued wank beneath her clinging tights?

The swivel chair was mounted on rollers below its five splayed feet. I began easing it back and forth behind the desk, thrusting and withdrawing my hips to force deeper in and out the hard shaft fucking her in the mouth.

And of course that did it. The lust searing through my belly exploded my cock into a spurting climax. The chair groaned as I half rose with a stifled shout from the seat. A choked gasp followed by hasty gulping sounds rose from between my knees. For an eternity, or so it seemed, my loins sprang as furiously as those of a twenty-year-old.

Busty Sally was already wearing a demure expression when she emerged fully dressed from under my desk. 'I heard it all, of course,' she said, smoothing down her black skirt. 'I'm sorry, Tom. I mean really sorry.' She grinned wickedly. 'Next time I guess I'll have to smuggle you into the building and stuff you down between my thighs beneath *my* desk!'

Once she was back in Irwin's office I went out and bought a cheap case to hold the belongings I'd been told to clear out. I crammed in ballpoints, papers, labels, boxes of clips and drawing pins, staplers, spare floppy disks, all the crap that clutters up office drawers. The Pirelli wall calendar of beaver-shot nudes was mine: I wasn't going to leave them that. The hanging charts of increased sales due to our advertising campaigns belonged properly to the firm. But the hell with that: I could use them as a self-selling point during the interview for my next job. I ripped them down and stuffed them in the case.

I looked at my watch. It was already after six and I wasn't through yet. Most of the staff would have left by now. I picked up the phone and called my wife.

'Darling,' I said, 'I'm afraid I've been kept a little late at the office. If the dinner's hot, I hope it won't spoil . . . but I'll be back as soon as I possibly can.'

'For God's sake, Tom' – Diana's voice was vitriolic – 'don't expect me to swallow that late-at-the-office shit yet again! What kind of a fool do you think I am? Who the hell is it this time?'

'Diana! Darling, I'm telling you—'

'Don't,' she raged. 'Let me tell you for once. This is the last time – I mean really the last fucking time – I'm going to swallow that corny old late-work chestnut! You hear me, Tom?'

She slammed down the receiver.

I heard her. I sighed, gently lowering mine to the cradle. She didn't know how right she was.

PART ONE

Ladies' Choice?

Chapter One

So there I was on the job market – Tom Silver, forty-one, five feet eleven and a half inches, dark, clean-shaven, said (when his wife was in a good mood) to have a slight resemblance to the actor Tom Cruise. Active for ten years as an account executive in the advertising business, with successful campaigns for brewers, bread-makers, Bongo-Bongo Coffee, Saucy Steaklets, Sneaker Shoes and Swimfit Slimwear (The Wet-Look That Leaves You Dry-Eyed) to his credit. Previously a news-agency reporter and printer's devil. A snip for any personnel manager looking for a keen ideas man with experience, integrity and all fingers on the consumers' pulse.

Not so.

I won't bore you with details, but three weeks after I let the Rogers agency go, personnel managers weren't exactly beating a path to my door. I mean the flowerbeds in our front garden had escaped being trampled by the feet of the jostling queues impatient to sign up yours truly.

Not to put too fine a point on it, the dozens of situations vacant display ads I culled from the business, finance and media sections of the quality press during those twenty-one days produced precisely nine replies, only four of which went so far as to suggest an interview. One of these was cancelled at the last minute because the job was already filled. Two promised to 'let me know' (and of course never did). But the last was the cruellest cut of all. '*Forty-one!*' the smirking oaf interrogating me crowed as he re-read my CV. 'But, my dear fellow!' He appeared aghast. 'We *never*, ever employ anyone as old as that. I mean to say, thirty-two is the absolute, ultimate age limit at which we're prepared to risk signing on a first-time staffer.'

'I'm not exactly first-time,' I said. 'I have a lot of experience. You have the success graphs of some of the accounts I handled in that folder.'

'You can't be serious, old-timer,' he said. He slipped the CV back inside and snapped the folder shut. 'Here, perhaps you could use this somewhere.' He shoved it towards me across the desk.

I wondered was there a blonde secretary hidden in *his* kneehole? If there was, I hope she bit him.

I tried new friends, twisted the arms of old friends, solicited such newspapermen as I still knew in Canary Wharf and even Fleet Street. No dice.

'Sorry, old boy. You know how it is: we have to have someone going with the wind these days.'

'If you ain't part of the yoof circuit, pal, you got nothing for us.'

'Good luck, Tom. Now, if you'll excuse me . . .'

'Perhaps if you were to try the provinces?'

Christ!

The Job Centre was equally hopeless. The only job I was actually offered was night watchman at a rubber glove factory in Slough. Five grand, bring sandwiches and provide your own transport, can you believe it!

I was down to the small-ads, ticking off possibles with a pencil and helping to run up a huge phone bill, when Diana made the suggestion that eventually offered a way out of the maze.

She'd been sweet and wifely and very supportive ever since she realized the late-at-the-office number was no joke this time. Now she dumped a sack of groceries onto the hall table, looked through the door of my study, and said: 'Tom, darling – why don't you quit beating your brains out amongst all that second-rate shit and turn the chore around, approach it from another angle?'

I was unshaven, my eyes were bloodshot, I had a headache. An unlit cigarette drooped from the corner of my mouth. I sat hunched over a mug of cold coffee at a table strewn with several acres of smudged newsprint. 'Turn it around?' I croaked. 'What the hell—?'

'Instead of spending all day reading the bloody things, why not write one?'

I stared at her.

'Instead of answering dozens,' she explained, 'insert one yourself and wait for *others* to answer *that.*'

'But, Diana . . . sweetie . . . no personnel manager in need of staff is going to waste his time combing through the fucking small-ads! The company's going to invest in a display panel, and *he's* going to wait for folks to contact him. It'd be a total waste of time to go that far down-market, I promise you. If I was to—'

'I don't mean advertise yourself as an account executive. I mean advertise yourself. Period.'

'If I'm not selling my profession, what I'm qualified to do, what I do well . . . what the hell *am* I selling then?' I grunted.

'I told you. You sell yourself – not as a smart-aleck copy-writer, a jazzy know-all. As a man.'

I frowned. Maybe she had something there. But . . . 'A man in what capacity' I asked.

'Just that,' Diana said. 'You're reasonably presentable, you have good manners, you dress well. I hate to admit it, but you are intelligent. That's quite enough already.'

'Diana,' I said, 'if I don't list my qualifications, my credentials, what the fuck do I put in the bloody ad? Even if what you say is true, it qualifies me in no way for any job that—'

'We're not talking about jobs,' she interrupted. 'Your qualifications are yourself.' And then, as I was about to interrupt in my turn: 'Your ad doesn't go in with the sit-vac and job-want dross: you put it in the personal column.'

I nodded slowly. 'Yeah? But again . . . as what? Selling what?'

'You're acting dumb,' my wife said. 'Among people with money, men tend to die younger than their wives. Because they've worked themselves to death amassing loot which is spent on Madame and/or the kids. Result: a lot of widows of a certain age with money to spare. Ladies who appreciate a presentable escort who can accompany them to restaurants,

13

theatres, exhibitions, concerts, the beach, whatever. Your ad must persuade them you're the guy they're looking for.'

I thought about it. 'Maybe. Bloody difficult to know what to put, though.'

'As little as possible. The weight of the message should be implicit rather than explicit, allusive rather than specific.'

'Ambiguous, you mean?'

'Not in the suggestive, smutty sense, absolutely not. Intriguing, certainly. Enough to make them curious, eager to know more – but above all discreet, serious, a quality approach.'

I grinned. 'A high-class carrot for up-market donkeys?'

'Something like that. With the key-word "class". That's why I turn thumbs down on ambiguous. The ad must never, ever suggest a gigolo, a stud for hire, a toy-boy looking for trade.'

I summoned up an artificial sigh. 'No sex for randy Tom, then?'

'Physically,' Diana said spitefully, 'the kind of woman we're looking for wouldn't interest even you!'

'Okay,' I soothed. 'Okay. But, darling, wouldn't it be much easier to get oneself signed up by one of these escort agencies? They're pretty thick on the ground, I believe. I mean let them do the casting; we only come into the picture when they have someone actually hooked.'

'No way.' Diana was firm. 'For one thing, it costs an arm and a leg just to get yourself on the books. Even then, there's no guarantee they'll actually find you work – and if they do, a huge percentage vanishes into their pocket before you get your cut. Secondly, they're the ones who decide the terms in which you're billed and sold. It's the agency itself which creates the image we hope will decide the client to bite.'

'Yes, I see that. Nevertheless, wouldn't it be an idea at least to check out—?'

'Lastly,' Diana pursued, 'I'm not at all sure you'd have the right to refuse a client you didn't think was right. Or if you did, they'd soon drop you, like cross you off the list. No – let me finish, Tom, please – what we need, what we must have, is total control. You're a professional copywriter: you're the one best qualified to sell the product the way we want it sold. It's got to be high-bracket selling too: if it's not ridiculously damned expensive, they're going to think it's not worth having anyway.'

I nodded. 'Undersell, and you rip off the quality label before they've even seen the product.'

'If they want the benefit of your company,' Diana said, 'it's going to cost them a bomb. And every single pound they pay is going to end up in one single bank account – ours!'

I was silent for a moment. I was beginning, almost in spite of myself, to ride along with the idea. Christ, it could be interesting in more ways than one! 'Something on your mind?' she asked.

'An idea.' I pushed back my chair, stretched my legs out in front of me, and linked my hands behind my head. 'We have two phones here. On two different lines, with two completely different numbers, right?'

She raised pencilled eyebrows. 'And so?'

'So mightn't it be an idea to turn around that old saying about killing two birds with one stone?'

She stared at me without speaking.

'Killing one bird with two stones,' I explained.

'I'm sorry. I still don't get it.'

I sighed. 'We write two different ads – each heavily into the quality bracket, but in totally different styles, each suggesting different . . . pleasures. We place them in different columns, maybe in different papers, with one of our lines as the reply number in one ad, and the second for the other. That halves the odds, you see: if she's not hooked by one, she could be by the other!'

'Brilliant,' Diana said. 'That's the first intelligent, positive thing you've said today.'

We started work on the two ads the same evening. The situation was not without a certain urgency. The buff envelopes with cellophane windows were piling up on my desk; the bank manager's hospitable desire to receive me in

15

his office was becoming more acute; if the cash flow didn't improve soon, we risked having no telephone numbers at all to quote in the ads.

'Two separate styles?' Diana said. 'But different in what way?'

'Mentally,' I said. 'In the type of personality we appeal to.'

'For instance?'

'Given that we're after ladies with money – and under-lining perhaps the word ladies – we quarry out two approaches likely to appeal to opposites in that category, bearing in mind each time, though, that it's a gent speaking.'

'What kind of gents?'

'Safe, reliable, intelligent, interesting – but above all trustworthy. And of course intriguing. Within those para-meters, it shouldn't be too difficult to frame two conflicting types, tailored for women with different interests but each of the same consumer class.'

'You talk as if this was an advertising campaign,' Diana said.

'It *is* a bloody advertising campaign,' I insisted. 'We find out what the customer wants and give it to her. Only this time it's a soft sell: the intrigue factor must whet the appetite, stimulate curiosity, make them crazy to know more. We do no more than scatter the seed; the flower is left to blossom in their imagination.'

'Poetic,' she said. 'And what two products, what types of gentlemanly advertiser do you see doing that?'

'The studious type for one. Obviously. A touch of the academic, spiced with a hint of the man-of-the-world. Nothing stodgy of course – but someone who can open a window on the important things in life and still be entertaining.'

'Okay, sold to the lady with the Peke on her lap and the chauffeur-driven Merc. And Number Two?'

'Equally intelligent, I would think, but veering more towards the sporty side. You know: the kind who enjoys listening to Mozart but can also play tennis. Women attrac-ted by that type tend to be a little more liberated socially.'

16

'But not, I hope, liberated to the point where—?'

'Certainly not,' I said firmly. 'We agreed that kind of ambiguity is a non-starter. The tone of the whole transaction must remain conventional, discreet and above board. The escort must appear to be – must actually be – someone you wouldn't mind introducing to your friends.'

'Darling, you're forgetting that *you* are the product; the escort is going to be *you*!' Diana said. 'If I was a rich lady, I wouldn't let you come within a mile of my friends.'

'You won't do that even now,' I said. 'At least not those with hips and D-cups!'

Before the newsreaders were shouting at us out of the box, we'd come up with two completed small-ads, each within the thirty-word limit we'd set ourselves – brevity, we had agreed, being the soul not only of wit. The first one read:

> GENTLEMAN, *thirties, tall, dark, univ. graduate, eager to accompany vivacious, intelligent ladies on visits to theatres, concerts, restaurants, exhibitions. Extensive wardrobe. Own transport. Complete discretion guaranteed (and the first telephone number).*

'Not bad,' Diana admitted. 'You think you could pass for a man in his thirties?'

'Try me,' I said. 'Forties sounds staid, almost square.'

'Why have you cut the word "university" like that?'

'Psychology. The whole word sounds a shade serious; shortened, it becomes almost a throwaway line. But it makes the academic point just the same.'

'Two other questions. There's a good, terse description of a desirable man. Why describe the sucker you hope to hook?'

I shrugged. 'Every woman likes to think herself vivacious and intelligent. It seems to me a plus point for the advertiser if he already agrees with her before they even meet. Must be the right kind of guy. Next question please?'

'You're a fucking cynic,' Diana said. 'Why the hell mention the wardrobe?'

17

'Because,' I explained, 'it implies different kinds of gear, in particular evening dress. Therefore a person of some sophistication. Therefore interesting. Therefore marketable.'

'You talk like one of those media bores in the advertising business,' my wife observed.

We had to spend a little more time over the second ad. The problem wasn't so much to find the right words to describe the second type of guy; it was more to maintain the polarity of two supposedly different individuals but ensure at the same time that each could believably be fitted to the real me. This was the final result:

EXUBERANT MALE, 37, sporting type also passionate
amateur literature, movies, music, available as occasional
escort for cultural, leisure excursions, social encounters and
outdoor activities. Any time, any day – but please book ahead.

'Yes, I like that,' Diana said. 'It suggests a strong character, much in demand – and the juxtaposition of amateur and passionate is clever: it implies a character in no way limited by a dull, nine-to-five job or too many home ties. I'd say that's one for the ladies who drive their own XJ-6 Jaguars!'

The only change she suggested was to take the word male out of capitals and make it lower-case. 'Exuberant is fine,' she said, 'but to me, emphasising male is going too far – a touch of the macho rearing its hairy head.'

She was right too. I rewrote the ad the way she wanted it.

And I deleted 'and outdoor activities' before she noticed there were in fact thirty-two words.

'Well, I think I might be interested in either of those types,' she said, reading through the finished copy again. 'Especially, I suppose, the second. I confess, reading it as the driver of a Jag, that I might well wonder to myself how well the writer would strip!'

I took her by the arm. 'Baby,' I growled, 'the bailiffs haven't repossessed the bed yet. Come upstairs and you can find find out for yourself right now, for free!'

Chapter Two

Diana was tallish and slender, with agreeably hand-filling breasts, a quite meaty backside but – surprisingly – very little in the way of hips. 'Darling, I'm afraid you'll have to put up with it,' she drawled just before we went to bed together for the first time. 'The pelvis is narrow: I've got nothing there really but a *hinge*!'

Otherwise it was a pretty sexy body, especially the legs, which were smashing. Between them was a generous bush of dark hair, silky in texture rather than the familiar wiry thatch.

We'd been married ten years – fairly successfully on the whole, though she could be spiky if provoked, particularly when it came to 'other women' or the suspicion of them.

I'd learned (if you'll allow the phrase) to ride that one out by limiting strictly the duration – if not the frequency – of my extra-marital activities. They were confined now to quickies, in the office or with like-minded enthusiasts with similar constraints. And although Diana suspected, or knew bloody well, about this kind of thing, although she screamed blue murder if I was 'kept late', she was prepared to overlook this or a least turn the blind eye. Even if it was overcooked, you see, I never actually missed dinner. And this proved – since clearly I couldn't be inviting them to dine or visiting a nightclub – that at least I wasn't actually 'having an *affaire* with some tart'.

I was surprised, though, that she had agreed – even suggested and approved – this escort caper. Even with the limitations we had imposed on it. Because, frankly, if you knew as much as I did about the sexual proclivities of unattached women of a certain age . . . well, suppose we let that one drift away with the tide, eh?

On this night, anyway, I was going to let her see just what all those feisty widows I would be so manfully repulsing would miss.

On this one occasion, however, for one reason or another, a certain hesitancy stopped us in our tracks once we actually reached the bedroom. It was probably because it was a deliberate move, arising directly from a cold-blooded discussion of physical characteristics, rather than a decision arising spontaneously from our own intimacy. Whatever, I found myself standing just inside the door, staring oafishly at my wife like a village idiot. Believe it or not, for that one moment I simply didn't know what to do!

Diana stood by the bed, looking my way with a slightly challenging glint in her brown eyes. For an instant I thought maybe she had been seized by a similar near-inhibition – a sense almost of adolescent embarrassment – as myself. Then of course I realized: it was I who had made the move. I was playing the piper . . . so it was up to me to call the tune!

And the tune had better be 'Parlez-moi d'Amour' – speak to me of love – if I wished to keep the wifely mind off all those voracious ladies with Jaguars. Otherwise she might find time to remember that in fact it was the person who *paid* the piper who called the tune . . .

The spell was broken and I strode towards her.

For the first time that evening – just as I was about to engineer its removal – I was aware of what Diana was wearing. I guess, before we'd worked out the small-ads, I'd been in too much of a loser condition to notice.

She stood with her legs planted apart and her arms folded, her whole attitude one of what I thought of as defiance. Okay, buster, you dealt the hand. Now let's see you play it.

The black leather skirt she had shoehorned herself into was very tight, the subdued illumination from the bedside lamps highlighting a soft curve of belly above the handprint of a mons. Dark crimson cashmere clung to her slim body above the black patent belt cinching her waist, and the long-sleeved, folded arms pushed beguiling slopes of breast up into the scooped-out neck of her sweater. Bordering these, black lace traced a seductive pattern on the cool, pale flesh.

Between the knee-length hem of the skirt and shiny, high-heeled red court shoes, black silk shadowed her elegant calves (stockings, suspender-stretched, I knew, and not boring tights).

I strode towards her. And then, perhaps because I still felt slightly ridiculous, a little *obvious* – what was I going to do? Rip off the sweater? Throw her on the bed – I said lamely: 'I think we need a drink.'

'The last bottle of champagne is already floating in melted ice in the bathroom washbasin,' Diana said.

I did throw her on the bed then. Laughing with relief, I fell across her, cradling the lace-edged breasts in my hands. 'You talk – and look – like a sexy mistress!' I said.

'Well, somebody has to,' Diana said.

I kissed her. We remained locked together, our tongues amicably wrestling, until her breath began to quicken. When it deepened too and the pelvis started to hinge up off the bed, I went to fetch the champagne.

When I returned with the brimming glasses, the crimson sweater had vanished (it's not possible to look alluring, dragging a tight woolly over one's head), the leather skirt revealed itself to be a wraparound, and the black silk ankles were neatly crossed.

Diana still wore the red shoes. She lay propped up on a pile of pillows with eyes half closed, red-nailed fingers shoring up the swelling breasts now revealed to be cupped entirely by lace. There were no panties visible above or below the black arch of her elastic suspender belt: the pubic hair was dark against white thighs, sombre as the tightly drawn-up silk sheathing her legs. I think she had applied fresh lipstick during my short absence. Certainly her lower lip – the mouth curved into a lazy smile – now glistened moistly.

I placed one of the glasses on the night table, sat down beside her, and offered the other up to those tempting lips.

She sipped, resting one friendly hand on my nearest

thigh. 'It's perfectly true,' she said, swallowing a more generous draught, 'medicinally or otherwise, it really does make you feel better. Don't you think?'

'I don't think; I know,' I said, reaching behind me for the second glass. 'But you looked pretty good tonight – even before I poured!'

The hand on my thigh twisted from the wrist, fingers brushing carelessly against that part of my fly that was already showing unmistakable signs of interest within.

'Mmmmmm!' Diana said. 'Otherwise rather than medicinally, perhaps!'

I drank, swung around to put both glasses gently on the night table, then turned back, leaned across, and lowered both hands to the black lace bra supporting her breasts. My palms and fingers cupped the warm weight of flesh straining against the indentations of the lace. 'Champagne,' I said, 'will no longer improve after twelve years. But there are some things' – the pads of my thumbs teased the nippled outlines crowning the cups of the bra – 'some things that only get more delicious year after year.'

A bit laboured, perhaps, but it was the best I could do with the breath suddenly caught in my throat. The fingers at my crotch, tracing the hardening outline of my tool, had suddenly gripped it hard through the stuff of my pants. My hips swivelled involuntarily towards her as the sliding grasp sent fiery shafts of lust spearing up into my loins.

Without removing my hands from the taut swell of my wife's breasts, I lowered my head to the cool flesh bared between the bra and the top of her suspender belt. My lips touched. My tongue circled moist arabesques around the dimpled depression where a tiny pulse beat furiously beneath the satined skin.

Diana's free hand was at my fly. Forcibly, almost savagely, she yanked down the zip. Without relinquishing her grip on my trousered tool, she thrust fierce fingers in to wrench aside shirt-tails and drag down the elastic waist of my Y-fronts.

Pulled abruptly into the open air, my hot and throbbing cock felt as hard as the granite of Cleopatra's Needle. Then

22

it was the balls, kneaded and softly rolled within the wrinkled sac as caressing fingertips skimmed the sensitive outer skin of the cock up and down the rigid core.

I was breathing hard. Beyond the curved arch of the tight-stretched suspender belt, a crescent of coral flesh sliced moistly through pubic hair in a welcoming smile.

I moved my head lower still, tongue leapfrogging the black elastic to home in on the silky thatch. Diana's hips arched momentarily up off the bed as the wet tip burrowed between sensitive, naked folds, tunnelling towards the hooded clitoris while my lips closed over the secret flesh flowering open to let me in.

My belt was unbuckled, the trousers and briefs jerked down to my knees as the hot hand milking my inflamed shaft increased its magic rhythm.

Diana's breath escaped from her lungs in hoarse gasps. Her whole body was trembling. My lips nibbled the creased outer labia of her cunt up into my mouth. At the same time, it seemed as if my tongue was being literally sucked down into the burning interior of her love canal.

I was shaking. The distended shaft of my masturbated cock felt as though it was about to burst from its restraining skin. My hands, having thrust up the lacy bra to spill out the fleshy swell of breasts, had now snaked down to Diana's belly, splaying wider still the lips of her cunt under the slavering attack of my tongue.

And then all at once her own hands were at my head, forcing me closer still but at the same time starting to thrust me way. 'Now, Tom!' she choked. 'For God's sake get naked; get out of those fucking clothes and give it to me! I want you inside me, hard up inside, right *now*!'

Panting, I heaved myself hastily away. One of my hands brushed against stubbled skin as I straightened up on the bed. 'My God,' I cried, 'and I haven't even shaved!'

'Never mind,' she said throatily. 'I don't mind a bit of rough trade now and then. But hurry, darling, do.'

I fled to the bathroom. Struggling out of men's clothes in a hurry is not the most romantic of activities – especially in the middle of a scene that's charged sexually already.

23

I'd already chucked the jacket. I eyed the electric razor (too obvious; no time). I ripped off shirt, socks, underwear, trousers, splashed water on the face, squirted deo, raced back into the bedroom. One minute fifty. Not bad, considering.

Diana was still propped up on the pillows. But now her eyes were closed. The bra had vanished, the nipples erect and rosy on the full breasts. She still wore the stockings and suspender belt, but the red shoes had gone, the leather wrap around had been definitively unwrapped. Her silk-sheathed legs were slightly apart, the pale thighs white against the suspender straps and the dark thatch of pubic hair.

Her right breast was supported by the splayed, red-nailed fingers of one hand. The other hand cupped her cunt, the forefinger lazily stirring the wet folds of flesh enveloping her clitoris.

Ten out of ten, I thought, for preserving the heightened atmosphere of an interrupted scene!

Naked and visibly, rigidly lustful, I approached the marital bed.

This time I knew what I was doing. Ten years is a long time – even when it comes to learning how to read a particular woman. And Diana was very particular. Once the threshold of interest was successfully passed, the rapids of yes-no-please-don't-now-hurry navigated, she became excessively demanding. You had to know – at once – which of several different patterns were on the order form. And if you guessed wrong there could be hell to pay – silences, withdrawal, sulks even. ('Nothing's the matter; there's nothing wrong with me' and 'God, why are men so *insensitive*?')

Tonight, though, I knew how to play it: I'd already been given the key. This was not one of those dreamy occasions when the foreplay passed imperceptibly, almost inevitably into what the shrinks term The Act. In this scenario, the foreplay was an autonomous, self-contained Act One. Act Two was conceived, as it were, In Another Part Of The City. And my bathroom dash was in effect the crush-bar interval

24

separating them. What was wanted now was the manly, master-of-the-house, authority syndrome. The positive 'do what you are told, I'm giving the orders' approach which psychologists say satisfies what they call the rape complex in women.

Put more simply, it amuses some women to be bossed. Sometimes.

Even if, in reality, it's the lady who makes the decisions.

There's a Jewish story which encapsulates this neatly enough.

Three Bishop's Avenue housewives are discussing their marriages, two of which are disasters – animated by quarrels, shout-ups, threatened walkouts, the lot. The third, however, is a haven of peace, calm and domestic bliss, and known to be so. The two angry ladies therefore ask their friend what is the secret of this placid existence.

'My dears, it's very simple,' she confides. 'My husband and I have a pact. It's as simple as that. When it comes to the decisions we all have to make, I confine myself to the minor ones, the unimportant ones, and he takes care of the serious stuff, the really important decisions. So there's nothing left for us to argue about.'

'But tell us, Hilde, tell us! Explain please,' they cry.

'Well,' she says, 'just for instance, I decide whether we should change David's Jag for a BMW. I decide whether I should have another sable coat, whether we should move to Stanmore or to Virginia Water, if it's worth keeping *both* villas in Marbella or not. I decide whether Simon should go to university or start work in his father's business, and things like that.'

'But, Hilde,' they expostulate, 'if those are the *un*-important decisions, what sort of things are there that David decides?'

'Oh,' she said. 'You know. Should we have a referendum on a common currency . . . whether it's worth spending all that money on defence . . . should the death penalty be brought back . . .'

That'll do for the interval.

Once at the bed, I moved heavily, swiftly onto it, seized

Diana's legs and prised them apart, then kneed the things wider still. I lowered myself over her, allowing a stubbled chin to graze one trembling breast before I buried my face in her neck.

I seized her wrists in one hand and forced her arms up above her head. With the other hand, I grabbed the hard shaft of my prick. Then, easing my hips up the rumpled covers, I nudged the swollen, bulbous head against the hot, wet, hungrily parted lips of her cunt.

Feeling the fiery clasp of that second mouth engulf the throbbing glans, I slid the hand palm downwards between our two bellies, spreading the first two fingers to splay the eager labia wider still.

'God, Tom, those big hands of yours,' Diana groaned. 'Don't ever let them shrink!'

I oscillated the hips from side to side, rotating them slightly, stirring the hard staff among the moist folds of inner flesh. Then abruptly I lunged.

Easily, greasily as a finger swallowed by an oiled rubber glove, my cock slid up into the burning embrace of her belly.

'Aaaaaahhh!' Diana breathed. Or words to that effect.

Fairly hard at first, I began pumping in and out of her, sliding the hard length of my tool up as far as it would go into the searing clasp of those ridged vaginal muscles I knew so well, letting the pubic bone and the hairy, hanging balls splat against her shamelessly exposed genital furrow with each stroke . . . then subtly reducing the rate and the force, slowly, slowly withdrawing the stem until only the very tip was retained by the suction of those blossoming labia.

Then – an instant's hiatus, a shuddering pause – and I was sliding it powerfully, slowly in again . . . further and further, deeper than deep, hotter and tighter in the violated depths of her violated flesh.

Diana had freed her wrists. Fingertips raked my naked back as her stockinged legs locked warmly over my calves. She was heaving fiercely up off the bed to meet my thrusts. Sweat ran between the big, resilient breasts I was now clawing with both hands.

'Oh Jesus, Tom,' she choked. 'Stuff it up higher, tighter! I want that cock so far up inside me that I can suck you off with my throat!'

I did my best. I rammed, I slammed. I fed it in inch by inch, so slowly, so forcefully that after a heart-thudding eternity it seemed there could not possibly by any space for a further advance . . . and then the last thrust proved us both liars and Diana yelped as my spearing shaft penetrated her savagely dilated inner flesh with a final, pulsating half-length.

The tension between us was so frantic now – an excitement tangible as the high, thin shrill of wind in distant telephone wires – that we both knew the climax was near.

We knew too that there would be gentler, more contemplative sex later that night. Stroking and sucking and kissing and the murmured caress, a still lustful but near satiated symphony of mutual desire. So there was no point in artificially prolonging what had already established its own rhythm, its inexorable passage to the predestined end.

Perfect sex is a tender plant. A wrong move, a misreading of the partner's need, a clumsy hesitation, can wither it on the branch.

Diana knew this as well as I did. In ten years, after all, one must learn *something*.

So this time it was she – sensing perhaps more acutely than I the *moment critique* – who deliberately provoked the sprint leading to the final hurdle.

Suddenly, I had a wild woman beneath me.

Streaming with sweat, a tornado of frantic limbs, she heaved manically beneath me, hissing like a snake. Her head flailed wildly on the pillows; her tongue squelched a maelstrom of lascivious pressure into the tunnel of my left ear; her breasts slid across my slippery chest as her obscenely impaled pelvis smacked again and again against my slaving hips.

And then with one last titanic effort she contrived to throw me over onto my back, at the same time spearing herself once more by squatting on my cock and riding me as furiously as a steeplechase jockey in a handicap.

27

She was already deep in the shuddering throes of orgasm, screaming aloud as her dark head tossed from side to side. 'Bastard!' she yelled. 'My fucking lover, give it to me now!'

There was, after all, nothing else I could do. Not in that situation. So I gave it to her.

It was some time later – my pulse was only beating at twice the normal rate and the champagne bottle was empty – that I said reflectively: 'You know, darling, if I had money – real money – I think I'd get an ordinary wife from a mail order company and set you up as my mistress: ten thousand a month, a Mayfair flat, a Ferrari and a Versace account – on the understanding, of course, that I'd be round your way at least seven times a week!'

Diana was flat out on the bed. She reached for my cock. 'Wait until the answers to your ads come flooding in,' she said.

Chapter Three

There were three calls on the Friday my first two small-ads appeared. This could have been promising – if it hadn't been for the contents of each call.

After a lot of discussion, Diana and I had decided to place the more 'serious' announcement in the personal column of the most intelligent of the quality dailies, leaving the sportier one for a weekly display in *Hunters And Fishers*. This rod-and-gun publication was in fact exactly the kind of country field-sports review that the title implied, but the thick wad of small-ads pages at the back was peppered with insertions from lonely-hearts advertisers, escort agencies, thinly disguised call-girl come-ons and marriage bureaux – clients who interpreted the title of the magazine in a social rather than a literal sense.

My first strike came from there; no lady, but an awfully dear fellow who was absolutely *dying* to meet a chum who sounded so *frightfully interesting* and he was certain that we MUST have something in common.

I told him that I could only think of one thing we had in common, but, thank you, I fancied I had a better use for it.

The second call – the daily this time – sounded as if it came from a left-wing university intellectual interested in relationships from an anthropological point of view. Really the *sole* approach, didn't I think? The voice was an alto bray and I was certain she had cropped hair. I declined politely.

Call Number Three – there were two, actually, one from each ad – was quite clearly a ranging shot fired by a Vice Squad type with no dirty bookshops to raid that day. Just a routine enquiry to check that I wasn't some professional stud-for-hire peddling his ass, as the cousins say.

The type's mistake was to use the same policewoman

for both calls. I told her to read the notices inside London's public telephone kiosks if she was interested in that kind of thing, and hung up on her.

Three strikes and out, I thought. I mean like zero out of ten for starters.

Luckily, I'd only just pushed the phone away when it rang up Number Four.

A pleasant enough voice, a bit husky. Getting on in life, perhaps? But with a certain assurance implying – it seemed to me – that there wouldn't be any hassle over whether or not there was enough in the kitty to settle this quarter's telephone bill.

The call was very short. The lady – she gave no name – would be interested to hear further details of my proposition. Since such matters were not a suitable subject for discussion over the telephone, she suggested that we meet.

Well, that was a start, anyway.

With pleasure, I intoned. Where could I call upon her?

But she wasn't having any of that. I mean like no address, thank you very much!

I didn't blame her. Voices can be misleading – especially the voices of professional con men. She wanted to make sure that I didn't have designer stubble – or, for that matter, that I did wear shoes – before she was giving an inch. She suggested that we should meet for tea at Fortnum and Mason's in Piccadilly. She gave me a time and a table number. So thank you and until tomorrow.

She was already installed when I arrived – fiftyish, thin, with sharp features and a chalky complexion. She wore a beaver toque and there was a fur coat thrown over the back of her chair. The only jewellery I could see, apart from a plain wedding ring, was a heart-shaped locket on a heavy gold chain.

Well, at least this was class! I bowed slightly and took the chair she indicated.

My spiel, my sales pitch, was honed and ready, but I had decided in advance – based solely on the voice I had heard – that I would advance nothing unasked; I would confine myself strictly to simple replies to the questions she posed.

You get the idea: discreet, professional, no embroidery, no attempt to play the personality boy.

Fine. Except she didn't ask any questions.

Not relating to the ad, that is. Just did I take sugar and milk, would I prefer cucumber or salmon sandwiches, had I seen this movie, that play, the Summer Exhibition at the Royal Academy?

I got the picture, of course. She wasn't going to bother herself with details until she had sight of the merchandise on offer. The tea party was no more than an opportunity for madam to decide whether or not she would be wasting her time – and money – if she pursued the matter further. And to give her an easy get-out if the answer was negative, without the risk of being pestered by bright-boy afterwards.

Very prudent, I thought. Businesslike and adult.

The meeting lasted all of ten minutes. Than she called for the bill and, waiting for her change, pushed a visiting card across the table.

Mrs Evelyn Porter. No address printed, but a line of neat handwriting citing an expensive apartment block in Kensington. And Evelyn? Could have been her own Christian name or that of a late husband. As unemphatic and down-key as the rest of her.

'I think – providing the terms are agreeable to me – that we may have business to discuss,' she said with a level stare (I was wearing a dark suit and a sober tie). 'Be at this address at three o'clock tomorrow afternoon.' She nodded at the card, rose swiftly to her feet, draped the fur coat over one arm, and swept out of the restaurant.

I was left halfway to my feet, struggling to avoid knocking my chair over. The waiter, who had noticed – as I had – that the scales of Mrs Porter's black handbag were from the largest, and most expensive part of the crocodile, had also noticed that she left no tip. As I righted myself, he permitted himself no more than a hint, the merest ghost of a half-raised eyebrow in my direction – a communication that expressed more clearly than words what each of us knew to be true: that our place in the world of Mrs Porter was decidedly outside the servants' entrance!

31

I fumbled coins from my pocket and slid them towards my cup and saucer. 'Thank you, indeed, sir. That is very kind,' the waiter said with a bow that stopped only just short of being a joke shared between us.

I went out through the other exit and left through the store, pausing only to buy Diana a box of *marrons glacés* that we couldn't afford.

There was nobody home when I arrived. Diana was visiting friends. A message on the screen of my word processor told me that there had been another phone call. Diana had tapped out:

DRAWLY (DROOPY?) LADY – POSSIBLE CLIENT, BUT SHE WASN'T GIVING ANYTHING AWAY TO ME, NOT EVEN HER NAME – WISHES YOU TO CALL HER BACK ASAP. WATCH YOUR STEP THERE, JACK!

I called the number. The code sounded as though it might be somewhere in the East End.

Interesting?

The phone was picked up on the first ring.

'Hal-lo, there! Beryl here.'

Diana had hit the nail on the head. The voice – hoarse, throaty, the syllables lazily drawn out – really was drawly. And it was a voice that did, immediately, for some reason, suggest a woman who could be droopy . . . a little slack, a trifle overweight maybe? Over-age too, perhaps? It made me think at once of shuttered rooms and cushions strewn about. Of incense, even. You know – the Turkish Delight syndrome, full of eastern promise as the ads used to say.

Frankly, in Diana's place, I'd have thought twice before I passed the message on!

I identified myself, and Beryl's voice said: 'Right. Come on over, now.'

'Perhaps you'd like me to give you a brief rundown on my terms and—'

'I said come on over. I want to *seeee* you, darling. Okay?'
I went on over.

The address was in the East End – a narrow side street off Spitalfields Market, not far from the Hawksmoor church, where the houses were still black from the days when steam trains ran into Liverpool Street station. Beryl's apartment was on the attic floor above three storeys of lawyers' offices, a tailor's fitting room and a street-level carpentry workshop. The creaking stairway was acrid with the smell of fresh sawdust.

The apartment wasn't precisely as I had imagined it, but it was certainly exotic. It covered the entire floor-plan of the old building – a single huge room with curtained-off alcoves for kitchen and bath and a skylight in one of the steeply sloping walls.

The glass of this was covered by a dark blue blanket and the only illumination was provided by a series of low-powered red and amber electric bulbs at different heights and an oil lamp cradled in a vast crystal chandelier at the far end of the room.

Much of the light was swallowed by the walls and ceiling, which were a uniform midnight blue, except for the lowest wall, inside the eaves, which was covered by a dark crimson tapestry. In front of this was an immense divan piled high with multicoloured cushions, most of them of oriental design. There were cushions on the floor too, and bright beanbag recliners, but most of the polished boards were strewn with an apparently haphazard collection of lacquered cabinets, low brass coffee tables, and shelves of different shape and height. Books, papers and CDs lay scattered around a built-in TV console and music centre, and there was indeed incense burning in a small brazier on a stone hearth.

Beryl was sprawled on the divan, half hidden among bead curtains and hangings of burnished silk and dark lace. She could have been anything between thirty-five and fifty, and she was not dressed – which is to say that she was not wearing actual clothes – but her ripe body was cocooned in diaphanous layers of rich material which could have come from anywhere between Tashkent and Samarkand, from Kashmir to Tibet. A black cigarette burned in the long jade holder jutting from her full lips.

'Come on over and let me see you,' the husky voice drawled. 'Sit.'

Feeling a little like a dog left off the lead, I advanced gingerly and found a beanbag not too far from the divan. I sat.

It seemed a long way down. And even though the divan was low, I had the sense of being inspected from a long way above. Clouds of perfumed smoke eddied out from among the draperies. I heard the silky rustle of materials in movement. 'Not *bad*!' my – er – hostess said.

I could see her more clearly now. She had levered herself upright and was leaning forward to return the compliment, peering through the amber gloom.

There was a lot of her. I judged her to be pretty tall too. But she was voluptuous not fat. Her flesh was taut and resilient and the swell of her breasts and mound of her belly among the billows of rich stuffs communicated an impression of sensual generosity. This was a woman who kept herself, as they say, in shape . . . and that shape was all curves. Beryl, one felt instinctively, looked exactly how she wanted to look.

'Perhaps, now,' I said, 'you'd like me to outline briefly what I have to offer. I mean, such terms and conditions as I propose are pretty simple, but I thought—'

'I can *see* what you have to offer,' Beryl interrupted. 'Why don't you come on over here and allow me to examine the details?'

'The . . . details?'

'Duality is everywhere,' Beryl said. 'If the sum of two disparate dualities is to symbiose into that Oneness that is the sole approach to the Great Unconscious, a certain amount of proximity is customarily thought advantageous.' She laughed – a surprisingly soprano trill. 'Come over here, where we can be in touch.'

I swallowed. This was certainly one for the book! 'If you wanted to make an appointment now,' I said, rising to my feet, 'I'm fairly certain that one day next week. I could find a window in my schedule . . .'

I let the sentence die its own death.

She had sat up suddenly straight – a big woman indeed among the layers of richness, with two very positive brown eyes staring fixedly at me through the swirls of smoke. 'Windows?' she repeated. 'Appointments? What are you talking about, man? You're already *here*, for God's sake! And we're wasting time. Now sit here and shut up.' She patted a tangle of twisted silks beside one pale, solid and unmistakably naked thigh which had emerged from the welter of colours kaleidoscoping the mattress.

I was lowering myself for the second time – telling myself, Wait, wait! Play it by ear! – when she cut in once more, echoing me again. 'Stop! I can't have you here, caparisoned in those absurd industrial epoch garments. Take them off at once, all of them!'

I stared at her, the mouth, I fancy, slightly open, the eyes probably bulging. Well, I mean . . .

'The tightness, the restriction, has already muddied your aura beyond recognition,' Beryl explained kindly. 'Now free yourself and strip . . . Here, you can ease yourself into this.' She tossed a bundle of something lightweight and garish my way.

I caught it with one hand. Silk again – with some kind of metallic sheen and incrustations depicting eastern images – birds? deities? *footbridges?* – in some harder, less smooth material.

I suppose I must have stood there like a dummy for several seconds – the scene, after all, wasn't exactly one that had featured largely in the scenario Diana and I had dreamed up – and then I let whatever it was that I was holding unroll.

Some kind of robe or shift, neck to ankle, I thought, with very wide, flowing sleeves and a Nehru-style rollneck. Just the job for encouraging the electro-magnetic fields and permitting the aura to expand. 'Get rid of that rubbish and put it on,' Beryl commanded.

I don't quite know why I obeyed so implicitly. There was,

of course, by now the very heavy undercurrent of sex which naturally enough intrigued me – I mean, wouldn't it you? – but what else could I have done without looking a complete berk? Announced stiffly, 'I'm afraid I'm not that sort of chap'? The sophisticated man-of-the-world with the high IQ who wrote the ad in the serious daily?

Do me a favour!

I was out from under the necktie, away from the shirt, jacket and trousers, and high above the shoes and socks before the black cigarette had incinerated another quarter-inch of its length (it was not, after all, the first time this particular request had been made). After that, it was hands above the head and allow the shift to slide down me like a caress. This seemed to me a less clumsy technique than trying – and possibly failing – to pull the small neckline up over my manly hips. And if her ladyship happened to remark, on the way, that the equipment with which I had providentially been furnished was in a state of partial elongation and putative rigidity . . . well, five gets you ten that this was not a hundred miles from the parameters that governed her own thinking.

By this time, you see, I was pretty sure I'd read this specific example of the other half right.

Everybody's tame anarchist rebel, probably with just enough to live on, tilting at all the easiest moral targets with the high-minded, patronising sneers of borrowed cultures just esoteric enough to intrigue, just daring and dangerous enough to blind the normal punter with pseudo-science.

Free love, of course. Anti-authority. The ultimate of in-group chic and heavily into things metaphysical, psychic, paranormal, you name it. The spiritual via the physical – or let's fuck, okay?

You must meet our friend Beryl. What a character! This is really a girl who has the courage to *live* her own innermost convictions!

Nothing wrong with that, of course. I mean fine – if it hadn't been done, publicly, already by Djuna Barnes and Violette LeDuc and Ottoline Morel and Zelda Fitzgerald in the twenties and thirties and forties and fifties ad infinitum.

I sat down on the edge of the bed. Beryl moved her ripe bulk over to make room for me, encouraging the proximity – her term, remember – with a hand falling heavily on my nearest thigh. There was a lot of light flashing from heavy, stoned rings on each finger. And, it must be admitted, a certain amount of electricity by now flashing around the nerves centered between this thigh and its mate. I noticed for the first time that a giant blow-up of a nineteenth-century illustration from the *Kamasutra*, fixed to one of the steeply walls, was leaning over the divan in a suggestive way.

The hand on my thigh moved.

It's a funny thing, but I suppose one of the reasons there have been so many taboos surrounding sex in the West for the past two or three hundred years is that we have packed away so tightly all the bits of us concerned with it. I mean when you think of jock-straps and brassières and elasticated tights and zip fasteners and hooks and eyes, it takes a pretty overt move on someone's part – what you might call a specifically decisive action or a causal transaction – before there's the faintest hint of a chance that the hidden treasures can be exposed to view, let alone enjoyed.

The looser clothes – saris and cheongsams and jellabas and robes of various kinds, favoured by the orientals – permit on the other hand a far freer interchange (shall we say?) of body parts. Permit isn't the right word either. Permission given implies a decision taken. It's the fact that chance can, literally, take a hand that counts here. Or there.

Face it, no human hand is going to *happen to* touch a cock shrouded beneath a chalk-stripe three-piece complete with belt and necktie, or graze a slope of tit ensconced within the reinforced satin palisade of a C-cup Playtex hidden by pearls and a twin-set.

With robes, though, anything can happen – and often does. Especially when lying on a low divan. Bodies shift. People have to move: a cigarette must be stubbed out, a drink reached for, a leg attacked by pins-and-needles eased. Each movement, in some slight way or other, affects the relative relationship of one body to another . . . so it's the most natural thing in the world, deliberately or by pure coincidence, for an upper arm swathed in soft material to lean momentarily against a veiled breast, for a hand resting casually on a thigh to find itself measurably nearer an unrestricted crotch. As the hand on my own thigh was in fact finding itself now...

The touch was at the same time exploratory and decisive. The pressure of the fingers was firm without being authoritative, bold without a sign of aggressiveness. The feeling was that of a positive individual whose behaviour could still be conditioned by the reaction of others.

It seemed the most natural thing in the world to cant my frame a little towards her, leaning her way so that the exploring hand might have easier access to a more ... intimate ... approach. If it so wished.

Apparently it did, for I was at once tinglingly aware of the back of a hand brushing against the tip of my throbbing and already hardened cock.

Beryl's eyes were half closed and there was a lazy smile curving her full lips, the lower of which, I saw, was generously bee-stung and glistening moistly in the subdued light.

From this position, leaning close, I could see her much more clearly, and much more of her. There was a lot to see. Dark hair, tightly curling, framed her face. Supported on one elbow, the big body so enticingly reclining among all those clouds of azure and vermilion and jade and gold suggested the pleasures of the seraglio with a breath-catching immediacy more voluptuous than the most clinical illustration by a master draughtsman. A swell of belly, shadowed by a dark hint of pubic hair between carelessly spread thighs, manifested itself against the pull of a more translucent silk spun with gold stars. Round breasts, heavy as ripe fruit, thrust out thicker voile and organza still dia-phanous enough to reveal the rouged nipples and areolas within. The superb fleshiness of the woman's hips and backside was implicit in the warm depression of the mattress sloping away from my knees.

I was breathing quickly now, aware that the robe I was wearing must have a wraparound mode because the back of the hand grazing my trembling cock-head was skin against heated skin. I stifled a small cry as the hand twisted and practised fingers wrapped firmly around my rigid shaft. One of my own hands, almost without conscious direction from my spinning head, stole out to drift down to the smooth curve of belly spilled towards me at the level of my knees. I caught my breath, exulting in the warm resilience of that carnally close surface pulsating against my fingers. Through several thicknesses of sheer material I felt wiry hairs rough against the heel of my hand as the pelvis rose involuntarily under my touch. My thigh was hard against a milk-white leg which had somehow freed itself from the swirls of drapery, and my cock now swelled harder still within the grip of the milking hand so deftly caressing.

It was then, as the excitement flaming through my loins threatened to rise up and choke me, that I lowered my head to the heaving slopes of those breasts so thrillingly upthrust towards me. At that moment, it seemed the only possible thing to do.

My head was pillowed on a shifting mass of flesh. I felt cool fingers cradle the nape of my neck as Beryl freed her other hand and subsided now flat out on her back. My whole body tingled as the entire burning complex of hips and thighs and buttocks and belly moved lazily against me.

Over the mundane sounds of life outside – a rasping saw, street noises, the whirr of sewing machines, brickwork struck with a metal tool – I could now hear over the subtle creak of the divan a wordless croon that was humming behind Beryl's parted lips. I closed my own mouth on silver muslin peaked over a painted nipple as taut as a baby's thumb, and was rewarded with a choked gasp of anticipation. I worked the filmy material with my mouth, sucking up the bud of flesh below to worry it with a wet tongue. Inches below my open eyes, a pulse beat wildly beneath the heated skin of Beryl's neck.

The grip on my shaft tightened, pulled, coaxing me – commanding me – closer, closer, higher. The divan creaked again as I moved.

I was staring down at lipstick and rouge and silvered

blue shadowing the slumbrous gaze of mascara-ed eyes.

Our mouths joined softly together . . . and suddenly everything was movement, with the liquid wrestle of hot tongues, the fleshy shaft of belly to belly, the shift of big breasts sliding beneath my weight and the roaring of blood behind the eyes as we strained and heaved.

I was never conscious of the details that followed this.

My hands were full of the fleshy mounds pillowing my chest, thumbs closed over nipples that were suddenly hot and bare. Somehow the rich profusion of stuffs miraculously parted and my hips were buoyed up nakedly on the padded cushions of a pelvis plastered against the trapped hand still pumping the head of my burning tool. I was aware of the hot blood thumping through my veins, the hoarse panting of snorted breath as we sucked and thrust, the eager shudders of the yielding frame now quivering beneath me . . .

And then all at once I was in her. There was no hint of a progression, of a series of manoeuvres from here to there. Beryl's two hands were clawing the cheeks of my buttocks, forcing my loins hard against her arching hips. She groaned deep in her throat behind our slaving mouths. And at the fiery center of my being I was swallowed, engulfed, my bursting cock sucked up into the searing wonder of inner flesh clasped scaldingly around it.

It was extraordinary. Especially at the tail end of an ordinary afternoon. It must have been some near-magical concurrence of circumstances, a special chemistry of the five senses, a physical ecstasy pushed beyond the point of no return – just the time, the place and the loved one all together, you may say – but it wasn't a loved one, the place was artificial as hell, and the time was, well, totally out of my hands. Whatever, there was unquestionably *something* about that afternoon. An absurd contrast, perhaps, between a bricklayer, a man with a saw, and the oriental extravagance of the smoky, low-key lighting, that super-abundance of rich materials and profusion of unexpected shapes, the affectation of the atmosphere as a whole plus the open invitation of the lush body so sexily exposed by the stranger on the divan . . .

Or maybe it wasn't just incense burning in the brazier.

Whatever the explanation, time ceased to exist for me. There was no today, no tomorrow, no yesterday. There wasn't even any me any more. There was only us . . . and this . . . and here . . .

It was as though I had been drawn inexorably to the edge of a vortex, stared down into the darkly whirling depths, then felt myself enmeshed, sucked under, swallowed in the maelstrom seething at its centre. So there was no beginning, no end, just now.

I was fucking like a crazy man. I was in a sexual limbo, plunging frenziedly in and out of the superbly quaking contours of hot flesh massed beneath me, billowing upwards against each thrust, flowering open at the centre to suck in the scorching prick tunnelling up into the dark.

I was a spearing instrument with no purpose, no existence apart from pleasuring the wide belly clamped in spasms against my hips, big quivering breasts hot against my chest. At the same time, loins flaming with lewd desire, I was the guest, the grateful receiver intoxicated by the joys of sex beyond logic or reason, rendered delirious by the opulent excesses of excited woman.

We came together, of course. What else could we have done? How else could such a fuck end?

It was a fairly titanic experience.

It seemed to me at first that my tool had exploded. The day went dark. I was totally swallowed up, engulfed within this palpitating universe of flesh; yet she, somehow, was by some physical osmosis drawn into me also to bloom at the centre of my being like a dark, exotic flower.

Afterwards, long afterwards, it seemed to me that my iron-hard cock had never spurted so forcefully, so much, or for so long.

Beryl appeared to recover more quickly than I did. Perhaps she did this every afternoon.

Naturally – there's always a down side, isn't there? – everything had to be analyzed and explained. I suffered, as politely as I could, a lot of stuff involving Karma and One-

41

ness and our respective auras and even, surprisingly, electro-magnetic fields of force. Par for the course with this kind of nympho-pseud, I thought. Still, it had been a hell of a good fuck!

Among other memorabilia, I discovered that Beryl had a thing. Wouldn't you know?

It seemed that she liked if possible to have a different man every day. It seemed she very rarely 'made love' (her term) with the same gentleman twice. Because, after all, she hardly ever found anyone interesting enough to warrant the exertion.

I made no comment and refused to ask the unspoken question.

Beryl of course was an artist. What else? When I asked what kind of work she did – and I could have written the script for her! – she replied gravely: 'My life is my work.'

I looked around the attic and nodded.

Nothing had been said about my ad – which was after all the reason for my being there in the first place – but somehow I didn't like to raise the subject myself. After all, as an escort of the kind I envisaged, if a client wanted to fuck, okay. But to ask for payment *just* for that seemed, well, a bit caddish, I thought.

When I was making I-really-ought-to-be-on-my-way noises, however, she said: 'I gathered from your announcement that you consider yourself in some way or another a professional. By the door, on your way out, you will see a small carved wooden chest on a stand. If you open that you will see that it is filled with banknotes. Please take what you consider sufficient before you close the door.'

I shook my head. 'Thank you,' I said. 'But to accept money would be to demean, to besmirch a beautiful experience.'

What would you have done?

There was nevertheless one thing I did have to do. A huge visitors' book lay open on a lectern beside the hearth which looked as though it had been wrested from a church pulpit. 'I'd be grateful if you'd fill in your name, darling,' Beryl said.

42

I complied. Why not? She had the ad anyway; she already had my number. I scrawled the necessary information in ruled columns headed *Name* and *Address* and *Profession* and even *Age*. The final column, much wider, occupied half the second page. It was headed *Remarks*.

'What about this last one?' I asked.

'Forget it,' Beryl said. 'I fill that one in myself, later.'

Chapter Four

'My terms are simple enough,' I told Mrs Porter. 'I charge fifty pounds an hour, with a minimum of three hours work on any given day. Longer sessions may be arranged, pro rata, by mutual agreement. There are no supplements to this tariff, which remains invariable whatever the hours of day or night chosen.'

'You provide your own transport?' Mrs Porter looked up from the eighteenth-century rosewood escritoire behind which she was sitting.

'Certainly,' I said. 'The client is responsible in no way whatsoever for any charges which arise outside the agreed hours of each session. During those hours, however, despite the possible 'social' nature of certain occasions, I remain one hundred percent your employee. I am available, without question, to do what you want, how you want, where you want and how often you want. And I undertake' – I smiled – 'to advance no opinions or comments on that employment unless they are specifically asked for.'

'Good,' Mrs Porter said briskly. 'You have certain stipulations, I suppose?'

I cleared my throat. 'Only one really. My loyalty and discretion regarding the terms of my employment and the details of anything that happens during it are total. It must be understood at the same time that clients may have no claim on my loyalties, or interests in my private life outside the time of such employment.'

'I am afraid I don't understand.'

'It's just an in-case-of,' I explained. 'To guard against possible misunderstandings. Suppose, to quote an extreme example, I had been for several months a regular employee of Client A . . . and was then approached to work also for

Client B, whom A not only knew but cordially detested . . . then the former would have no right to attempt to influence me or prevent me accepting that second job.'

'I see.' Mrs Porter opened a drawer and took out a cheque book in a Morocco holder. 'I am prepared to offer you a trial run of three hours from Wednesday of next week at noon. There is a city luncheon and the opening of a flower show which I prefer not to attend alone. On this initial occasion I am prepared to pay you in advance. Will you accept a cheque or do you prefer cash?'

Diana and I had discussed this one. Although, in the state of our affairs, waiting for a cheque to be cleared would be a drag, we had decided against cash payments. 'It looks too much like a wide boy, black market or tax-dodging scheme,' my wife had said. And I had agreed that first impressions and an appearance of trustworthiness were all important.

'Thank you, madam,' I said now. 'Whichever is more convenient to you.'

'A cheque then.' Mrs Porter nodded and began to write.

I looked around the room again. It was spacious, with a high, moulded ceiling – typical of this Edwardian mansion block with its polished woods, shining brass and uniformed porters behind a glassed-in desk at the entrance. Such furniture as I could see was mostly period stuff in show-room condition. Behind the desk, French windows opened onto a wide balcony bright with flowers in expensive urns. And beyond that were private gardens heavy with chestnut trees in bloom.

It was going to be an easier place – and an easier meeting – to describe than my hectic docklands sortie and its eastern promise so dramatically fulfilled!

I had thrown that one away when Diana asked. An overlong, over-lush description of the homo-exotic, quasi-oriental attic, followed by: 'A nutter, sweetie, who wanted to see if our Karmas matched.' Which was at least partly true. Then I had shrugged. 'One cab fare down the drain – but it shows, I guess, that you can't win 'em all.'

'Well, at least it seems as if you can win with Mrs Porter,'

Diana said after I had told her that one. 'She didn't query the rates at all?'

'Not a word,' I said.

She nodded. 'I thought we had it about right for the market,' she said.

There had in fact been quite bit of discussion about what I was going to charge. First of all, we had agreed that whatever the hourly sum was, it had to be inclusive. No extras to frighten the clients and – inevitably – provoke disputes. The rate therefore, with its guaranteed three-hour minimum, must be elastic enough to cover unexpected eventualities, expensive enough to give the impression that this was high-class, top-drawer merchandise on offer . . . but not so outrageous that half the possible clientele would be put off before we even started.

'As to the quality of the goods on offer,' Diana said, 'and whether the service is sufficiently high-class to justify the price – well that, my sweet, will be entirely up to you!'

We had settled on the fifty after analyzing the fees of several different types of expert who provided a specialized service requiring a specific amount of time per client – and thus accountable in terms of hours. Among others we had checked out hypnotherapists, masseurs, certain types of psychiatrist, advanced individual language teachers, translators and official interpreters. The hourly rate for most of them varied between forty-five and sixty. Apart from the fact that it was a nice, round, simple sum, fifty seemed to us an equitable – in particular a *believable* – amount rather than an undercut rate or a price high enough to be a bad joke.

In fact it seemed the right flavour of carrot, because we did get quite a number of bites during the first two weeks the ads appeared.

Only one caller described the rates as 'ridiculously high' and tried angrily to talk them down, and this was an eighty-year-old Scotswoman who owned *a whole house* in Belgrave Square and swanned around London from Prunier to Cartier in a chauffeur-driven Rolls – which had a yellow and black twin sister garaged at her Georgian country property in Herefordshire.

The others included a female barrister who sounded quite young, the widow of a Harley Street surgeon, a woman who had inherited an antique shop in Brighton, an elderly county type (probably a breeder of racehorses, I thought) and a retired hospital matron. There were one or two others who had sounded interested but failed to call back. And of course the odd, expected nuisance caller and Can-I-Suck-Your-Cock? gigglers.

Plus Mrs Porter, who was the first person I actually worked for.

Who did indeed have a Jaguar – the model which calls itself a Daimler Sovereign to be exact – and a chauffeur in a brown uniform with polished boots and a peaked cap.

Her city luncheon was a very high-powered affair. It was held in a private, members-only restaurant overlooking the river not far from Tower Bridge, and at least half the men there I knew by sight and recognized as MPs, captains of industry, press lords and suchlike. The food was five-star, most of the conversation – electronics, takeovers, the financing of mineral-producing, third-world republics – above my head. But I kept my end up as well as I could.

The crunch came with the coffee and brandy. The luncheon was quite a small affair, about twenty men and around a dozen women. But it seemed it was a once-a-month event . . . and a ritual had established itself from which there was no escape.

At the conclusion of the meal, every man present was expected to rise in turn and say a few words – not exactly a speech, but something apposite, very short, and if possible witty. Every man including non-member guests such as myself.

I fell back, not for the first time, on the old maxim: when faced with the impossible, tell a funny story.

I said that there were so many distinguished men present, expert in so many different fields, that it reminded me of the day when the Archbishop of Canterbury and the Roman Catholic Archbishop of Westminster were obliged to share a taxi after some function because there was a cab-drivers' strike that day. As they settle back on the rear seat, the Archbishop of Canterbury says: 'It seems to me very right and proper, my dear Cardinal, that we should share this conveyance. We have after all a great deal in common: we are both men of the cloth; each of us spends his life, does he not, spreading the Word of God?'

'Indeed we do,' the Cardinal agrees warmly. 'You in your way, and I in His.'

It appeared to go down all right, and I noticed Mrs Porter's brittle features relax into a satisfied smile.

After that the flower show was a doddle. I bowed and scraped and offered my arm, making the right noises to the right people and treating Mrs P like the Queen of Sheba.

She introduced me when necessary simply as Mr Thomas Silver – with no background and no tag. She wasn't the type of person one dared to ask: 'Who's your friend? What does he do?'

The important thing was that she made a five-hour rendezvous for the following week. Dinner at the Ivy and a box at the RSC.

By the time I left her apartment, we had been together twenty minutes over the three hours. I made no mention of this . . . and I observed that she noticed I made no mention.

'I felt it important,' I told Diana, 'to establish a kind of confidence between us right at the outset. You know – who's going to bother about a few quid this way or that. Not everyone who agrees to take me on, after all, is going to become a regular client.'

It was indirectly through Mrs Porter, nevertheless, that I met my most *irregular* client.

It was after my third outing with her (*Troilus and Cressida* had been followed by *Coriolanus*) and I had already worked for the surgeon's widow, the matron and (twice) the young barrister. It was almost midnight when I left the mansion block and went to collect the Volkswagen from the underground parking lot off Cromwell Road, and at first I didn't notice the woman standing by the railings in Harrington Gardens, half hidden in the pool of shadow between two streetlamps. When I did, I thought only that it was a bit late for a business girl to be out, especially in this area.

She emerged into the light as I approached – a young blonde with shoulder-length hair. I was about to pass by with a polite smile and a no thanks when she called me by name.

I stopped and turned towards her. 'I'm sorry, I don't think . . . ?'

'Forgive me,' she said breathlessly. 'I know it's, well, not the thing . . . but I couldn't think of any other way . . . I'd no idea how to get in touch with you, and I knew you were going out with Mrs Porter tonight, and I thought . . . perhaps if I dared contact you when you left?'

I was intrigued. I studied the woman more closely. There was in fact something vaguely familiar about her – nothing more definite than that – but I was at a loss to place her as . . . what? Someone from a shop? An acquaintance of Diana's? A person briefly met at the office? In a pub? 'There's something I can do for you?' I asked.

'I hope so,' she said. 'It's so difficult. You must excuse me, but . . . is it true that you are in fact – I don't know how to put it – I mean someone told me that you have some sort of, well, a kind of escort business. Can that be so?'

I smiled. 'It's no secret. Not exactly a business; a one-man show. But yes, that is true. In what way can I . . . ?'

'I want your help,' she said. 'But I had no idea how to get in touch with you.'

'Look,' I said, 'there's a late café open in Gloucester Road. Why not come with me, make yourself comfortable, and tell me about it over a coffee?'

'That would be most kind,' she said.

Beneath the garish café lights, surrounded by the noisy, boisterous post-pub drinkers, I saw that she was older than I had thought, more like thirty than twenty. She had fine features, discreet make-up, quiet clothes and superbly cut hair.

Her name was Carol Dagois. And as soon as I heard the first part, I remembered where I had seen her. At Mrs Porter's luncheon that first time. She had been in charge of the waiters and waitresses at the riverside restaurant – a quietly efficient organizer, discreetly in the background but always at hand, ready with the lift of an eyebrow or a professional word to correct a mistake, supply something missing or answer a question. A treasure, in fact – and all the more valuable since her presence was felt rather than noticed. The kind of person who made businesses run smoothly.

What she wanted, in fact, was simply to employ me. But in a rather special way.

Briefly, the restaurant was owned, and the superb food prepared, by a well-known Italian chef named Geraldo Porrelli. He was married to a Scotswoman and they had three school-age children. Carol – Porrelli's great strength professionally, as I had seen for myself – had been working with him for six or seven years, during five of which, although she was very friendly with Signora Porrelli, she had in fact been the boss's mistress.

Okay. Secretaries do it too! So what?

Well, it seemed she loved the man very much ... so much that she would do anything to avoid hurting him.

Such as breaking up his family, for instance, with the resulting traumas for Mama and the children.

Carol was, on the other hand, unwilling to terminate the relationship. And Porrelli himself was adamant that she must stay with him. Whether for sentimental reasons or something rather less personal I didn't like to ask.

The problem with this until-now comfortable threesome was that Carol, in spite of all the care they took, was fairly sure that the wife had begun to suspect that 'something was going on'.

And such suspicions must at all costs, for the sake of all concerned, be shown to be entirely without foundation.

So how to prove a negative?

How can you show, convincingly, that something *isn't* happening?

By demonstrating, Porrelli and his lady considered, that something else was.

In short, they wished to employ me in a particular role: to play the apple of Carol's sexy eye.

51

They – Porrelli himself, I assumed – would shell out the usual rates on an unspecified number of occasions if I would squire the lady-love around town, visit the Porrelli home with her, be seen as a couple here and there, and in general behave as though life was a conspiracy to keep the two of us out of bed.

Oho, you may say, but you are running into a moral question here. First, as a married man yourself, you risk upsetting your own wife if you make this charade as public as the employers wish. Secondly, by agreeing to the plan, you compound, not a felony but at least a transgression of the laws of marriage – and involve yourself in a scheme designed to deceive someone else's wife and confirm the guy in his infidelity.

True. But if I didn't agree to act as Porrelli's bird dog, the marriage was likely to end up on the rocks anyway.

So what does one do?

I didn't waste too high a proportion of the night wrestling with the ethics of the problem.

I stared through the swirls of cigarette smoke at this attractive blonde. Her face was drawn, the expression concerned. She had explained the situation simply, briefly, with an air of evident sincerity and a warmth of feeling both for her lover and his wife. Now she was staring down at her untouched coffee in silence, involuntarily twisting a plain gold ring around the middle finger of her left hand.

Abruptly, she raised her head and met my eye. Over the clatter of crockery, the hiss of the Expresso machine and the rowdy ground swell of late-night conversation, I just managed to make out the single word she uttered.

'Please!'

I hesitated. Diana and I had agreed to keep sex, even indirectly, out of my escort scene. On the other hand, this was only pretending. Also, these were the only clients, so far, who had suggested anything resembling a semi-permanent contract. I mean like there was *money* involved.

I nodded. 'I'll do what I can to help,' I told her.

We said goodnight and I went home. There was one thing I had meant to ask her which somehow got forgotten.

She had only seen me once before, at the riverside luncheon, and I certainly hadn't had a card with a copy of my small-ad on it pinned to my lapel. So how had she known that I was in the escort business? How come she knew Mrs Porter was a client? How was it she had realized we were going to the theatre and would be back late that night?

Someone, somewhere, somehow, must have talked. Certainly not Mrs P. So who, and why? Carol Dagois hadn't mentioned it at all. Never mind – I must remember to ask her sometime. In the meantime, a job was a job, whoever had been responsible for igniting the original idea!

There was however one other factor in the equation that Carol had omitted to mention.

Namely, that not only was she the longtime mistress of Signor Geraldo Porrelli; she was also a raving nympho with a roving eye who fucked, as they say, like a rabbit.

But I didn't find that out until later.

Chapter Five

It started off in the most normal way possible. I collected Carol from her apartment in Chelsea Cloisters – one of those pre-war egg-box blocks packed with one-room flats equipped with a kitchenette that folded into the wall and bathroom you had to go into sideways.

It was her day off from the restaurant, and she was to deliver a package to the Porrelli home on behalf of her boss. We went in my Golf convertible, the top down because it was sunny and warm.

The house too was a riverside property, in Putney, not far from the bridge over the Thames. I parked outside the gates and remained at the wheel while Carol took the package inside. Five minutes later she came out with Porrelli's wife – a gaunt woman with no make-up and sad eyes – and introduced me with a pretty good attempt at enthusiasm. Not as Tom Silver, of course: Roland Harris was the name we had chosen. Don't ask me why.

I smiled. I leaned over to shake hands. The boss's wife said how lucky it was that Carol should have such nice weather on her day off if we were going for a drive. Carol climbed back into the car. I smiled again, said nice-to-meet-you, and waved goodbye. We drove off.

First nail in coffin designed to the bury the idea of hanky-panky between hubby and his Number Two.

I hadn't met the man yet, but he had told Carol that his wife was having lunch with a friend at the restaurant overlooking the Hyde Park end of the Serpentine. It was important not to risk overkill, the message said, but there was no reason why we shouldn't – purely by chance because after all it was a lovely day – just happen to pass by there for a pre-lunch drink at the bar. Maybe even decide to eat there if the chemistry could be shown to be working. We would not, of course, notice Signora P among the crowd, but we would play love at first sight in a high enough register to make sure she noticed us. Second nail . . . and then nothing for several days apart perhaps from an odd word dropped at home by Porrelli himself. ('I'm just a little concerned about Carol; she seems lost in the clouds half the time. Not herself at all. I hope she's not sickening for something.')

The restaurant was animated. Wavelets on the lake glittered in the bright sunshine as the skiffs glided offshore. There were people bathing in the lido and shopgirls sharing sandwiches on the grassy slopes of Kensington Gardens.

Very nice, very pleasant – *and* I was being paid for it!

The fact that our particular charade was not played precisely as written arose because someone had added a couple of pages to my copy of the script without warning me first.

It was really, as Bountiful Beryl had observed not long before, a matter of proximity.

'We don't really have to go for a drive,' Carol had said once we were out of sight of the house in Putney. 'There isn't time if we're going to be at the Serpentine early enough to get a table. And what's the point anyway? Who's going to notice if we quarter the West End street by street?'

'What would you like to do?' I asked. The time after all was hers; I was just the hired help.

'Why don't we just go back to the flat and have a coffee and a glass of champagne?' Carol suggested. 'Kind of a pre-apéritif . . . and there's a bottle of Krug in the fridge as it happens.'

'Anything you say,' I agreed. We crossed the river and headed back towards Chelsea.

The coffee – as would be expected – was good, the champagne super. I'd hardly had time, really, to register Carol as a person. Apart from that meeting at the late-night café, she had simply been Mrs Dagois – one client among an increasing number of others. Facing her now in the close quarters of the tiny flatlet, I was obliged to take stock in a little more detail. She was indeed very slender, with excellent legs. She carried herself well, with that tight, almost reined-in quality that very slim, tall women often have. Her breasts, small, pointed, made little impression on the lightweight wool two-piece that she wore. Her pale hair, burnished and beautifully set, was as usual impeccable.

Sitting opposite her almost knee to knee in the two armchairs filling the cramped space between the dining table, a sideboard and the foldaway bed, I noticed a certain tightness, a reserved quality about her thin features, an air almost of nervous tension that complemented the restrained stance of her body as a whole. It was practically – I thought, eyeing the ghost of a frown shadowimg her forehead, a misty look veiling her eyes – practically as if she was deliberately keeping a tight control of herself, waiting with suppressed impatience for something to happen.

She was.

Less than half the champagne had gone when she rose restlessly, took a step towards the window, turned suddenly, and said: 'You'll have to excuse me. I have to change into something else before we go to lunch.'

Odd, I thought. Porrelli's wife had already seen what she was wearing. Wouldn't it strike her as curious, seeing the woman only a couple of hours later in a different outfit? Curious enough even for rats to be smelled? Then I realized: perhaps I was underestimating the lady's intelligence. Might another woman not suspect, noticing the wardrobe change, that it signified the couple of hours in between had been spent in bed? Was Carol in fact driving in a sophisticated nail number three? Aloud, half rising, I simply said: 'Would you like me to turn my back or look out of the window?'

'No,' she said. 'I wouldn't.'

There was something about her voice that made me open my eyes. 'You sit right there in that chair,' she said, 'and pour us another couple of drinks.'

I sat. I poured. She turned her own back to open a built-in wall cupboard. I saw rows of dresses, coats, blouses

57

hanging on a rail; transparent drawers full of underclothes and nylons.

Without removing anything from the rail, without disturbing a hair of that immaculate coiffure, Carol had shrugged off the woollen top. Her back was bare. She wore nothing under it. She swung around. Her eyes were wide now and I could see that she was breathing fast. Staring fixedly at me, she leaned fowards, small breasts peaked below her chest, and slid the fingers of each hand under the waistband of her skirt.

Without shifting her gaze, she eased the skirt down, over her hips, past tightly clenched buttocks, below the thighs.

She stepped out of the skirt and straightened in front of my chair, wearing high-heeled shoes, dark stockings stretched high, and a brown lace suspender belt tightly clasped around her slender waist and plastered to the flat plane of her belly.

I took in the near nudity with a single glance. Her big nipples, hard and prominent, jutted from darkened areolas large enough to cover half the area of her breasts. The flare of pubic hair sprouting boldly beneath the arch of the suspender belt was the colour of sand. The taut skin which fanned from the corners of her eyes was without blemish though there were faint indentations at the corners of her mouth, which was widening, astonishingly, into one of the most lascivious smiles I had ever seen.

Above the tight breasts that rose and fell with the acceleration of her breathing, I could see beneath the firm skin the quick-pulsed rhythm of her beating heart.

I was still holding the glass of champagne. For some reason or other, I swallowed a final gulp and lowered the glass to a coffee table.

Carol's eyes widened still further – an unfathomable depth in the inscrutable dark of her distended pupils, the melting brown of the irises outside. Without removing this equivocal, challenging regard from her face, she moved forward, placed an elegant leg on either side of my knees, and lowered herself to straddle my thighs. Her hands rose up and she began deftly to undo the knot of my tie.

Warmth flooded the area of my loins as her weight settled. I could feel the springy rasp of pubic hair through the trousers covering my suddenly stiffening tool, hot breath playing on my face.

Her fingers pulled the tail end of the tie through the unlooped knot. My shirt buttons were open. The hips on my lap swivelled very slightly from side to side, rolling the length of my cock against the top of my thigh.

The thin face was very close to mine. The indentations on either side of the mouth deepened as the smile widened. She wore the subtlest veneer of pale foundation, itself disguised by the most discreet blush of powder and rouge above. Whatever brand she used, it was clearly as expensive – and as discreet – as the elusive hint of perfume wafted to me by the heat of her almost naked body.

'We-ell?' Carol said gently – and I was astonished to find that the tone of her voice had dropped almost half an octave.

I cannot deny it: I was still – quivering with suspense though the loins might be – quite dizzy with amazement. That this diffident, quietly efficient, businesslike lady should metamorphose into a raging sexpot . . . well, as I said, this had been omitted from the original scenario.

'Very well indeed, thank you!' I replied breathlessly. 'But—?'

I lost the sense after that because her head swooped nearer still and she kissed me.

The quality of that first kiss was as surprising as the deeper voice.

Hot lips clamped voraciously over my mouth, forcing it open to let in the burning tip of a hungry tongue. My ears were flattened to my skull by the pressure of two hands holding my head in a vice-like grip. The hard tips of two small breasts smashed against my unexpectedly bared chest. Hips and thighs ground savagely down on the swollen shaft of my cock.

Forced against the back of the easy chair, I was aware of the deepened breathing heaving those tight little breasts spasmodically against my naked chest. And the sudden startling need searing through the rigid column of that imprisoned cock.

For some reason, I was abruptly convulsed by a gust of laughter. Carol snatched her head away and stared angrily into my eyes. 'Something funny?' she enquired.

'N-not really,' I choked. 'Just that old schoolboy Confucius joke: "When rape is inevitable . . . lie back and enjoy it"!'

She laughed then herself – a deep, hoarse, unrelievedly bawdy chuckle.

'Very well,' she said. 'I'm not all that sure about rape – but inevitable is certainly the word, so lie back there and let a girl get on with the work!'

With a single swift movement, she slid backward to my knees, dropped to a squatting position on the floor, and wrenched my aching thighs apart. Shuffling forward, she knelt herself, ripped open the zipper of my fly, unbuckled my belt and splayed open the front of my trousers.

An instant later, two hands were scrabbling at my loins, shirt and pants were thrust aside, and hard fingers touched my flesh. I felt the air of the apartment cool against my inflamed cock.

Less than half an instant after that, the cool air was replaced by fiery heat.

She had lowered her head to close her mouth over the spearing shaft of my stiffened tool.

Holding it in position with one hand, she tightened her lips as firmly as an elastic band and began lowering and raising her head with practised ease, sliding that oral caress up and down the throbbing staff as she sucked and thrust.

I lay back as I had been told.

I stared down the reclining length of my half-stripped body, savouring her salacious gaze as she eyed the thick, hard shaft alternately pulling out her clinging lips and then thrusting them back in again after each lewdly pumping stroke. Her tongue swirled hotly around the ultra-sensitive skin below my blood-engorged cock-head. Sharp teeth grazed agonizingly against the veined stiffness swelling the base of the tool. With her free hand, she had dragged out the hairy sac cradling my balls, softly kneading the fragile glands as she gobbled and licked.

As the tempo of her milking clasp increased and the exquisite pressure of that mouth tightened, my splayed legs involuntarily scissored with the mounting excitement, clenching and then releasing the ribs and hips of my panting mistress.

I was lost in the lustful, hot throb of the sensual universe threatening to convulse my genitals.

Carol suddenly straightened her back, releasing my cock from her slavering mouth. She sat on her heels, holding it away from my loins, stiffly upright as it speared from my sprawled frame. Sunlight slanting in through the apartment window stained the purplish, distended head, gleamed wetly on the ridged surface of the swollen skin and silvered a thread of saliva looped between her half-open mouth and the moistly quivering tool she held.

She drew in a long breath. 'It's beautiful,' she whispered. 'I love it!'

And then, in one lithe but complex movement, she rose to her feet, swung one slender leg over my half-prone body, and turned to face away from me.

She stood with both feet on the ground between my heels. Bending her knees slowly, she lowered her hips towards my aching prick. 'It's too good,' she breathed, 'to leave on its own, out in the open!'

Reaching back between her thighs, Carol seized the shaft again and guided the spearing tip towards the sandy vaginal furrow whose hairs were already moist and darkly matted.

I watched, fascinated, while the two round, creamy globes of her buttocks, splayed beneath the tight indentation of the suspender belt clamped around her waist, settled heavily on my hips.

And my cock, shining still with moisture, vanished slowly between them – first the swollen head, then the shaft, and finally the dark-thatched hairs around the base swallowed in the burning clasp of her invisible pussy.

I lay with the whole length of my tool sucked into the tunnelled flesh of her cunt.

Very deliberately, keeping the staff embedded within her hot and quivering belly, Carol began rising up and down, her weight spread evenly on her two feet, screwing my desire to screaming point as her body caressed my hard cock as smoothly, as wetly as a masturbating hand.

I don't know how long we fucked like that but finally she fell forward onto her hands and knees, pitching to the floor in front of me with the whole lean contours of her backside and the hairy furrow of her genital cleft lewdly exposed to me.

It was a riveting sight – especially remembering the quiet, well-spoken employer in the little wool two-piece who had brought me here and the activities which had immediately preceded the move.

But in such circumstances, agreeable as they are, a gentleman can hardly remain a passive watcher, a voyeur: action is called for if opportunity is not to be wasted and the partner deceived.

I levered myself into a sitting position, half rose, then fell forward onto my own hands and knees immediately behind her. On the way, somehow, I contrived to kick off my savaged trousers and underpants. The open shirt would have to wait.

Carol looked over her shoulder and smiled at me – a naughty schoolgirl grin of such lustful complicity that the hardened cock, pointing stiffly at the floor between my tense thighs, at once extended itself further still and jerked a few degrees higher up towards my belly.

The parted labia, nestled in glistening coral intimacy among the damp pubic hair furring the crack between Carol's buttocks, were also smiling a welcome. I edged forward, kneed apart her legs and aimed the head of my cock at the dark space separating those lips.

Flexing my hips, I lunged powerfully forward.

The moment she felt the velvet tip touch the quivering skin of her secret flesh, the slender blonde hunched herself backwards, impaling herself accurately on my spearing shaft.

I was again swallowed within the heated, wet-mouthed clasp of that shuddering, excited body.

I began at once treating it with the deference it deserved . . . not pounding into it with thrusts so forceful that my pelvis splatted uncomfortably against the clenched cheeks of the backside and jerked the small breasts hanging below the chest, but gently, with long, smooth strokes as silky as the caress of the inner secretions permitting them.

I pulled out to the ultimate extremity of my distended cock-head after each thrust, then fed the tool back in again, millimetre by millimetre, in a single, long mesmeric plunge that buried it to the hilt in Carol's quaking belly and startled a gasp of ecstasy from her each time the tip slid home.

I leaned over her back, feeling the ridged column of her spine react to my weight, the muscled pads of her hips clench as I reached my hands around to cup those hanging tits.

It was as I was increasing (I hope subtly) the speed and power and penetration of my strokes that I noticed Carol twist her head sideways as she panted and groaned.

Since this seemed an unnecessary and even awkward move, I turned my own head . . . and saw that a narrow, full-length wall mirror in a frame had been unhooked and laid sideways along the floor.

Leaning against the feet of a chest of drawers, this elongated looking-glass now reflected a strip of carpet – and our two naked, lewdly copulating bodies sprawled jerking above it!

Very well, I thought. So the lady really is a tramp! A voyeur herself, turned on by watching herself being fucked! Okay then, I'll give her something to watch.

Accelerating suddenly, I clenched my hands on the tight flesh of her buttocks, splaying them still further apart as the staff wedged into her belly slammed hard up into that inner flesh.

Choking out a sudden small cry under the onslaught, she collapsed face downwards after the first few lunges, shuddering on the floor – the head still twisted towards the mirror – as I fucked with increasing fury in between her widely parted thighs.

I had been slaving away there for some minutes – might as well give her value for money – and the tension in my loins was threatening to send me soaring up dangerously near the moment of truth when I decided it might be better to flip the coin over to the other side.

With a last glance at the mirror – splendid, I thought, in my nudity, because somehow the shirt too had now vanished – I withdraw and, seizing her by the hips, twisted her around and flung her down on her back with her ravished loins angled towards the glass.

This time, I leaped on her and started fucking her in earnest, hands clawed into those tight buttocks heaving her up against my pounding hips, chest grinding down the small breasts with their thuggish nipples erect, cock pistoned in and out of her flaming cunt.

Almost at once, eyes squinted down the sweating perspective of the coupled bodies mirrored in the glass, her parted legs rose up as if hauled on wires and she scissored her calves over my back. I had just enough time to reflect that the life of a missionary, after all, might have held certain compensations when the sight of my thick staff plowing into her – unless it was the reflection of my own hairy arse and balls pumping away – triggered the climax she was waiting for.

For what seemed a small eternity, she drummed her heels on the floor, mouthing out gasped obscenities as her thin frame spasmed and her head rolled wildly from side to side on the carpet.

Later, after I had dumped her in one of the chairs and pushed her knees back and up until they touched her breasts, I knelt in front of her and repeated the compliment, sucking her until she jerked into Number Two with a squeal of animal delight.

I have often noticed that thin girls, model types who one might expect, when undressed, to be nothing but muscles and bones are, in fact, astonishingly 'cushioned' when it comes to the arts of love. Whether or not it's the very tonus of those muscles, or a natural taut resilience that takes the place of pillowed flesh, quite often the tactile thrill of these slender ladies is as sensually lush, as they thrust and squirm, as the fleshiest of roly-polies.

Carol herself proved this, arching up fiercely in the steam as we fucked under a tepid shower in the bathtub before it was necessary to dress again. But it was during the *coup de grâce* awarded to me personally that I became aware of the voluptuous possibilities of even the leanest hips.

It was when I was flat on my back on the table. My cock was as tall – and as rigid – as the Eiffel Tower. She sat astride the upper part of my thighs, the base of my shaft caressed by the open, gaping lips of her welcoming cunt. And above the warm French kiss of those folds of flesh, the upper half of my quivering tool was skimmed and milked and manipulated by the wanking fingers of her two expert hands.

I choked, soaring towards oblivion, as I felt myself tossed off in a delirious, sexy dream that left every nerve end in my body concentrated in the one bursting instrument so exquisitely played on by those orchestrated hands.

The release, when it came, was volcanic.

There was a roaring in my ears. The centre of my body literally heaved itself up off the table as those magic fingers drew me to the edge . . . and over.

The labia half wrapped so hotly around the base of my prick seemed almost to suck as Carol thrust her hips towards me. A hoarse cry escaped my lips as the core of the shaft jerked galvanically, shooting a load of white-hot semen high into the air in fountained spurts.

Carol wiped a drop from her chin with the back of one hand, massaging three more sliding between her breasts into her heated skin. 'I always think' – she said with a crooked smile as the squirts died away and I collapsed against the polished wood – 'that the last one is the best. From every point of view.'

'From my point of view right now,' I croaked, 'I'd like to think that your "last one" was no more than the beginning of an indefinite series!'

If Signora Porrelli was covertly watching us during lunch

65

with the detailed attention we hoped for, she could hardly have failed to come to the conclusion that we were . . . well, intimate.

The expression on my face however was due at least in part to the fact that, under cover of the crisp white tablecloth, Carol had kicked off a shoe, stretched out a leg, and was rolling my cock against the crotch of my pants with the toes of one stockinged foot.

PART TWO

Instincts – Basic and Otherwise

Chapter Six

Weeks passed and I squired a variety of clients around, some weeks busier than others, while the balance of the family bank account rose steadily. The most regular employers included Mrs Porter (luncheons and theatre); the surgeon's widow (hospital visits, a medical conference); Carol, of course; the horse-breeding lady (point-to-points, racing, thoroughbred sales), and the Brighton antique dealer (the Chelsea Antique Fair, the V&A, auction rooms). I won't bore you with the details.

The most surprising client (excepting Carol, of course!) was the young lawyer, who seemed to welcome an escort to professional meetings because it protected her from 'sexual harassment' – which is to say bottom-pinching and more serious passes from randy old solicitors. I had no idea whether or not she had a boyfriend of her own.

Before that particular astonishment, however, I was faced with the problem which had always been on the cards – even if the pack hadn't yet been shuffled and the cards dealt.

The client 'of a certain age', that is, who eventually allowed herself to come out into the open and admit that she was less interested in lunch and the theatre than the kind of scene usually referred to as indoor sports.

The artist responsible for the scenario was the hospital matron with time on her hands following her early retirement.

She was about fifty, a smallish, brisk lady with steel-grey hair and large round spectacles. It was difficult to say what kind of figure she had, because she wore fairly loose clothes rather severely cut, but her face, though weathered a little, was animated and quite pretty in its way.

The problem presented itself when we were due to go to

a movie première for which someone had given her tickets.

It was a wet night. A log fire burned in the grate of her living room. Outside the ground-floor window of her small Croydon terrace house, rain bounced high off the streaming sidewalk and rattled on the bonnet and top of my parked convertible.

We had already eaten (shepherd's pie and a glass of Beaujolais) and she was stacking the dishes in the small kitchen when she looked over her shoulder and called: 'Goodness, it really is a filthy night, isn't it?'

'Terrible,' I agreed.

'I was just thinking . . . I know it would be very naughty of me . . . but it's an awfully long run all the way to the West End. Do you think . . . I mean would you mind awfully . . . ?'

'Would I mind what? Do you mean if we didn't go?'

'Exactly,' she said gratefully. 'You know I'd really rather not. With the weather and all – and I'm not awfully attracted to these science-fiction films anyway.'

'No problem,' I said, not knowing that this was a lie.

'Naturally I'd pay you for the whole time, as we agreed,' she said hastily. 'But would it bore you to sobs if we just . . . well, just stayed here at home for the evening?'

'Certainly not.' I was grateful enough myself. The idea of driving up to Leicester Square, finding a place to park, sitting through the movie, bringing her back to Croydon and then heading back home *again* in this downpour had not been filling me entirely with joy.

'I could make us some real coffee,' she said. 'I'm afraid there isn't any brandy but I have a bottle of whisky that's supposed to be good. I'm sorry, but—'

'You don't have to apologize,' I said. 'Look, I told you the first time – you're paying for my company, my time: how you choose to spend that time is entirely – and wholly – your business.'

She smiled. Without the spectacles it really was a pretty face. 'That's very understanding of you,' she said. 'I'll go and make the coffee.'

While she was out of the room, I noticed that the première invitations were propped up behind a silver candlestick on the mantlepiece. For some reason, I took one down and idly scanned the printed message.

The film was showing all right – but the invitations were to a première three days ago.

Oh-ho!

The ex-matron – her name was Muriel Savage – bustled back into the living room carrying a tray laden with a silver coffee pot, porcelain demitasses, sugar in a silver bowl. She placed the tray on a low table in front of the fire, drew up two armchairs, and fetched glasses and an unopened bottle from the sideboard.

I shot a swift glance at the label. Sixteen-year-old Lagavullin, the finest – and most expensive – of the Islay malts!

Well, well, I thought. It made a change from a second oh-ho.

We talked. There was a wide-screen television but she didn't offer to switch it on.

The coffee was good. The whisky burned its insidious charm through my body. I noticed that she was matching me, shot for shot. Did this mean that she was an enthusiastic drinker ... or that she was steeling herself to the point where she dared make the break?

I waited, luxuriating in the comfort and warmth, inner as well as outer.

Muriel came to the point after we had ranged through the worst parts of world news, the scandal of the current health service, the excellence of the BBC's wildlife documentaries. It was the thorny subject of unemployment that gave her the opening.

'Everyone lucky enough to have a job finds themselves faced with problems, these days,' she said. Her voice was only slightly slurred but she must have been pretty high by now; I had a pretty good buzz on myself. 'What kind of difficulties do you have in your present ... profession? Difficult clients, I imagine? People who don't know what they want – or ask too much?'

'So far I've been very fortunate,' I stalled. 'Nothing but perfect ladies!'

'You haven't ever been asked to provide . . . well, rather more than the . . . regular . . . service?'

Here it comes! I thought. Aloud, I chickened out and said: 'Er – how do you mean?'

'You're a good-looking young man,' she said. And she must have been pissed to go that far, in these circumstances, a respectable lady like her. She wasn't even blushing! 'Surely some deprived widow or spinster who has lost hope must have . . . well, made you a commercial prop— A proposition?'

'No,' I said truthfully. 'At least' – smile – 'not yet!'

She turned away, pretending to shake the coffee pot to see if there was any left inside. 'Well somebody's asking you now,' she said. And, yes, she *was* blushing, eyes above the pink cheeks shining.

I didn't know what to do. Or say. I had agreed with Diana that this kind of situation must not arise. Beryl and Carol were, after all, one-off episodes: nobody had asked me first. Here, on the other hand – there was no question about it – if I fucked her during the time she had paid for, I would be playing the whore. ('It would not, m'Lord, be an exaggeration to describe the defendant, Thomas Silver, as a male prostitute . . .') If I refused, on the other hand, with some stiff-necked, corny line about not being that sort of person, it would be a crushing blow to this nice lady's pride. And I would certanly have to refuse the fee she had been going to give me anyway.

Could I do that to her? After the Lagavullin?

Could I do anything to her – I mean like get it up and (crude thought) give her her money's worth? Was I sure enough of my libido to agree?

'Look,' I began, 'Mrs Savage—'

'*Miss* Savage.'

Oh, Christ! There was nothing like rubbing the salt in, was there? 'I'm truly sorry,' I said contritely. 'I really can't tell you—'

She misread me. 'You mean you won't?' she cut in. 'I quite understand. Why should you?'

She was crying now, back turned, shoulders shaking,

hands held to her burning face. I thought of all the lonely women in London, in the whole bloody world, who would give anything – their money, their pride, their self-respect, their reputation – to have, just once, A Man. Or maybe twice.

I thought: how can one – once the situation arises – be such a shit (such a *cad* in fact) as to humiliate a person this much?

I approached her back. I put my arms around her. I laid my face against her hot, damp cheek. 'Muriel,' I said gently. 'I am not refusing. I was apologizing for being a clumsy fool. Of course I would like . . . I should be honoured . . . that is to say I'd very much like to . . . to make love to you.'

It was beginning to be true too: with my arms wrapped around her from behind, I could feel that she had in fact very good breasts. Just in time I stopped myself thinking she *still* had.

The idea, too, that I was probably about to hop into bed with a *total* stranger – someone who hadn't actually turned me on, someone I wasn't even horny about – was beginning to excite me. There was a definite stiffness lengthening that part of me nearest her plump little bottom.

'You don't have to,' she said tearfully. 'It was just that . . . forgive me . . . I like you; I find you attractive. And, God, I want to be loved!'

'There's no question of have to,' I said. 'I want to.'

'Naturally, I should expect to . . . I mean some different scale of . . . of fees—'

'Muriel, look,' I interrupted, 'there's absolutely no question of any extra . . .'

I let the sentence die. Once money was mentioned, the situation risked becoming embarrassing. Better, I thought, to transform the relationship into a jokey one – two mates having a giggle together – while there was still time.

I spun her around and kissed the tip of her nose. 'We have a contract, a deal,' I smiled. 'Remember my sales pitch: "there are no supplements and the tariff remains invariable".' I placed my hands on her waist, just below the weight of those breasts. 'You are paying me to stay away from home until one o'clock in the morning. During this time I'm free to do whatever you want, wherever you want, right? But let me underline free. I'll accept the fee for my time because we agreed that. But there is to be absolutely no question, not the merest shade of a hint, that any of that money . . . that you are in any way *paying me* to make love to you. I'm doing that because I want to, because I think you are a very sexy lady – and because, to be honest, it excites me to hell that you care enough to ask me!'

She freed herself from my embrace. She was blushing again. 'You're very sweet,' she said softly. 'And very understanding.' She walked to the sitting-room door. 'Even if it isn't true, I appreciate the sensitivity, the elegance with which you contrive to let me keep my self respect!'

She walked out into the tiny hallway. At the foot of the short, steep flight of stairs, she turned and smiled. 'In the front room,' she said. 'Give me five minutes.'

She scampered up the stairs.

I treated myself to a final shot of the whisky before I went up. I didn't need it. The house was a two-up-and-two-down, with a bathroom built out at the back. When I emerged – thinking it would save time, awkwardness and possibly embarrassment if I left all my clothes in there – I saw that the stage had been set with considerable delicacy. There was another fire burning in the small front bedroom; heavy crimson damask curtains had been drawn; a silver tray with more whisky, tumblers, even a soda siphon was on one bedside table, an amber-shaded, low-key lamp with a silk shade on the other. The warm, intimate illumination was animated by dancing highlights lanced out by the flames leaping in the fireplace.

Muriel was lying in the wide bed with her back to the door. The corner of a flowered duvet, drawn up only to her waist, was turned down on the bedside nearest the door.

She had really handled things awfully well, I reflected, thinking of her use of the out-of-date première invitations, the second fire already burning, the sophistication implied by the choice of malt whisky. She might – presumably after

74

a lifetime of devoted work – have found herself one of the world's lonely women, but she had the guts to do something about it.

There was also – a plus point I noticed with pleasure – a certain positive assurance, a straight-forward and common-sense approach to her own preparations, despite the contrived nature of the evening as a whole.

Too many girls, once bed has been understood, appear from bathrooms, dressing rooms, studies, wherever, still for some reason wearing a bra and pants. As if they didn't know that they were going to be fucked and naked within the next minute and a quarter! But Muriel, manless though she claimed to be, was above such absurd, such hypocritical demonstrations of false modesty. Perhaps she had studied enough bodies in her hospital work not to place too high a value on their prudish concealment.

Breathing rather fast, she was nevertheless dressed in nothing more than a dab of Givenchy's *Ysatis* behind each ear.

I lifted the duvet corner and slid my own nude body into the bed.

She caught her breath as she felt the mattress subside under my weight.

I edged towards her, savouring as I swept an arm over her hips that delicious first sensual impression of a scented, naked woman – taut breasts swelling against the forearm, the curve of warm belly, wiry hair grazing the palm, and the tool hard against cool, resilient bottom cheeks.

For an instant I held the warm and eager length of her against me. And then, taking me completely by surprise, I heard a sudden exhalation of breath and she had twisted herself forcibly around to face me. Her arms crossed behind my head. The whole fleshy complex of her small. voluptuous frame plastered itself against my chest, my hips, my belly, my rigid, quivering cock. A plump thigh forced itself between my legs.

Before I had time even to react, a wet mouth was reaching up to my face and I felt Muriel's hot little tongue force itself between my lips.

That was enough to harden my tool still more, and I felt again the graze of pubic hair as she squirmed against it. I slid an arm between her waist and the mattress, clamped a hand to the small of her back. I held her tight against me as our tongues writhed in the hot cavern of our mouths.

Once you are naked in bed with a woman – or anywhere else for that matter – all previous categories of relationship are automatically annulled. Muriel Savage – *Miss* Muriel Savage – the respectable, retired spinster who happened to be a client, who happened to have orchestrated a situation which could have turned awkward, who happened to have told lies and happened to be slightly drunk . . . that Muriel Savage no longer existed. For me would never exist again.

This was my girl and I was in bed with her and we were going to fuck.

Her breath was coming in gasps that were faster still. Somewhere on the left side of her belly, a muscle tremored. The knee wedged between my thighs rose apparently of its own accord and forced up my balls, flattening the cock tighter still between us.

I was breathing hard myself. The kiss was exciting. The lady might be randy and in search of male company at the moment, but this certainly wasn't the first time she had been – shall we say close? – to a member of the opposite sex.

I took her in both hands and turned her over until she was lying on her back. Supporting myself on one elbow, I leaned over her and cupped a breast with an eager hand.

She was looking up at me with that flat, expressionless, almost vacant stare which settles on a woman's features when she can think of nothing but: What's he going to do next? Will it be right? Will I have to show him?

For myself, now that I could look at her properly, I could see even in the dim light wavering through the room that her figure, although she was small, was gorgeous. A credit in any case to her age. The breasts were full, standing well up from her prone chest, the waist pliant and smooth, the hips and belly fashioned from resilient flesh. So far as I could tell under the bedclothes the legs were pretty good too. I leaned closer and said – truthfully – 'I think you're wonderful. You turn me on. I want you like crazy!'

She smiled, the eyes misty now. Cool fingers suddenly appeared, to wrap around my tool. Her other hand rose up to touch my face, then curled around to the nape of my neck, pressing gently, drawing my head closer. We kissed again.

It was during that second kiss – the fitful light playing with a magic touch over what I could see of her bare body, the fire crackling behind us, rain pelting down outside – that I became aware of the huge reserves of energy and enthusiasm imprisoned within this enigmatic woman. She was quivering with suppressed desire from head to toe. Every available inch of muscle and tissue and flesh and vibrant skin seemed to rise from the mattress to touch me wherever and however it could. Her swelling breasts buoyed up the chest in which my heart was beating so fast. Below the soft, palpitating curve of her cool belly, those intrusive fingers stirred the wet head of my cock among the burning thatch of her pubic hair.

Between the unspoken testimonies of lustful desire communicated by our wrestling tongues, I wondered if all those lonely women I'd been thinking of harboured within them such an untapped reservoir of physical need, such a drowning tide of urgency craving relief.

If they did, I thought, the male population of the world was remarkably dumb: all those hesitant and unadventurous gentlemen – to coin a phrase – simply didn't know what they were missing!

By the time we broke apart for the second time, Muriel's breathing had become hoarse and deep. Her legs spread themselves wide and somehow my own found themselves sinking between them. The cock-head now throbbed and swelled within the scalding clasp of genital flesh. I had twisted the upper part of my body enough to paw those two delicious breasts, thrusting up their naked weight so that I could suck up the nipples one after the other, paying gentle respect to the rubbery buds and their wrinkled surrounds with tongue and teeth.

77

Muriel's curvy frame was tensed tight as a bowstring, belly sliding and hips arched off the bed as she gasped and groaned. We had projected ourselves into that storm of wrestling passion that promotes a raging need that can go only in one direction, will be satisfied with only a single goal.

There was no question here of foreplay – that fascinating, tantalizing shall-we-shan't-we alternation of advance and retreat, of seizure and caress that assumes but cannot always guarantee the high, thin shrill of desire in the nerves that urges one irresistibly towards what we used as kids, to call 'the whole way'. The desire here was so sudden and so complete that we couldn't have stopped the fierce coupling of our pulsating, supercharged bodies if we had wanted to. From my position between her shuddering legs, I made a single, decisive lunge towards Muriel's hips.

The cock-head, already throbbing between walls of warm, wet flesh, slid into her as smoothly and easily as an oiled finger into a rubber glove.

The entire length of my burning tool was swallowed, engulfed in the darkly sucking depths of my client's quivering belly.

Muriel's breath exhaled in a sobbing groan as she lifted her hips to accept the invading shaft. There was sweat between her voluptuous breasts. Ferociously, she arched up to meet each of my plundering, pistoned strokes.

It was clear that for her, at this moment anyway, the world held only one imperative: she wanted it, needed it – demanded it – in her, all of it, as hard and as high as it could get.

I did my best to oblige.

Driven by the compulsive, urgent demons of our shared lust, we rocked together into the most powerful, thrilling, beautifully balanced fuck it was possible to imagine.

My experience – although in a sense I suppose you could call it all-embracing – is of course limited. But, such as it is, it has already brought me into contact (interpret that any way you want) with the most extraordinary diversity in the matter of the female pudendum. Put another way, I am in a position to say that there's a hell of a difference between one cunt and another.

My researches have led me to establish, nevertheless, that this multiplicity of private parts can be divided, broadly speaking, into four main categories.

On my personal scoreboard these are marked as The Slit, The Pout, The Rose and The Gash. They relate, I should add, to cunts in a non-excited state.

The Slit, it seems to me, tends to suggest the little girl who has never grown up. That is to say the actual organ is virtually invisible: even the outer labia are hidden; the smooth skin at the base of the belly and the top of the thighs is interrupted simply by a gap, with only a fringe of hair to mark the site. And the sight. The effect is similar to the lips of the mouth during a repressed smile.

The pouting cunt exposes the outer labia (and sometimes a thin crescent even of the inner) as a coral-coloured wrinkle of flesh visible always as the central point, the main accent, of the pubic hair. In The Rose, the cunt is the perfect oval, the flesh less folded, the outer labia more defined still, virtually ready – it seems – to flower into its receptive mode.

The fourth category is the rarest. In this the actual aperture – if I may so unromantically term it – is much more extensive, seeming at first glance sometimes to stretch virtually from the navel to the anus! The folds – whorls in extreme cases or even vortices – are more pronounced, though less evidently *inner* flesh, and they are far less likely to be hidden by pubic hair. The structure, which in no way affects the tightness of the vaginal clasp within, is much favoured by cameramen shooting erotic movies: it gives a much more intimate view of the subject when, for instance, a girl is lying on her back with her legs apart, wanking.

Unusually, so far as Muriel was concerned, I found myself in bed, actually fucking, without having had even a glimpse of her cunt.

So far as I could tell from the messages flashed by my cock – and the fingertips now dabbling in the wet depths of her bush – it should have been a cross between a slightly exaggerated Rose and a minor Gash.

Interesting – if ever we found time to uncouple and the space for me to look!

For the moment, all our energies, all our concentration and all our desire were tuned to the intoxicating, see-saw rhythm our straining bodies had perfected, and the dizzying clasp of flesh on excited flesh.

'Oh, God! Oh, yes! Oh, *please*!' Muriel gasped once. 'Why are you so good to me?'

'Because you turn me on,' I whispered into her ear between plunges. And then, because it often excites respectable ladies in the throes of passion to hear you 'talk dirty' and use the forbidden words: 'Because you're the best fuck in the whole bloody world.'

I had to stop myself saying 'in South Croydon'. I reckoned that would be carrying the jokiness a shade too far.

I suppose it cannot in fact have been much more than ten minutes after my entrance, fifteen at the maximum, that the small bedroom with its low-key lighting and its welcoming fire was vibrating with the evidence of our shared lust: choked off gasps of breath, the accelerating creak of bedsprings, the slap of flesh on flesh, the rasp of starched linen as I flung off the duvet to allow her legs to twine around my back. But during that time the intensity of our mutual compulsion reached a high that some couples would be lucky to attain after a whole day and night of urgent exercise. The lady was certainly not – as the song says – a tramp. But, my God, the randiness, the eagerness of her physical need, had transformed her into the most compelling, the most bawdy and lewdly salacious partner it was possible to imagine.

At the end of our shared odyssey towards the infinite, it was she who lost her grip on reality first – legs scissoring, belly and breasts spasmed in the tempest of her release, wet mouth working as she screamed out her joy, And I, whose shuddering orgasm, triggered by this exhibition of female abandon, continued the longest, spewing the proof of my own sensual demands up into the tight grasp of her belly in never-ending spurts.

It was after we had recovered our breath and the crackle of the fire was again audible over the labouring of our lungs that Muriel showed a side of her nature even more jokey than my own.

Sitting up in bed with her legs splayed wide and her savaged cunt gaping red among the drenched hairs of her cunt, she reached for the bottle and splashed half a tumbler of whisky into each of the bedside glasses. 'It's just eleven-thirty,' she told me. 'Since you're obliged contractually to remain here until one, how do you think we could usefully spend the time we have left?'

'How was the movie?' Diana asked when at last I dragged myself home. It was just after two.

This was a question I had been waiting for, and I reckoned I had to box a trifle crafty. You never knew what papers she might have read, what radio or television news she might have heard. 'She made a mistake about the dates,' I said, shaking my head at the well-known tendency of retired hospital matrons to get things wrong. 'The bloody première was three days ago!'

'So what did you do?'

'Oh, we saw the movie, but it was without all the tinsel and the media and the stars.'

'Wasn't that a relief?'

'I guess so,' I acknowledged, sighing. 'But you know I'm not an enormous fan for those damned science-fiction epics – no matter how clever the special effects are.'

'Poor darling,' Diana said sympathetically. 'Into every escort's life a little rain must fall!'

'At any rate,' I said – quite truthfully – 'it was a better way to spend an evening than sitting in front of a South Croydon coal fire talking about life in *Emergency Ward 10*!'

Chapter Seven

You were going to ask me about the antique dealer? Or if you weren't, you should have been, because this – apart from Carol and the barrister of course – was really one of the most curious, and perverse, of the cases which fell outside the orbit of normal escort duties.

My ads had been running for several weeks before the lady rang, and by this time I was building up a fair-sized clientele; so it was ten days before I could find the time to go all the way to Brighton to meet her.

That could have been time – and money – lost, because I never charged transport for a first, exploratory rendez-vous. It was essential, Diana kept emphasizing, that I should steer absolutely clear of anything remotely suggesting the money-grabber.

She was a big-titted country type in her mid-thirties who wore a too-tight sweater and a mini-skirt – sort of a slutty Sloane. I would have thought she'd have men crawling all over her and I wondered what she was up to. The name on the brass plate outside the shop read Kate Fitzallan.

It was with Fitz, as she liked to be called, that one of the difficulties of the extra-mural – shall we say? – side of the escort business manifested itself at its strongest. One could not, after all, make a pass at clients off one's own bat. Not when one was being paid. One had to wait to be asked, to be propositioned oneself, even if one in fact fancied the lady like crazy. And this led to kind of an artificial situation. Because until the joint was jumping one was playing a passive rôle and what the client really wanted, in most cases, was the strong, silent, overtly masculine type – Schwarzenegger with brains or Clint Eastwood with his cock out – the kind of guy who would growl, 'Take your clothes off!' before the first Bloody Mary had been sunk.

This was not at first evident with Fitz, although she said yes, agreed to my terms, and made a date within ten minutes of my arrival. It was only during our second meeting, ten days later, that she broached the subject of her secret desires.

I say secret. They were only secret in the sense that she didn't wear a lapel badge announcing *I Want To Be Fucked*. What she actually wanted was straight out of the Freudian textbook.

She was candid enough about it, too, once the title of the piece had rolled up on screen.

On our first date, I had escorted her to London, sat silent during a conference with two valuers and the Assistant Keeper of Furniture at the Victoria and Albert Museum, shared dinner with her at the Savoy Grill, and then taken her home. Eleven hours, thank you very much, and a fair day's work, even though the second of the one hundred-mile-plus London-Brighton-London drives was in my own time.

The second rendezvous was at the Hotel Metropole. We met in the American Bar – I think it was: American Bars have fitted carpets; Lounge Bars have fitted carpets with cigarette burns. We really did drink Bloody Marys, too.

After lunch, we were supposed to meet an auctioneer from one of the big continental houses, but Fitz wanted to collect something to show him, so we called back home on the way. Her shop was in the Lanes, a warren of narrow alleys a block from the oiled blondes strewing the coarse sand of the beach. It shared the old quarter with other antiquarians, numismatologists, purveyors of bric-a-brac, print shops and dealers in stamps, cigarette cards and ancient maps. The windows were leaded, the lighting was low-key, and the atmosphere redolent of polished wood, freshly cleaned brasswork and oriental carpets. The maisonette upstairs was comfortable in the style of deep-buttoned leather, heavy velvet drapes and eighteenth-century engravings framed between exposed beams supporting the white walls. Pottery from Staffordshire,

Bristol, Chelsea and even Meissen (all of it clearly for sale) strewed shelves, glass cases, inlaid cabinets, occasional tables and the surface of a huge early Victorian sideboard, but otherwise the sitting room could have been the den of any country solicitor in Hereford, Ludlow, Lavenham or Exeter.

Fitz emerged from a surprisingly large and modern kitchen four and a quarter minutes after our arrival, carrying a butler's tray loaded with champagne cocktails: brandy, Veuve Clicquot and three drops of Angostura bitters, agitated by crystal swizzle-sticks.

She waved me to an armchair, than walked to the window and stared down at the tourists crowding The Lanes. 'I consider you to be agreeable company. Tom,' she said without preamble. 'You are intelligent and I find myself stimulated when we are together.' She took a sip from her glass. 'The trouble is, I do not find myself stimulated enough.'

Is this going to be it? I thought.

Mrs Fitz swung around and fixed me with a challenging glare.

'I want to know, at this moment, yes or no, whether you are prepared – given suitable financial encouragement – to go to bed with me?'

I almost choked on my mouthful of champagne cocktail.

I mean this kind of suggestion was always on the cards, with any client, but I hadn't expected anyone – especially Fitz – to put it quite so baldly.

This wasn't a case similar to the matron's either – a matter of sympathy (I liked to think), of doing a friend a good turn at a time of need. I was specifically being offered extra money: if I was to accept, I'd very definitely put myself in the stud-for-hire category – something that Diana, money or no money, would under no circumstances tolerate.

If she knew.

Well, Fitz certainly wasn't going to tell her. And neither was I.

There remained nevertheless, and perhaps most

importantly, the moral question as it affected myself. Could I live with myself? Could I accept Tom Silver as the kind of character I had always imagined he was, could I sustain my own image of him – randy, opportunist, sometimes tricky and deceitful but basically honourable and honest – if I allowed myself to be paid to fuck this lady?

I looked at her over the rim of my glass. At the lush red lips and the shadowed valley of her cleavage framed by the vee of her blouse. I looked at her too-short skirt and the creamy, butter-soft gleam of her half-exposed thighs. My cock was stiff already.

Just the same . . .

'Well?' Fitz whispered.

I hesitated.

She knew weakness when she saw it. 'I'll double your fee,' she said.

I rose to my feet. We needed the money. 'I'm doing it for Di,' I told myself.

I put down my glass. I closed my hands gently over her upper arms. She was solidly built. The arms were slender but the breasts were big mounds beneath the pleats of her little-girl blouse.

I tightened my grip, staring deep between the blackened lashes.

'Shall we go . . . upstairs?' I said.

The bedroom overlooked a miniature walled garden at the rear of the building. I saw a trellis of roses, geraniums in urns, hanging baskets of lobelia over a flagged walk. 'Look, I'll be as blunt as you,' I said. 'We hardly know one another. I know I like you. Period. Perhaps you could give—'

'You want a character key?' she cut in. 'I'm not going to give you a blueprint, darling. Imagination on your side is part of the deal. But I'll quote you something – an anecdote – which had a great effect on me as a girl and has remained with me as a memory ever since.' She drained her glass of champagne and put it down on a three-glass, heart-shaped dressing table. 'It was when I was fourteen years old,' she said. 'We had a house in the country. My father was a doctor. There was a full-time gardener – a big man with rather cruel lips and black hair on the backs of his hands. One hot day in the tool shed, he ripped down my gym tunic, tore open my blouse and put one of those hands up my skirt when I wasn't looking.'

She paused, staring down at the roses and lobelia.

'And . . . ?' I prompted.

'My father's footsteps frightened him off. And he never came near me again, although I was looking all the time!'

I nodded. Classic example of childhood trauma resulting in a rape complex. 'Take your clothes off,' I growled.

A swift glance from those lidded eyes, and she obediently slipped out of the pink jacket and began fumbling with the front of the pleated blouse. 'Quickly,' I said. 'I've been waiting all day: I want to see you naked!'

That was true enough. How this was going to develop was beginning to interest me.

Suddenly she was breathing fast. Her big breasts rose and fell. 'And the skirt,' I said. 'I want to see you stripped bare!'

'Yes,' she mumbled. 'Oh, yes!' With downcast eyes, she pushed the short skirt down over her hips and thighs and stepped out of it. She was wearing dark tights pulled tightly up to the waist. 'And take those off,' I grated. 'Next time I see you, you will be wearing stockings, suspenders and open-legged French knickers. I want your cunt to be immediately available.'

Mrs Fitz was nodding frenziedly, mouthing words I couldn't catch. She peeled off the tights. 'Now the blouse, and the bra if you're wearing one,' I said. 'I want those great tits out in the open; I want you to hold them up for me to see.'

This was going down rather well. Her face had crumpled. She was almost in tears. The breasts certainly were huge – pear-shaped and full. My fingers itched to heft their weight.

'Good,' I approved. 'Big tits that are bare turn me on. I'm already getting hard.'

I wasn't kidding. I was as stiff as a post as I ordered her around.

I said: 'Now get down on your knees, unbuckle my belt, and open the zip of my trousers. You are going to suck my cock.'

The breasts with their outsize brown nipples, which she had been holding up towards me as ordered, subsided under their own heavy burden as she reached for my crotch. She lowered herself to the carpet. Her breath came in a series of short, quavering gasps. The hands fumbling for the buckle of my belt, I noticed, were shaking.

I felt cool air stir the hairs of my bush as slender fingers groped inside my fly.

And, yes, there was no doubt about it: the sight of this total stranger cowering slavelike at my feet, naked and quivering at my command, in some way still obscure to me, *was* a hell of a turn-on. I could hardly wait to bury myself between her smooth thighs. However, I wasn't here to please myself. I had work to do.

Big lips closed over the head of my cock and I felt heat, pressure and a sucking wetness as she started rocking back and forth on her heels, tongue swirling on the sensitive underside each time she withdrew her mouth to plunge in again on another stroke.

She was cradling my balls with one hand, red-nailed fingers of the other clenched tight over the pubic hair at the base of my prick while she sucked and slaved.

A few minutes later – I was standing with feet spread and knees slightly bent to give her easier access – I felt the tension in my loins beginning to mount, and I reckoned it wise to distance myself at least for the moment. I couldn't afford to go off yet – I was a professional.

Disengaging myself roughly, I made no comment on the sucking – which had in fact been expert – and ordered: 'Get up off the floor and lie on that bed!'

She gave me a quick glance, a swift upward flick of the painted eyes, as she levered her lush body with its swinging breasts upright. Her lower lip was quivering, but the glance was an okay signal: it was all part of the game; the lady was enjoying herself.

She moved towards the bed, a wide Victorian affair with

a beautifully fashioned brass head and foot separated by a mauve silk eiderdown.

Feigning impatience, I strode towards her. Just before she reached the bedside, I grabbed her and lifted her nude body from the floor. 'I said *lie* on the bloody bed!' I snapped.

I flung her onto the eiderdown on her back.

She bounced on the bedsprings, big breasts quivering, a gash of pink cunt flesh among the dark fleece between her legs.

As she landed, her breath exhaled in a delighted gasp and her hands flew up to steady her breasts. Not only was the lady enjoying herself: I sensed that she was having a ball!

For Phase Two I decided to vary the tempo: remembering the gardener, I'd keep her waiting.

There was no black hair on the backs of my hands, but I'd always considered – heigh-ho, Silver! – that I stripped pretty well.

Seeing Fitz lying defenceless on that bed, the whole luscious mass of flesh at my mercy, was almost enough to make me come on the spot.

I would expose what I had little by little, I thought, allowing her to feast her eyes on the male machinery destined to subjugate and humiliate her later!

I felt a little like a stripper in a Soho club as I fingered open my shirt, unravelled my tie and shrugged out of my jacket – except that instead of a crowd of beery Covent Garden porters I was being ogled by a naked lady antique dealer spread-eagled on a bed in her own home.

Her eyes opened wide as I transferred my attention to the trousers – already unbelted and open at the crotch. I stepped out of them.

The shirt was undone, but I let it hang. There was a certain forbidden quality about male underwear, especially, I imagined, if *you* imagined you were a schoolgirl of fourteen.

Keeping my own eyes fixed on the nude figure sprawled on the bed, I reached under the shirt-tails, grasped the elasticated waistband of my underpants, and drew them slowly down to my knees. My rigid cock, freed of the restriction, sprang up and thrust the material of my shirt out in a menacing peak. Fitz uttered a small gasp and caught her lower lip between her teeth. Unblinking, those eyes vectored in lasciviously on the bulge at my loins.

Very slowly, I peeled off the shirt and let it drop to the floor.

My cock stood out from my bush, suffused a dark red, rigid as a flagstaff, the distended, purplish head quivering eight or nine inches above my hairy balls.

I still wore socks and the pants were still swathed around my knees. These traces of underwear, I felt, emphasized the male nakedness above and the spearing shaft so soon to violate the shivering lips of a female cunt and force its way up into the soft and secret belly flesh of the naked woman on the bed.

For a moment longer I remained immobile, a ravisher regarding his victim. Then I strode to the bed, somehow ridding myself of the underpants on the way, and knelt up beside her. I seized her hips, positioning her roughly in the centre of the big bed, and placed my hands flat on the inside of her thighs, forcing her trembling legs apart. I dropped down between them, allowing the weight of my marauding hips to grind against her pelvis as I reached between us for my cock. I seized the head and forced it between the warm, wet lips of an eager cunt, lunging suddenly, powerfully forward to force the whole shaft far up within the wet caress of her hotly clasping vagina. She squealed then, thrashing her hips from side to side, squirming wildly in a pretend attempt to keep me out – but in fact ecstatic as her energies only locked my hard staff further in.

I began to fuck her in earnest, battering against her apparently ravished pussy with a power and force that had her gibbering on the mattress as I thrust and withdrew.

I make no boasts, I stake no claims, I allow myself no reflections on the nature of the encounter. A question of chemistry perhaps – or simply two enthusiasts thrown together in the right place, at the right time.

The fact remains, all fantasies and rôle-playing and paid-for pleasure apart, this transformed itself – for both of us, I hope – into an absolutely super fuck.

It's difficult to explain, but all preconceived notions went out the window, our relationship was simply him-and-her.

Her skin was peach-bloom soft and resilient as a baby's. The tonus, the muscular thrust and give of her fleshy body, was as thrilling as any woman I'd ever fucked. Buoyed up on those generous breasts, supported on the lissom tenderness of an unrestricted belly, imprisoned by suddenly loving arms, I wallowed and exulted in the embrace of lustful, all-conquering flesh.

Cocooned in that bottomless swell of softness and warmth, dizzied by the sliding caress of skin surface on surface, I allowed myself – literally – to be carried away on a tide of sensual ease.

Until the clamour of thrilling nerves tensed in my loins warned once again that a few more strokes – very few, the accelerating tension flaming through my genitals signalled – would send me soaring over the edge of the sexual precipice into the abyss of joy.

Roughly, almost brutally, I withdrew and left her gasping.

'Get up on your hands and knees: I'm going to fuck you like the bitch you are,' I rasped.

Trembling, she clambered into position, darting a fearful glance over her shoulder as I seized her by the hips, knelt up behind her and dragged the milky globes of her backside towards me. I thrust my aching cock into the cunt gaping darkly between her clenched buttocks. Leaning forward over her back, I slapped her bottom hard and then began pistoning in and out of her again with redoubled speed and force.

The big breasts hanging below her chest swung to and fro each time the impact of my pelvis jolted her hips forward. I felt for the swelling mounds of flesh and caught the erect and rubbery nipples savagely between my forefingers and thumbs.

She was groaning with ecstasy now, the hoarse voice humming from crescendo to gasped crescendo each time the force of my rear assault drove the breath from her lungs.

I continued ploughing in and out of her like a crazy man. The cheeks of her arse reddened under the battering of my hips; long weals crisscrossed her hips and back where my fingers had clenched her soft flesh. Her head hung down as she squinted past breasts and belly to savour the sight of my balls slapping against her savaged cunt.

And then suddenly Fitz climaxed. There was no build-up, no warning: she simply collapsed face down with an inarticulate cry and lay spent on the mauve eiderdown, her whole soft body shuddering uncontrollably as she came in an endless series of diminishing spasms.

Trapped inside her as she fell, I think I came too, but the shared intimacy of that lewd and lustful fuck was so intense that there was really no Fitz and no me – only the delirious joy of the thundering blood and the nerves singing in the passionate dark.

Before I left, my hostess offered to double the fee as promised.

Although in a sense I reckoned I'd earned it, I refused. I told her, smiling – and truthfully – that it had been a real pleasure.

Then she showed the more sensitive side of her nature. 'Come on, honey,' she breathed. 'I'll give you a cheque for the sum you quoted, to make it right with the wife, okay? But you take the rest in cash and keep it for yourself – a secret between you and me!' And she raised a hand to touch my face, then slipped a roll of banknotes into my breast pocket.

It was on the way out that I played – in every sense – my masterstroke. We were going downstairs, Fitz, fully dressed, leading the way.

There was a half-landing before the last flight leading down to the shop, and a newel post at the angle, where the polished wood bannisters turned through a right angle.

Without any warning, hard again at the thought, I threw her forward across this, yanked the skirt up to her waist, hauled the tights to her knees, and rammed it into her again from behind.

'So how was lunch at the famous Hotel Metropole?' Diana asked when finally I had dragged myself home.

'Too much!' I replied – truthfully again – in a sated voice.

Chapter Eight

I must have led a sheltered life, because I had never met anyone like Fanny Elmore. She was, I suppose, what would once have been called a hoyden. That is to say she was bouncy, exuberant, jokey, relentlessly jolly and altogther what a previous generation would have called *unfeminine, my dear*. She was also, to compound each of the above sins, thirty-seven years old.

Fanny – what else could she have been called? – was the kind of person who would end a boring account of some girlish escapade with a giggling: 'I bet everyone thought we were absolutely *mad*!'

'My granny used to call me a tomboy,' she told me once, 'because I wore trousers when one didn't.'

I met her through the small-ads – the sportier one, naturally.

Once I had quoted the terms, she came straight to the point. She wanted me to accompany her to a movie – 'take me to the pictures,' she called it. The performance, she imagined, would be the usual three hours, but it would be an idea if we had 'a spot of chinwag' first, so she would pay in addition for a fourth. Unsuspectingly, I agreed.

We met in a vegetarian restaurant off Leicester Square – carrot juice and peanut brittle – and she tried to explain more precisely what she wanted. Precision, though, was not a quality which came naturally to her, and when – later – I discovered what she actually meant, it came as, well, a bit of a surprise.

Fanny was tall, and sturdily built. She had beefy hips, an agreeably small waist, and a shelf of breast as formidable as the prow of an eighteenth-century three-decker. She sat, I guessed, rather well on a horse. No trousers today, though:

95

she wore brogues, a heather mixture tweed skirt and jacket, and an oatmeal-coloured shirt with bone buttons. Her hair – mouse with highlights – was cut short and her features, reddened a little by wind and weather, were plain but regular. If I hadn't found out that Daddy was Lord-Lieutenant of one of the shires (an Earl too, as it happens) and the family was loaded, I'd have taken her for an unmarried schoolmistress or the boss of some charitable organization connected with the social services.

'I suppose it was really all a question of the wrong kind of school, being shut away all those years,' she said awkwardly when she was trying to explain why she was hiring a man to take her to the cinema. 'And then Switzerland of course.'

'Of course,' I echoed blankly.

'No, but I mean really,' she explained, seeing nothing but incomprehension on the Silver face, 'it was as if . . . well, actually, I kind of missed out on my youth, my adolescence, you see.'

I cleared my throat. I saw not. I thought it best, for the moment, to reserve comment.

'There was a book, once,' Fanny said, 'called *I Lost My Girlish Laughter*. Or was it a film? Well, the thing is, I never had any of that. Girlish laughter, I mean. What with Mummy's work on the Bench, and the estate and everything . . . I jolly well never got around to doing what all the other girls did in their teens.'

I nodded. Most certainly no comment here!

'Dances, I mean. Nightclubs.' She shivered pleasurably at the forbidden thought. 'The theatre, boating parties on the river, fancy-dress balls, that kind of thing.' Fanny sighed. 'So I thought to myself,' she said in a burst of confidence, 'well, now that I've got a bit of time to myself, I'll damned well fill in the gaps before it's too jolly late! I'll live my teenage life *now*!'

I nodded again. Thus the cinema. 'I think you're absolutely right,' I said.

She glanced at a gold wristwatch. 'The programme starts at four,' she said. 'Shall we go?'

The huge cinema was two hundred yards away. Engulfed within its 1930s Wurlitzer baroque, we were flashed into the Dress Circle by a uniformed usherette with a torch. It was mid-afternoon, the movie had already been running a couple of weeks, the place was half empty. 'No, no!' Fanny hissed as we started down the carpeted, steeply raked stairway. 'The back row; it must be the back now.'

'Okay,' I said to the usherette, 'we'll stay up here.' She sighed theatrically, lanced the beam of her flashlight along the row. About two hundred yards away, a couple were wrapped together. Otherwise, the crescent of upturned seats was uninhabited. We slid along to the centre and sat.

Fanny might, as she put it, have missed out on the adolescent life of her contemporaries, but she certainly knew *what* teenage girls did in her epoch. My buttocks had scarcely settled on the velour seat when her head was heavy on my shoulder. She took my nearest arm and twined it around her waist. At the same time the hand nearest me alighted on top of my thigh.

Evidently, I thought, if this was expected of me, I must join in the game. Silver the Snogger, Demon Lover of the Dress Circle!

I tightened the arm around her waist, stretching the hand up towards the jutting prow of her blouse. Despite the size, the bosom was firm and warm and resilient. Much more surprising, the taut flesh was bare against my fingertips!

Somehow, the bone buttons of the blouse had slipped through their buttonholes – and if there had been a bra, or bust-bodice as she might have called it, this had mysteriously vanished.

My breath quickened as I cradled the weight of that breast. My fingers automatically teased the rubbery bud of an erect nipple. Fanny caught her breath. The hand on my thigh clenched, groped for, and quickly found through the stuff of my trousers the long shaft of my tool. If it hadn't been hard before, it certainly was now as the invading fingers rolled and breath hissed hotly in my ear.

Christ, we were locked together in the back row of a

movie house, in as heated an embrace as any schoolkids cutting afternoon class to do some fieldwork on the facts of life!

My fly was unzipped – she was certainly adept for a sex-deprived ex-teenager! – and urgent fingers scrabbled aside undergarments to lock around the burning stem of my cock.

Expert too. The stiffened, throbbing staff was out in the open air, lewdly speared out from my loins as her fingers started skimming the outer skin tantalizingly up and down the hardened core.

I turned towards her, breathing hard, determined – you could say – to keep up my end. A wet kiss, to quote the sub-teenagers, and her tongue was forcing itself fiercely between my lips.

I brought across my free hand, with the idea of paying attention to the second bared breast, but it was seized in an iron grip and carried downwards. Groaning softly behind our wrestling tongues Fanny writhed on her seat . . . and the hand was thrust beneath a hitched-up skirt, between thick wool stockings and coolly trembling thighs. Forced in between skin and silk, my fingers brushed damp, wiry hair, grazed hot flesh and sank into the fiery maw pulsating at the base of Fanny's voracious belly.

The three rows in front of us were empty. Screened from view by the tall wooden barrier separating our seats from the semicircular promenade, cheeks hollowed and hands working, we were locked in a bout of masturbatory frenzy before the pre-credit titles rolling up on the huge screen below had got even as far as the director's name!

Three reels into the story, she was pumping my tool so hard up and down with that deliriously familiar milking action that I was scared the audience four rows ahead of us were going to turn around and shush us because the squelch of lubricated flesh was drowning the dialogue.

We were still kissing – in between gasps, coming up for air. My outer hand, the one at the end of the arm squeezed around her, was working overtime on the nipple of the nearest breast, naked and heavily trembling at my touch.

The inner one was lost in the hot, wet, hungry depths of Fanny's cunt. I explored the warmly sliding folds of flesh, mashed the clitoris, charted the complex geography of those sinewy isthmuses and peninsulas which seem differently arranged in every pussy in the world, and finally burrowed hot and deep within the ridged, muscular contractions of her tightly clasping love canal. At times (thinking of those forbidden gay movies of fist fucking), I felt as though I must be buried inside her up to the elbow! I was afraid the ticking of my watch in there would bring her off before she was good and ready.

Good she was. I do not think this was the first time she had been 'taken to the pictures'. I wondered how many hopeful Lotharios had been taken for a ride.

Fanny's whole big frame was shuddering with passionate desire. Had she ever, I reflected, actually been fucked? Or was she waiting until she was grown-up?

For a manic instant, I toyed with the thought of grabbing her hips and shifting her across to sit on my lap, skewered on my throbbing prick. But sanity – and the fear of being skewered myself in the beam of the usherette's flashlight – prevailed. In any case it was clear that my date was winding up, like a baseball pitcher for the third throw, to a monumental orgasm that was going to explode at any minute.

Any second, I thought frenziedly as the hand jerking my cock accelerated to an unbearable speed. My heart was trying to break out of my chest; my breath was stifled in my throat.

Fanny convulsed. Her entire frame shook with a series of violent spasms. Her belly contracted so fiercely that I felt I was risking a broken wrist and I was afraid for my watch. She verbalized the release with a single choked-off shout. Fortunately the babyfaced mouth of Sylvester Stallone or whoever opened at that instant to bellow a bloodcurdling battle cry, so I hoped the audience took the noise either for an excess spectator reaction from an impressionable fan or an echo of the soundtrack itself.

I wasn't in a position to spend much time on the

problem, because Fanny's practised hand had raced me to a shattering climax parallel with her own. Still grasped tight in her piston-like fingers, my tossed-off cock squirted its scalding load high into the air between us as my loins blew up. Some of the drops spurted high enough to reflect the brilliance of the light beaming from the projection room before they splashed down over the empty seat in front of me.

The movie still had fifteen minutes to run. She kept her hand wrapped around me until the titles rolled, released me for a choc-ice when the house lights went up – and homed in again, working throughout the supporting programme.

We stood on the sidewalk outside the cinema when the show was over. Theatregoers heading for an early dinner thronged Leicester Square. Traffic was stalled beneath the sodium lights. Fanny refused a drink, shook my hand heartily – if a trifle stickily – and said: 'Thanks awfully. That was really a *stunning* afternoon! I can't tell you . . . I mean, gosh, it was honestly a pleasure to meet you!' Nodding once, she smiled, turned away, and strode towards the Underground.

When she was a few paces away, she looked over her shoulder and called: 'I'll probably call you again in a few days.'

But she never did.

Chapter Nine

The barrister then? Okay, the barrister. I'd been playing the small-ad field for some weeks when she rang. Curiously, I knew her . . . or, rather, I knew of her. A drinking mate of mine, Andy Tarrant, had met her some years ago when she was fresh out of law school, articled to some legal firm with chambers in the Inner Temple. Andy was in a racket running parallel with my old stamping ground: he was a hotshot promoter and publicity wizard in the pop-record business. I recalled vaguely that he'd engineered some brief kind of *affaire* with the lady*, so I thought I'd give him a call to fill myself in and see what the score was – or had been when he was around.

But the blower was never unhitched when I rang; even his answering machine was silent. Andy's office told me he was in the US of A, pushing some Heavy Metal rock group, and would not be back for a month, so I'd have to meet M. Collett, QC, unbriefed and on my jack.

That was her name: Minerva Collett. She was rather glamorous in a quiet way. Chestnut hair arranged in neat waves, fine-drawn features and very wide brown eyes, a trim figure in good clothes. I remembered that Andy had termed her a graduate of the low-heels-and-country-walks school. But she was very intelligent, well-read, amusing and knowledgeable about movies, the theatre, sport. About as far from a musty solicitor's office as you could get!

We met at her place, a red-brick Edwardian mansion block between Gloucester Road and Earls Court – familiar territory as it happens, only a few hundred yards from Mrs Porter's square.

*See *Scandalous Liaisons*

It was a nice flat: large, airy rooms with period furniture, polished pine floors, good rugs. French windows in the living room opened onto a small balcony overlooking a railed-in square with sycamore trees.

'I think, Mr Silver,' Minerva said after we had been chatting of this and that for almost an hour, 'that you may be just the person I'm looking for.' She smiled; she had an attractive, rather deep voice. 'I'd better explain. My work is very important to me. I am fortunate to have as many briefs as I can handle. More than enough, I sometimes think, to fill the time I have available. But I also like to go out. Quite often, professionally, I *have* to go out. And on such occasions – perhaps I am old-fashioned – I prefer a male companion, an escort if you like.'

I did like. I liked very much. I was beginning to find this lady lawyer most attractive. *Watch it, Silver! Diana's Rule Number One: passes must on no account be made at clients, however alluring they may be.*

Minerva said: 'I have no wish to get married. On the other hand my workload at the moment is heavy enough to rule out any permanent . . . relationship . . . any possibility of a' – another smile – 'a boyfriend.'

She looked out of the window, frowning. Rays of morning sunlight were slanting between the branches of the sycamore trees. 'If I restrict myself, nevertheless, to playing the field, as they say, in my search for companions – well I risk being thought available or 'fast' on the one hand, and subject on the other to "sexual harassment" from priapic colleagues!'

Smile Number Three. 'That is why I answered your advertisement, Mr Silver: precisely because I am *not* looking for a man! Now I find you agreeable company, easy to be with, and we have certain tastes in common. Will you accept my offer of occasional . . . employment?'

My turn to smile. 'I should be delighted,' I said. 'Maybe I'm a little old-fashioned myself; I open doors for ladies and stand up when they come into a room!'

'I had already noticed that,' Minerva said. 'Splendid, then. Shall we say next Friday?'

102

'With pleasure.'

I had already committed my own workload over the next couple of weeks to memory, so that I didn't have to go through that servants' entrance charade of consulting a diary with wetted thumb. Stay up there in the top drawer, Diana said; you're an employee but not a skivvy!

'You may accompany me to – and alleviate my boredom at – a city luncheon given by the Lord Mayor at the Mansion House,' Minerva said.

The majority of the clients of course were Mrs Porters – widows and old ladies who liked the idea of being squired around by a younger man, perhaps to stick two fingers up at tea-party rivals, and were prepared to pay for it. I don't aim to bore you with these: it's only the one-off or raunchy minority who make a tale worth telling. I hope so, anyway.

Minerva Collett was certainly a minority. She was by far the most atractive client my ads had brought me. When I said that luncheon with her at the Mansion House would be a pleasure, I was understating the truth. And for me at any rate there wasn't shadow of boredom on the horizon.

There was nevertheless, despite a lively conversation on media hypocrisy back at her apartment afterwards, something about her that I found particularly intriguing – something quite apart from from her attractiveness, physical and mental, as a woman.

I couldn't exactly place it; there was nothing I could identify as a departure point for this impression. But I had the feeling that somewhere, somehow, despite her openness, there was a reserve, a holding back.

Of what? Don't ask me. It was no more than a hunch – and she certainly owed me no confidences in relation to her private or professional life. But the impression remained.

In short, I didn't entirely believe the reasons she had given for hiring me. At any rate, I didn't believe they were the only reasons.

On the other hand, what reasons *could* there be? A woman as intelligent and attractive as she was could get as many presentable squires as she wanted as easily as picking ripe fruit off a tree. Without shelling out fifty quid an hour too.

She had nevertheless made this point that she was not looking for a relationship with a guy. Okay, so this left my own position unchanged and as defined. Unless of course she was playing double-bluff and was using the idea that she was against relationships to mask the fact that she did want one. Perhaps with a particular individual? In other words that I was being used as a decoy? Or was this too wily a manoeuvre even for a lawyer?

It depended on whether or not she had confided in anyone that I was a paid courtier. And why.

I was going round in circles, chasing an answer that probably didn't exist to a non-existent problem!

What the hell, I thought. Relax. The money's good and the lady is fun to be with.

There was a problem, however – and a secret. And there was an answer. But I didn't find this out until our third encounter.

The second had been another lunch and the opening of an art gallery. The third was an evening affair, and it involved dinner at her apartment. She wanted, she said, an informed, intelligent opinion on a tricky case she was pleading. She would lay before me the arguments advanced by the prosecution and oppose them with the defence of her client. The idea, I suppose, was to get an objective view of the case as it might appear to a juryman before she determined her approach.

Fine. The money was still good. I'd do my best to be impartial.

Dinner was okay – not too adventurous but well presented: a salad of endive and roquette, a roast guinea-fowl, cheese, kiwis with rather an interesting ginger sauce. Malt whisky before, a good Burgundy with. The two sides of the law case came with the coffee and Calvados.

Minerva outlined the pros and cons clearly and succinctly – rather more briefly than I had anticipated. I told her that, on those facts, to a jury of people like me, the prosecution didn't have a chance of a conviction. She nodded and appeared to be pleased with that opinion.

Par for the course, so far. But there was still a lot of evening left. I mean like nine of the eighteen holes still to play.

And what if the game turned out not to be golf?

We were on the second Calvados when the answer to that was delivered to my door.

Minerva was sitting on the sofa, looking rather demure. She wore a soft, camel-coloured suede jacket over black corduroy pants and a creamy sweater too loose to outline her breasts. No make-up was visible on her face and the only jewellery she wore was a heart-shaped locket on a heavy gold chain.

It was ten minutes short of ten o'clock. Normally, in the case of a proper guest who had furnished an answer to a question as requested, it would have been time to lever oneself upright, murmur thanks for an agreeable evening, and say that, by Jove, it was almost ten! Time to toddle off home to the wife, don't you know.

But I wasn't a proper guest. I wasn't a guest at all. And I had been paid for a visit from seven-thirty to eleven-thirty.

I remained sprawled in my deep leather armchair, sipping. And waiting.

Abruptly Minerva drained her glass and set it beside her empty coffee cup on an occasional table. 'Excuse me,' she said. 'I'll be back in a moment.'

She rose to her feet and walked out into the long hallway. I heard a door close. Water ran. Another door.

Suddenly hit by the alcohol? I hoped not, although she had had been – rather surprisingly, I thought – knocking them back a bit ever since dinner was served. I had quite a buzz on myself: that agreeable, faintly dizzy feeling when you seem to be walking through the world on a sheet of glass about a foot above the floor.

Time passed. In another room, a clock chimed the hour. I poured myself another Calvados. I drank. I replaced the glass on the table. I was aware of movement. A current of air perhaps? I raised my eyes.

I almost choked, half rising to my feet as I swallowed fiery spirit.

Minerva was leaning against the wall just inside the hall doorway. She was wearing a floor-length, near-transparent extravagance in some smoky, cheap material, fastened only at the waist by a tie-belt of the same lightweight stuff.

She was stark-naked beneath it, a shadowy pubic triangle and the rosy tips of small, elegant breasts showing clearly through. Her pose, with one hip out-thrust and the burnished head thrown back, was a caricature of some 1930s Hollywood sex queen being ogled by the photographers.

Of the discreet, conventional young professional in the suede jacket who had invited me to dinner, only the locket and chain, dangled between those breasts, remained.

There was rouge on her cheeks, mascara and false lashes framed her eyes, and her mouth blazed red now with an overload of lipstick.

The mouth opened. 'You've been asked for – and given – your opinion once tonight,' she drawled. 'Now I'm asking for a second opinion. What do you think of this?'

She swept a languid hand down the length of her barely covered body.

I remained transfixed, staring wordlessly with my mouth half open.

The négligée, or whatever it was called, was ghastly. Apart from being cheap and vulgar, it was flashy in the worst sense; it was bunny-girl sex without the finesse, the strip-club come-on minus the delicacy. It was knickers and pink champagne and it was the absolute end.

I didn't know what to say – or what I was expected to say.

'It's frightful, isn't it?' Minerva said in her normal conversational voice. 'I always think this kind of rubbish looks as though it came from one of those *lingerie* – she pronounced the word with distaste – 'shops in Shaftesbury Avenue that specialize in open-crotch panties.'

I swallowed. I cleared my throat. 'Since you ask . . .' I began.

'Destroy it!' she snapped, the voice suddenly hard.

'I'm sorry . . . I beg your pardon . . . ?'

'Rip it off me. Tear it away. I want you to strip me naked and . . . and violate me. Now.'

There was I, Sex-King Silver, the Smoothie – non-plussed! Well, I mean, really . . .

'Minerva wants you to rape her, to despoil her,' she explained, switching neatly to the third person singular – to distance her conscious self from the fantasy sexpot, I supposed. 'She deserves all she gets, the filthy little slut. *Now tear this cheap trash off my back!*'

I had walked gingerly up to her. Now I reached out a tentative hand. She nodded.

Okay, I thought. You wanted it, you asked for it, if this is really what I'm being paid for – tonight anyway – this is what you're going to get!

I locked both hands over the flimsy material forming the négligée's vee neck – there were even gold sequin stars on the hems, for God's sake! – and I ripped downwards with all my strength.

The thing literally disintegrated under my attack, falling away from her body to pool at her feet as the breasts and belly and pubic area slid lewdly into view.

Over the rasp of tearing nylon, or whatever it was, her breath exhaled in a keening cry that could have been interpreted – even if it wasn't exactly a yes – into an excited affirmative.

I picked her up then, flung her over my shoulder in a fireman's lift, and strode into the long corridor.

It was one of those flats dating from the days of easy living, with four or five bedrooms. I'd thought of chucking her down on the settee in front of the occasional table, but one of the doors in the passageway – there were four on each side – was open, and I followed the signs.

A chintzy bedroom – one of the spares, perhaps – with a marble-topped commode, huge bird's-eye maple wardrobe, chest of drawers, and a divan bed with a padded, flower-covered head.

I threw her naked on this.

'Oh, God,' she whimpered, 'you must punish me for

being a dirty little slut and trying to seduce you – a married man! – with cheap, sexy clothes. Hit me, slap me, make me suffer.'

I was a little dazed. I knew of course about the rape complex and female fantasies. But this was the first time I'd been brought face to face with the syndrome in such brutal detail – and with so little warning.

I had already 'placed' Minerva in fact (such is the egotism of the macho male!). She was a 'nice' girl. None of the liberal or bohemian affectations characterizing the media and showbiz folk I normally mixed with. Probably from a reasonably well-heeled professional background, private school, good university and all that. Outwardly, she doubtless lived by a code of behaviour with 'correct' manners inherited from her parents. A type common to untold thousands, even today, of vicars' daughters, the female progeny of country squires, the apples of the rheumy eyes of retired army officers whose frigid wives propagated the heresy that sex, like the other bodily functions, was a bit nasty really, almost dirty in a way.

And with it the downright lie that nice girls 'don't behave like that'.

Except of course that they bloody well do – they're as randy, as horny, as lascivious as anyone, anywhere. Once the particular trigger that turns them on has been squeezed.

As soon as I had mastered my astonishment, all this came back to me. I realized that all those bottled-up sex urges had to be released somehow, all the inherited taboos overcome once the safety-valve blew. And at the same time – especially in a profession as proper as the law – the naughty girl, whose basic urges were as strong as anyone else's, had to be reprimanded, punished for stepping out of line, for daring to rebel.

With of course, in extreme cases, the self-justifying, subconscious get-out: *Mummy, I couldn't help it. He made me do it.*

Once she was on the bed, I ripped open my fly and jumped up beside her. Kneeing apart her ready thighs, I hauled out my cock, which was by now as stiff as a plank.

After all, forgetting the lurid scenario, this was a beautiful, very sexy woman. The legs were slender and tapered, the hips and waist pliant, the small, sharp breasts deliciously holdable.

And of course those refined and classic features, contorted now in a fury of lustful desire.

As she squirmed helplessly beneath me, I seized the cock, fell upon her, and rammed it in to her as hard as I could.

I grabbed her wrists, forced both arms up above her head, and held them there while I flexed my hips and plunged that tool savagely in and out of her wet, receptive pussy, fucking deep and dark up into her trembling belly.

The words were coming fast now, forcing their way past the breath groaning in her throat. 'Oh, Jesus; oh, God! That's right, you bastard: humiliate me . . . fuck me until I come! Make me suck your big, hard cock! Bugger me. Force it up into my backside . . .'

'Keep your foul mouth shut until I tell you to suck!' I shouted – and I released one hand to slap her face, hard.

I hit her five times – fast, stinging blows, three on the right cheek, two on the left – and she came at once. It was a dramatic orgasm too. Impaled on my spearing tool, she hurled herself from side to side on the bed, half crying, half laughing – presumably with joy – as her limbs jerked and the neat chestnut head flailed from side to side on the pillows.

While she was calming down, I withdrew and took off my own clothes. It wasn't long, though, before the wide brown eyes began to mist over anew and the scarlet lower lip to tremble.

I was back on scene, dead on cue. Her need, it seemed, had yet to be satisfied; her thirst for violation slaked.

She was propped up on one elbow, her head hung in shame. 'Sit up straight, bitch,' I growled harshly. 'And wipe that muck off your mouth: you're going to suck my prick until I come.'

'Oh, ye-e-es!' she cried in a choked scream. 'Oh, *please!*'

Nice girls fuck like crazy, I said, as long as you're familiar with the trigger that sets them off. Minerva Collett had it all sewn up in her own quiet way: she provided the trigger herself, at a time of her own choosing. And the sexual encounter it provoked was the kind that automatically furnished her with the punishment she felt she deserved for daring to press that trigger!

No need, therefore, for years of expensive analysis to sort herself psychologically out to her own satisfaction. Smart, eh? The result, maybe, of a legal training?

I stood at the bedside with a hard-on that felt as tall as Nelson's Column. I made her kneel up and take it in her mouth, and then I reached down to seize her nipples in the thumb and forefinger of each hand, tweaking them savagely as I reopened the verbal barrage.

'You will keep that in your mouth,' I rasped, 'and you will use your lips and your dirty little tongue until they have made me ejaculate. And if I feel the least grate of a tooth, the smallest discomfort on my sensitive skin, I'll beat you until you scream. Go on,' I yelled. 'Harder, deeper – you can do better than that. Suck my prick harder until you bring me off!'

Better she did do, too. And, very clearly, this wasn't the first time. On my scale, Minerva scored four out of five, very close to being rated as an expert.

Far back in her throat, she groaned – Christ, she actually *growled!* – around the pulsating staff gagging her mouth. Indicative, I thought, that my use of the term ejaculation sent her leaping almost out of her skin. And, to tell the truth, it turned me on like crazy too, to see her gulping and choking once her expertise had brought her face to face, as you might say, with the reality.

Later, I knelt on the bed myself and slapped her energetically on the bottom as I dragged her, on all fours, bodily back towards me. I leaned over, felt beneath her, and slapped the pointed breasts hanging there too before I forced my way in from behind.

'You will keep that arse raised *right up*, so that I can bugger you like the dirty tramp that you are,' I cried as she squealed and writhed.

Technically, this might have been a violation, but it could scarcely have been termed anal rape, judging from the force with which she thrust herself back against each of my strokes. Apart from which, it provoked a release even more abandoned than the first.

After that – one more surprise in an evening crammed with amazement – I was unexpectedly reduced to the ranks – the ranks of a voyeur rather than a protagonist, to be exact.

Minerva had leaped off the bed and hurried to the dressing table. From a bottom drawer, she drew out a jumbo-size vibro-massager. I didn't even realize what it was at first. It had a foot-long shaft covered in black neoprene like one of those powerful lamps they sell to motorists. But instead of the usual cone-shaped head with the round reflector, this gadget had a pivoted head equipped on various surfaces with a hard plastic knob, a suction cup, two metal electrodes and a pad of black rubber spines as spiky as a pincushion. 'Now you must watch,' she croaked. 'I'm going to humiliate *myself* – right here in front of you. I want you to see me at my most vile.'

She plugged in the vibrator and switched it on.

For an instant the bedroom was silent apart from the insistent buzz of the machine and the hoarse gasps of her breath. I stood by the window. Bars of light fanned out across the road below as a car passed the building. I heard the swish of tyres. It must have started to rain.

There was an open box of cigars on the chest of drawers. I took one, peeled off the band, and lit it. I leaned indolently against the wall, puffing smoke. This, I reckoned, should square with Minerva's image of the rogue male: a figure of authority, remote, magisterial, regarding dismissively, perhaps even contemptuously, while the naughty girl dirtied herself.

It was extraordinary. I was unable to relate this abandoned, lewdly demented creature, this lustfully perverse nympho, with the intelligent, well-bred barrister who had been my solicitous hostess such a short time – such a very short time – before.

111

Oh well, I reflected, I guess it takes all sorts! And the spiel I handed my clients did say that I was available to do 'whatever you want, wherever you want, in any way you want'.

Minerva was sprawled naked on the bed, buttocks on the edge of the mattress, heels on the floor. She was supporting herself on one elbow, chin on chest as she stared down between her erect nipples at the tufts of hair marking the base of her belly. The vibrator, held in her free hand, hovered nearby. White letters on the black casing spelled out the legend *Yamahito Techno*.

Japanese of course. Wouldn't you know!

The rubber suction cup of the machine was poised, humming, just above the crease at the top of her thigh. She lowered the cup until it touched her flesh. At once her legs twitched and she caught her breath with an audible gasp.

She guided the splatting rim of the cup slowly towards her crotch. When it found the first line of pubic hair, she moved it across to the other side, watching with a kind of dreamy fascination the tremor of flesh produced by the vibrating head.

Slowly again she traversed the chestnut thatch, sliding the cup from side to side, caressing, teasing, titillating the entire pubic zone as the mechanical shiver of the rubber approached her most intimate area. Thanks to my own vibrations, the lips of her cunt, pouting amongst the damply matted hair, had flowered open and still gaped obscenely between her thighs. At the apex of the inner labia, the swollen hood of her clitoris glowed, throbbing with an inner life of its own.

Suddenly she cried aloud; her legs jerked up, jackknifing towards her hips. The head of the vibrator had nudged the upper limit of her exposed cunt.

Her eyes were closed. Her mouth had fallen open. In a sensual daze, she slid the machine away, stroked it several times over her bush, advancing, retreating, always approaching but never again quite reaching the quivering flesh of those eager coral lips. Her hips squirmed on the bed. In a dreamlike rhythm, her pelvis rotated, buttocks rolling from side to side under the insidious advance of the electric caress.

With her free hand, she snapped abruptly into decisive movement. Fingers splayed, she spread wide the outer lips of her cunt. The vibrator head homed in on wet and glistening flesh.

This time the effect was galvanic. A violent spasm quaked the soft plane of her belly. The smooth skin shuddered and she arched momentarily up off the bed.

Swivelling the machine now, she aimed the black rubber spines downwards and moved the switch indicator to *Maximum*. The burr of the accelerating motor rose up the scale. She forced the vibrating spines hard against her clitoris.

A harsh exclamation forced itself from her throat. She began writhing snakelike from side to side, opening and closing her thighs spasmodically. Stifled animal cries echoed within her as the pulsating machine head hummed all over her pussy, swarming once more over the pubic hair, tracing the trembling margin of the outer lips, compressing the inner to mash the clitoris against her pelvic bone.

Minerva was going out of her skull. Her hips were thrashing up and down on the soaking mattress as if she was being fucked by an invisible stud. The breath snorted from her nostrils.

The raping rubber throbbed relentlessly between the folds of flesh exposed to my view. The spasms shaking her whole nude frame became more frequent, more forceful.

I heard a deep groan, another, a third . . . and then, cramming the vibrator head within her cunt in manic determination, she uttered a long-drawn-out, wailing cry, doubled up with her knees almost touching her breasts and – casting aside the machine – rolled over onto her side with her hands covering her face.

When the stifled sobs had died away, I silently approached the bed and switched the vibrator off. I laid one hand gently on her shoulder.

Lowering her hands, she twisted her head to look up at me. 'Tom Silver,' she said, 'you're a lovely man!'

And there once again – to hell with the naked body and the tear-stained face – was the quiet-voiced, respectable lawyer who'd invited me to dinner . . . how many hundred years ago?

'I think I should get you a drink,' I said.

Back in the sitting room, wearing a man's pyjamas and a blue silk kimono, she made more coffee. 'I've stopped trying to rationalize the compulsion,' she told me. 'I have accepted that the need must be a subconscious rebellion – against my background, my upbringing, my blameless image as a people's advocate. But I don't let many people into the secret!'

'I appreciate the confidence,' I said. 'Just the same, I'd like you to know that . . . I mean, as far as I'm concerned . . . Well, Christ, I had a ball too, you know!'

'You don't have to tell me,' Minerva smiled. 'I know. I'll quote you my favourite line: you can't fake lust!'

Before I left, she said: 'I'd still like to see you. But only from time to time. Part of my thing, you see, is that I play the field. I have to . . . well, to abase myself in front of *different* men. But of course I don't have many partners, and they have to be chosen – er – carefully, as you can imagine.' She put up a hand to touch my face. 'And whatever else happens between us, you'll always be one of them, Tom.'

'On the house, next time, baby,' I grinned. 'And you'd better take that hand away from my cheek, otherwise you risk being before the Bench yourself for sexual harassment!'

Chapter Ten

Eve Lorrimer came to me courtesy of Mrs Porter. Which is to say that, late one night, after we had returned from the Covent Garden Opera, Mrs P said: 'Oh, by the way, Tom – there's a young friend of mine I think you might be able to help.'

'Naturally,' I said, the eyebrows slightly raised, 'anything I can do . . .'

'Professionally, of course,' Mrs P added. 'She's a little timid about answering your advertisement herself – God knows why – so I thought the best thing to do would be simply to put the two of you in touch, and leave you to sort it out.'

'That's very kind of you,' I said. 'I'll call her of course if you'd like to give me her number.'

'Good.' Mrs Porter handed me a visiting card with figures scrawled on the back. 'It's no more than a couple of business lunches, I fancy . . . but you never know!' She favoured me with a smile that was, for her, almost arch.

I didn't think anything of that at the time, but the lady knew perfectly well that I was married, and it was only later that I recalled with hindsight the particular quality of that smile.

Eve Lorrimer was quite something. She was dark, svelte, very expensively dressed in the very latest fashion, the thoroughbred racehorse type. She was also, clearly, a very keen business type, for she had a high-powered executive job with an American agency specializing in rag-trade promotions. Naturally, therefore, we had mutual acquaintances among members of my own ex-profession. There was one other thing: she couldn't have been a day over thirty.

So what was a super-efficient bimbo like that doing with

a male-order escort living off small-ads in *Hunters And Fishers* and *The Sunday Review*?

Fortunately, tightly reined-in glamour girl though she was, Eve was the kind of person you could put the question to directly.

I put it, almost in those words, the first time we met, in her apartment – an ultra-modern, white hide, stainless-steel penthouse in a new block only a hundred yards from the American Embassy.

'Not all that complicated,' she replied. 'I have to go to a certain number of functions, half business, half social. Cocktail parties, press receptions that pretend to be private affairs, dinners occasionally with "people who matter". You know.'

'And you prefer to be accompanied . . . ?'

'There's a hell of a lot of lobbying goes on in this kind of situation,' Eve said. 'More business is transacted, often, than at official conferences. You find out who's in whose pocket, which media barons can be . . . guided towards . . . a favourable handling of one's product, which big-time buyer is going to be where when collections are shown. Even, sometimes, how to organize a parliamentary question in the house which could draw attention to a brand image. Gossip here is everything.'

'I know,' I said. 'I had a bit of that myself . . . Once.'

'Really?' she said, without following up the remark. 'Well, when business comes up at a semi-private session, it helps if an interested party – especially a woman alone – is accompanied by a fellow guest who clearly has nothing whatever to do with that business. It emphasises the social aspect; it whitewashes, as it were, any approaches I might make to others; and of course, if it could be interpreted as a relationship, it keeps off the wolves, the gropers, the plain randy, and customers with both eyes fixed firmly on the main chance.' She smiled. 'Me!'

Her voice was a definite soprano, but without the shrill quality sometimes associated with the upper end of the scale. The laugh was surprisingly deep: she must have had a range of two octaves.

'So' she said, 'since you're the kind of person I could believably be going out with . . .' She left the sentence unfinished.

'I'm flattered,' I said, because that seemed to be the comment required by this cool and self-assured and utterly composed bird-of-paradise.

'It's just good business,' Eve said.

There was lunch at Keats, in Hampstead – very good, very expensive – during which, clearly, she was finding out what opinions I had, what tastes, what literary and artistic background – and was I likely to embarrass her by trotting out unacceptable ones at the wrong time. She paid the minimum three hours but the lunch only lasted one and a half.

'Got a policy conference with J. Walter T. in Berkely Square,' she told me, signalling a taxi in Haverstock Hill. 'Never does to turn up late.'

She waved, the door slammed, the taxi sped downhill. I was left standing on the pavement feeling like a spare bed. To tell you the truth, I was a little scared of her.

The first 'function' I squired her to was a hectic party in another penthouse not far from Cunningham's Oyster Bar in Curzon Street. There were about fifty guests, mostly gossip-column stuff with gilded ladies wearing the latest and men, some of them heterosexual, with designer stubble in casual clothes that looked as if they had just been unearthed in the attic but probably cost a fortune.

Here were the chattering classes at their shrillest, nobody actually listening to anything that was said, but waiting impatiently for a gap into which they could lance their own next sally or barbed witticism. I saw women from *Harpers* and *Vogue* and *Elle*, a sprinkling of minor starlets with aggressive boobs, Canary Wharf scribblers, television people, members of the London literary mafia, the linkman from *News At Ten*, and the like. Waiters in white jackets swooped among these 'personalities' bearing trays of brimming champagne glasses, quails' eggs, petits-fours, oyster patties, you name it. The noise was deafening. I never did find out the name of our hosts or what the party was in aid of, but Eve seemed satisfied with an MP she chatted up after I had heard the words, 'Beat it, love, for three minutes,' shot from one side of her luscious mouth.

It was toward the end of the socially acceptable time to stay, not far short of eight o'clock, that I began to notice a slight – how shall I put it? – a slight *imbalance* in the behaviour of certain factions within the party. To put it more precisely, the party itself, or most of it that was left, began splitting up into factions. Instead of the normal swirling, shrieking chaos – with everyone looking over the shoulder of their vis-à-vis to see if there was anyone more interesting or influential within reach – there was a definite tendency for people to coagulate into small groups. The heads-bent, murmured confidences of cliques and claques signalling *Keep out – Private!* with their backs.

Guests were leaving. Luvvies cooed, 'Darling-*such*-fun!' and 'How-clever-of-you' (though I still couldn't identify a host or hostess). All around me I heard 'See you on Tuesday, then, at . . .' But there were now at least five separate cells, each of anything from half a dozen to ten guests, who demonstrably shared some specific interest.

Or taste? Or political opinion? Or secret?

I was intrigued. Eve had temporarily vanished again, so there was no one I could ask. I made myself as inconspicuous as possible in a window seat framed by heavy damask curtains and tried to work out some common denominator which might unite the elements of this symbiosis.

Were they all into the same subject? Could there be five or six *different* subjects producing such a phenomenon at one party, even a large one? If they were all into the same thing, on the other hand, why separate groups rather than one big one?

And the composition of these groups? Two, the largest, were composed almost entirely of super-chic women, mostly over forty, with a sprinkling of gays. A third, female only, looked more serious. In one collection, mainly male, a distinguished grey-haired fifty-year-old who could have been a lawyer or surgeon appeared to be issuing low-voiced instructions or maybe an explanation. Another, Sloane Rangers and yuppies, produced chortles and some giggling – but very low-key, practically discreet in fact. The only thing I could find in common was an atmosphere, not exactly furtive but definitely secretive. That was it: they were all behaving like some kind of plotters!

Although many guests had now left, the groups, collectively, were still a minority. Two of them – the surgeon's in one case, women in the other (but not the chic ones: more like lady librarians who hoped to win the Booker Prize) – had drifted, in a seemingly casual fashion, towards long corridors which led, to right and left, off the huge salon in which the food and drink were served.

Perfectly normal, no doubt. The apartment after all was enormous – seven bathrooms, I'd heard someone say earlier – but it appeared a trifle, well, odd, to me just the same. It was turning a brawling, par-for-the-course, state-of-the-art gossip-column function into a mystery investigation!

I wanted to take a leak anyway, so as I wasn't being talked to or at by anyone, I eased myself towards the nearest passageway – the one taken by the surgeon and the librarians. Surely, I thought, somewhere along here one of those seven havens of rest should be located?

I was right. At the far end naturally. Around a corner. But when I turned, I saw to my astonishment that neither of the groups preceding me was visible. The passage – heavy cream doors with panels picked out in gold – was empty.

Several of the doors I passed, however – there were half a dozen on each side – acted as sounding boards for low-voiced conversations on the far side.

There were three doors leading off the bathroom. God knows why I chose the wrong one after I had finished my business in there. Maybe I lost my sense of direction admiring the pale blue sunken jacuzzi or the thalassotherapy equipment coiled up in the glass shower stall.

Whatever the reason, I didn't leave by the door I came in by.

I opened it quietly . . . and found that I was staring not at the corridor but into a bedroom.

The librarians were crowded in there, perched on chairs, leaning against flock-sprayed walls, reclining on a white fur rug covering the king-size bed. I opened my mouth to excuse the intrusion – then froze. Two things stopped me dead in my tracks, peering through the partly opened door.

The first was that the women – for the most part heavily-built, studious-looking, bespectacled – were without exception naked from the waist upwards.

Secondly, they were being addressed – lectured perhaps? – by a speaker.

And the speaker was my Mrs Porter.

I was thunderstruck. *Mrs Porter?* What the *hell* was she doing here? I hadn't seen her at the party. Hardly surprising. Jet-set functions were not exactly her style. But nor was acting the school-marm in front of a crowd of half-nude librarians!

Not the stiff-necked, super-correct, conventional Evelyn Porter, my first – and still my most proper – client!

Forget the mystery, the questions. Whatever the answers, I had evidently stumbled by mistake on something very strictly private.

So how could I get out of it undiscovered?

I concentrated. Mercifully, nobody seemed to have noticed the opening door. It was only open a crack. None of the women had turned round: they were all too intent on the words of Mrs P.

Twisting millimetre by millimetre, I turned the heavy gilt door handle. I heard Mrs Porter intone: '. . . let you know that, for the moment, the temple will remain available to members on weekdays, but it will be closed on Saturdays and Sundays. Quorum sessions will continue . . .'

Noiselessly, the door homed in against its jamb.

As carefully as I had turned it before, I eased the handle back to its original position. Not the faintest click. And the door was securely closed once more. That's one of the infuriating things about life: expensive stuff, paid for by people who are loaded, tends to be better designed, better finished, and to work more efficiently than the down-market material.

But I was thankful for it that evening in Curzon Street.

I found the right door and left the luxurious bathroom. My mind was in a whirl as I headed back towards the salon. What the devil was all this talk about temples? What did the woman's reference to quorums mean? It sounded halfway between some kind of cranky religious cult and a meeting of the Parliamentary Labour Party.

So why would it be ladies only – and why for God's sake the bare tits?

I turned the corner in the passageway.

For the second time I froze. A second group of females – the chic ones this time – were coming my way. Chatting in the usual shrill, high-pitched fashion, they crowded into the first room on the left. The door closed. The voices excitedly continued. A little less shrill of course.

Were they too going to bare their breasts?

There was no bathroom beside that room, so I had no means of finding out.

Nor, for the same reason, was I able to eavesdrop on the surgeon and his friends, though the male-voice choir continued as I passed the door of their particular hideaway.

I went back to the salon. Waiters were whisking starched white cloths from the serving tables and stacking empty champagne bottles in a hamper. Despite the government warnings, the air was foetid with cigarette smoke. I rescued Eve from the writer of a weekly column on the media, and we got out of there.

Naturally – or perhaps just to make myself feel important – I said nothing of my discovery.

It was two days later that Mrs Porter phoned me herself. Nothing to do with the cocktail party, of course. She wanted me to escort her to a conference – in St. Albans, if you please! – of female journalists. Women against the exclusion of female columnists as political commentators, or something like that. Equally of course, I made no reference whatever to the party.

I arrived a little early. There can be a lot of traffic on –
and off – the M1 motorway at that time of day. It was while
I was waiting for her to get ready, and helping myself, as
ordered, to a drink, that I happened to stroll past her desk
and saw the open cheque book lying there. No doubt it
had been left there in preparation for the payment of my
account, which she always liked to settle at the beginning
of each encounter rather than at the end. Money at the
end, she confided once, underlined the commercial nature
of the rendezvous. Whereas if such embarrassing details had
already been dealt with, we could say goodbye-see-you-
soon when the date was over, just as if we were real friends.

Anyway, I suppose because I was still intrigued by the
idea of Mrs P in some kind of double role, I very rudely
picked up the cheque book and glanced at it. Not the act of
a gent, Silver; about on a par with reading somebody else's
letters, no?

I looked only at the last entry before the cheque bearing
my name that was waiting to be signed.

As in everything else, Mrs Porter was meticulous to a
fault when it came to transactions – especially in the matter,
I had noticed, of cheque counterfoils. I tend to forget, tell
myself I'll do it later, then scream blue murder because I
can remember neither who the cheque was for nor what
the sum was, so it's impossible for me to calculate how
much I have left in the account. Mrs P, on the other hand,
in immaculate copperplate handwriting, invariably noted
the date, the amount, the precise details of the transaction,
and the person or organization named on the cheque.

This counterfoil, dated two days before, noted that the
payee had been Eve Lorrimer ('A young friend I think you
might be able to help').

The sum paid was inscribed globally – but immediately
above there was a breakdown, dividing it into three separate
payments for three different transactions.

The three sums quoted corresponded exactly to Eve's
settlement with me after our first meeting, the bill she paid
for lunch at Keats in Hampstead, and what I had been paid
to escort her to the cocktail party.

A coincidence? It was possible: there were no explanations against those three sums; just the amount each time. But it would have to be a particularly long arm in this case.

Remembering the 'almost arch' smile with which Mrs Porter had suggested Eve as a client, recalling especially that extraordinary scene I had witnessed unseen from the bathroom, it seemed to me highly probable that Mrs Porter was *paying* Eve Lorrimer – or at any rate reimbursing her – to become a client of mine!

Why? Well, *that* would be a question that demanded a pretty good answer!

For the moment it looked suspiciously like Women Against Thomas Silver.

PART THREE

The Web Tangles

Chapter Eleven

They say life goes in circles. The seventeenth-century Italian historian Giambattista Vico was convinced that civilization itself went in circles – religious, heroic and humanist eras endlessly repeated, in that order. Ask James Joyce about that.

At a certain moment in my own escort saga I started to wonder if the grandiloquence of this theory could be sufficiently banalized as to apply to the personal civilization of one individual, to whit, Silver, T.

I mean, forgetting the humdrum Mrs Porters and the others who really did want just an escort, just look at the extra-marital adventures I'd lived through since the small-ads first appeared. Oriental, never-twice-with-the-same-guy Beryl and Nympho Carol certainly made a religion out of sex – one way or the other! Muriel and Mrs Fitz, women of a certain age who wanted a man in their beds and had the guts to do something positive about it, certainly qualified as heroic. And, to round off the litany, Fanny (who wanted to go back to her childhood) and Minerva (who wished to escape hers) surely fitted into the human category?

The reflection, and the possibility of some cyclic phenomenon controlling my own destiny, was prompted by the unexpected appearance at my place one morning of Secretary Sally.

She, after all, had at least been present at the start of the small-ad era – in the kneehole of my desk the day I was fired.

Did her re-entry into my life cycle pre-suppose the apparition in the handset of my phone of another Beryl, another Carol?

What the hell – life's full of surprises, isn't it? Come to think of it, how could I ever have used the word humdrum to describe a woman giving a lecture about temples to a bedroom full of half-naked librarians?

More about that – and the hiring of Eve Lorrimer – later.

Sally was looking good. Short skirt, tight jumper, white boots and just the right amount of lipstick to make the lower lip glisten.

She manifested herself suddenly in the doorway of my study. I was sitting at my desk, happily writing cheques to pay bills (a new experience for me). I hadn't heard anyone knock and the bell had not rung, but the front door was unlocked: Diana had gone shopping.

'Sally!' I exclaimed. 'What a surprise – what a nice surprise. What can I do for you?'

'I've been fired,' she announced.

'Good God!' I blurted out. 'So the wheel does turn full circle?'

'How's that again, Tom?'

'Nothing,' I said. 'Just a thought.'

'I've come to ask a favour,' Sally said.

'If it's a question of loot, love,' I began, 'I'm sorry but—'

'It isn't. I wouldn't do that to you, fellow-firee! I think I've probably landed another job, a better one, but I need a hotshot letter of recommendation, glowing to the point of incandescence, to clinch the deal.'

'Couldn't Irwin do that for you? Why were you sacked? Redundancy?'

She looked out of the window. It was raining. 'N-not exactly,' she said.

I grinned. 'You were caught at the wrong time, at the wrong desk – or under it. Is that it?'

'Something like that,' Sally said.

'Well of course I'll do what I can,' I promised. 'But I'm not sure it'll carry much weight. After all, from a personnel manager's p.o.v. I'm jobless myself.'

'I was your secretary too. You wouldn't be lying if you said I did a good job . . .'

'I certainly wouldn't! A desk job too!'

'. . . and in any case I've brought a sheet of Rogers Agency notepaper. The new job's nothing to do with the advertising business – thank God! – and there isn't a chance they'll know you're no longer there.'

'That's my girl!' I said.

I wrote a pretty sizzling recommendation – but not so extravagant that a PM would leap to his or her phone and call Rogers to ask was she *really* that marvellous?

We were desperately sorry to lose her for personal reasons, I said (she had told me that the new job was nearer where she lived). She had been with the company for X years and never failed to give complete satisfaction (that would be worth a smile to any man who knew Sally). Indeed, through her loyalty and sense of initiative she had on many occasions proved a godsend in the case of an emergency when one of the senior partners had been temporarily absent.

'I'm not going to read it through,' I said, handing her the typed and signed sheet. 'There's a risk I might believe what I say and offer you a job myself!'

'Not bloody likely,' Sally said. 'We'd never get the work done!' She folded the paper, slipped it into an addressed envelope, and stowed that in her handbag. 'Still, it's decent of you, Tom, and thanks a lot . . . I tell you what!' Suddenly those experienced lips opened in a huge smile. 'Why don't I say thank you in a practical way? A reward for services rendered – by rendering a different kind of service?'

I blanched. She was unbuckling the belt holding up the short skirt.

'Sally!' I cried. 'It's sweet of you, but I can't . . . not here . . . I mean, Christ, Diana will be back at any moment and—'

'Not a chance,' Sally said calmly. 'She's at the hairdresser's. I saw her go in as I walked up the High Street. She won't be back for at least an hour.'

'Sweetie, we *mustn't* . . . !'

The skirt and belt dropped to the floor. No panties, of course. Par for the course in fact.

I swallowed. 'Sally . . .' I began again, despairingly.

She had pushed aside the word processor and planted her neat little bottom in the space this provided. She hitched the high heels of the white boots over the edge of the desk and wrapped her arms around her bare knees to keep them close up near her chest.

I stared aghast – I think that's the word – at the image replacing my machine.

Beyond my chair, immediately above the kneehole, the boots splayed wide, the backs of two thighs jackknifed up, the swell of two buttocks flattened against the leather desk top – and between them, obscenely exposed in this non-sexual situation, Sally's pubis and bush and cunt.

And talking of cunts – who wasn't right then? – Sally was a pouter. She was showing me everything she'd got. And she had plenty. The private view was entrancing, but I wished to hell the exhibition had opened later. Or on another day, in another country. With a different invitation list.

I stared helplessly at the vision ornamenting my desk. I knew Sally, I knew what turned her on: this was one hundred percent her scene. The risk of discovery was half the fun.

She was in fact already turned on: between the swollen, fleshy folds of her outer labia, just below the hood sheathing her clitoris, a pearl of moisture glistened within the inner lips.

She was staring me full in the face. The compressed buttocks squirmed from side to side. 'Come on, Tom,' she urged. 'It's your turn after all. How many times have I been kneeling under your desk giving you head? Here's a chance for me to turn the tables and have you on your knees underneath me, showing the world what *your* lips and tongue can do!'

The flesh at the corners of her mischievous eyes crinkled. 'For old times suck,' she coaxed.

God knows why, or how, but I was down on the floor with my face only inches from that eager pussy, the chair rolled aside and the breath beginning to quicken in my throat.

Sally was like that. Persuasive, whatever the odds.

Or could it have been my subconscious – or my con-science? – screaming: For Pete's sake, man, do something! If it's inevitable, get it over with fast . . .

'You don't even need to unzip your fly,' Sally encouraged. 'You can leap to your feet, brush the back of your hand over your mouth and say: "Darling, what a surprise! How nice to see you back from the hairdresser's so soon!" '

'Bitch,' I grated. 'Sexy little cow.' But my lips, pursed to pronounce the 'w' of cow, were already pouting still further, poised to close over those other pouting lips so invitingly, so moistly near.

Sally laughed. And suddenly caught her breath as my mouth closed over the folds of flesh gashing the blonde vee thatching her loins. She uttered a small cry, feeling my tongue thrust apart the sliding pads of that secret entrance, lashing the clenched orifice wide, wide to let the raping tip home on the palpitating, sinewy button of her unsheathed clitoris. Her backside gyrated among the bills and envelopes on my desk, offering the salty gap between her thighs more freely still to my invading mouth.

My pulses raced. Could it be that the fear of Diana surprising us – sucking off some little tramp in our own fucking *house*, goddammit! – was acting as an extra spur to me too?

My hands came up, one on either side of Sally's wet cunt, splaying the lips still wider apart but at the same time cradling the cunt as a whole, shaping it into a lustfully gaping oval, hotly ready to receive my spearing tongue. Sally squealed, tensing the muscles of her belly as the tip burrowed deep in the throbbing tunnel of her vagina.

She unwound the arms from around her knees, allowing them to fall apart and open her loins more lewdly still to my lustful, slavering, slobbering approach. Her hands flew down between her thighs to grab my head and force my face even more savagely into her quivering cunt.

I nibbled and licked and sucked and tunnelled and explored the dark mystery of her inner belly. Sally whooped and groaned above me, sliding her skewered pelvis to and fro across the polished surface of the desk. I was a mad magician, a sorcerer casting spells without a magic wand.

The wand itself, trapped at the top of my left trouser leg, was rigid and hard as iron. For some insane reason, I remembered a favourite line of an American friend, extolling the cunt of his wife. 'When I see that pussy,' he said, 'man, I just want to dive in there and beat my way upstream like a trout!' Abruptly I was seized by a compulsion. By God, I knew what he meant! The hell with cunnilingus: my cock was screaming for a fuck!

The hell with closed zips too. I released her cunt, freed my slaving lips and tongue, and rose to my feet like a rocketing pheasant, scrabbling for the tag at the top of my fly.

Downstairs, the front door slammed.

I stood transfixed, staring at the obscenely exposed figure on my desk. 'Jesus!' I hissed. 'Diana! What the *fuck* are we going to do?'

'Relax, sweetie,' Sally whispered calmly. 'Hurry down to the hall and stall her there.' She slid off the desk and picked up her belt, skirt and handbag. 'You've got a side door, haven't you, beyond the kitchen? Good. I'll creep downstairs and let myself out that way while you coo sweet nothings and help with the shopping bags.'

At the door, she turned and grinned. 'See you,' she said. 'And at least you've seen me!'

I ran to the landing. 'Darling, what a surprise,' I croaked, leaning over the bannisters. 'How nice to see you back from the hairdresser so soon . . .'

'Bloody man had overbooked,' Diana said. 'I had to put off the appointment until Friday. Come and help me with all this stuff, would you?'

Later – we were having lunch – she said casually: 'Had a visitor this morning, did you?'

'N-no,' I stammered, feeling the ants already running up my spine. 'Why do you ask?'

'There's a woman's glove on the hall table,' she said. 'A white glove. Not one of mine.'

I shook my head dumbly, shrugged. My mouth was dry.

'Must have been some friend who called by, heard you were working, and decided not to disturb you,' Diana said.

Later that afternoon I went out to a call box and phoned Sally at home. 'You idiot,' I fumed. 'You could have ruined bloody everything! You left a white glove on my hall table.'

'Glove?' Sally echoed. 'What are you talking about? What glove? I haven't worn gloves since I left school!'

So somebody *had* come secretly into the house. And seen us together? And then sloped off?

Interesting.

Especially if there was going to be some kind of follow-up. From someone.

That would depend on whether or not it was someone who wished to make trouble.

What, astonishingly enough, was even more interesting – to me at any rate – was that when I came home I entered by the side door . . . and it was I who caught Diana in flagrante. In a manner of speaking, that is.

She was on the phone. 'You're a fool,' I heard her say angrily. 'I *told* you never to come here. Never. I suppose you realized Tom was in, and ran away. But, little stupid, you had to go and leave one of your gloves in the hall! Of course, I had no idea you'd be indiscreet enough to come. I'd no idea the glove was yours. And I had to fake it like crazy in case Tom—'

And it was then that she heard me coming and put down the phone.

The side door, then, had been connected, on the same day, with two separate . . . what? Infidelities? Infelicities anyway.

Maybe we should keep it locked.

Chapter Twelve

So there we were, Diana and I, lying down to watch this video on the bedroom set, each of us with a drink in one hand.

I was on Scotch; gin and tonic for the wife.

Our 'free' hands, as it happens, were occupied too – hers wrapped in a friendly way around my tool, mine cupped over her silky crotch – because the video was an erotic one.

That's what it said on the cassette anyway, though I'm not sure this might not have been contravening the law governing description of a product. Oxford define erotic as, 'of or causing sexual love, esp. tending to arouse sexual desire or excitement'.

The object of items sold under this label has of course nothing whatever to do with sexual love: they are designed to stimulate lust. A truer description would therefore be obscene ('offensively indecent, esp. by offending accepted sexual morality'), but I don't think manufacturers, even today, would dare market anything openly described in this way – even in Germany, where the tape was made.

Okay, so my wife and I were propped up on pillows in our bedroom, watching a hard-porn movie. We didn't need to have our love aroused, sexually or otherwise: we were lucky enough to have that already. We were watching the tape, lent to us by a friend of Diana's, because it was reputed to be 'super-hard' and the friend wanted to know what we thought of it. Or so she said.

I wasn't all that keen at first. There had been Carol at lunchtime (Ouf!) and a boring post-modern play with the surgeon's widow in the earlier part of the evening. But Diana had persisted. 'Oh, come on, darling,' she coaxed. 'Just once. Just to please Linda.' She grinned. 'Just for fun!'

And, since I couldn't explain that, apart from being bushed mentally by the fringe theatre, I was also double-bushed physically because of Carol, I had finally agreed.

After all, I didn't *have* to look at the bloody screen; I could always look at Di.

In fact the film – it was called *Fountains Of Lust* believe it or not – was at least interesting, if only because of the quantity, as well as the quality, of the fucking experienced by the individuals involved!

I mean, Christ, I could see at once that Carol was just a *beginner* when it came to lust . . .

We were looking at a normal room, normally furnished, with here and there half a dozen characters, three of each sex. Two of the females had been having it off together and were now somewhere in the background, still sucking and stroking away. It was the third girl who was, well, quite extraordinary. Not so much because of what she did as what was done to – and with – her.

She was very beautiful, not more than twenty, we thought. A slender brunette with super legs, an exquisite little waist and perfectly shaped, resilient, full-ish but not especially large breasts. She was really *pretty* too, with angelic features and the kind of smile most guys hope to see over a candle-lit restaurant dinner table.

Come to think of it, as an extra bonus, she had a pretty good arse on her as well.

Real pin-up material, and not what you expect to see in a porn context.

So anyway . . .

The movie director wasn't going to bother with any time-wasting crap about undressing or foreplay, not even behind the titles. Dammit, the thing was about lust, wasn't it?

So there's this sensational chick, face down on the floor. Naked of course, but not flat out: she's supported on her knees and elbows, so that her head and shoulders are raised and her backside is in the air, leaving the belly and breasts a few inches above the carpet.

Right. Well, immediately in front of her there's an armchair. And in the armchair there's a belly – male, nude – and a pair of hairy legs, spread wide with heels on the floor.

At the base of the belly there's a dense, dark thatch – and from this there spears a very large, very thick, darkly throbbing cock. The girl's tender lips, of course, are closed over the veined and rigid shaft of this.

Behind her, between her spread thighs, there is the kneeling lower half of a third figure. Also naked, also hairy, also male.

Can't see much of his cock because – even with his two hands on her buttocks, splaying them wide apart – the shaft is buried between the delicious cheeks of that arse.

I describe that threesome as though it was a tableau, a movie still or a painting even. But that's just to put you in the picture, as it were.

In reality, it was all movement, every element of each character, dizzy with movement – a balanced, visually smooth, action and reaction of contoured flesh masses in perfect reciprocation. Each of them imposed his or her personal rhythm, but the trio, viewed objectively, worked immaculately as a single, complex but individual unit.

From time to time the brunette freed one hand, raising it to grasp the stem of the hard staff gagging her mouth while she withdrew far enough to nibble the extremity of the glans, lick the sensitive underside or swirl her tongue around the engorged and purple head. But for the most part she concentrated on a dreamy, near mechanical piston-slide up and down the oiled shaft – the dark head with its neatly waved hair bobbing compulsively as cheeks hollowed and lips worked their lazily slaving routine.

From time to time, tilting back her head, she raised her eyes to shoot a swift glance up (and out of shot) at the stud she was sucking, flesh crinkling at the corners of what must have been a conspiratorial smile. The man himself moved little, tensing the muscles of his belly, occasionally shifting his buttocks to deepen his penetration of that delicate mouth.

The guy behind, on the other hand, was all action. He was slamming his inflamed prick into her as hard and as fast he could go, hips smacking against her bottom with a forceful impact that jerked her forward on her knees with every plunging stroke.

At first I couldn't be sure whether or not he was sodomizing the girl, but after a few minutes that was no longer a mystery. Diana grabbed my arm. 'Look!' she breathed. 'You can see – each time he draws back for the longer, harder stroke!' And, yes, we could see: as the cock withdrew, just beyond the quivering curve of the nearer buttock, the swollen lip of a hairless cunt was pulled out into sight – to be driven back in as the cock lunged forward on the following powerful stroke.

So that was clear: it was super-energetic, but it was no more than a straight fuck, even if it was from a rear entry. There's nothing kinky about Gordon, my dear!

What was especially impressive about this three-dimensional perpetual-motion machine was its effect – from the mechanical, purely physical point of view – on the girl.

On her actual body that is, not in any evident psychological or emotional fashion.

The force, the impetus of the long, hard thrusts fucking into her from behind – together with the reverse movements, at the other extremity, of her cock-sucking head – were enough to shudder and shake the central part of her into a heaving, compulsive motion that adopted a violent, almost dancing life of its own, quite apart from the actions of the two men skewering her cruelly from in front and behind.

The shock of each ferocious thrust – the pelvis splatting against her backside, the penis tunnelled far up inside her violated belly – was enough to jolt her forward on her knees, hinge the hips forward in a momentary spasm, and slap into involuntary movement the flesh beneath. The soft weight of the impaled belly shot forward towards the hanging tits, the breasts themselves flapped forward below her labouring chest, jerked their swelling mass on and then relaxed to hang ready for next battering assault. On and on and on; stroke after relentless stroke.

Linda was right: it really was an extraordinary sight. Those three, as the Duke Ellington song has it, were rockin' in rhythm!

Most extraordinary of all, though, at least to me, was the unbelievable extent of this scene. I mean what performers! Each of the men was in constant and thrilling contact with excited female flesh; the brunette was being remorselessly, forcefully banged, yet neither guy had come and she showed no signs whatever of discomfort or fatigue, despite the fact that this had been going on continuously for well over ten minutes. And this was no faked up montage, shot in many different takes then cobbled together in a cutting room. This was a single shot and the camera hadn't moved. What we were watching – the girl uncomplainingly, perhaps enjoyably, shaken and convulsed, each man in his own way tense as a drawn bowstring – was reality. And it had been going on, exactly like that, with no interruption and no variation of pace, for all that time.

It may not sound much, well over ten minutes. But you should have seen them . . . and gauged the energy each was dispensing, in one way or another. I mean like bravo, bravo!

A third man joined the guy in the armchair. Bare as the others, he half stood, one knee lodged on the seat of the chair, with a hard, stiff cock as thick as the others jutting from his hairy loins to wave immediately in front of the girl's intent face.

Without hesitation, without pausing for an instant in her rhythmic head and shoulders oscillation or her expert handling of the sitting man's tool, she simply raised a hand again to coax the intruding penis nearer still to the one she was so avidly sucking. Jolted spasmodically still by the power of the thrusts slamming into her from behind, she began swivelling her head sideways in time with the triple rhythm the three of them had established, incorporating the extra cock in her matchless expertise by a swift suck, a double flick of the tongue prick to prick, an occasional entry of the new shaft into her mouth as her face turned that way.

You may have noticed: I said the interloper half stood; I

mentioned only the lower half of the original pair; I said that the brunette smiled up at the first man out of shot.

This was because we never saw the upper half of these gentlemen. All three of the girls – the skewered brunette and the two blonde lesbians still busy in the background – were in full view all the time, all recognizable, all with their pretty faces in shot. The blondes couldn't have been more than five years older than the girl on the floor. But the faces of the men were never seen at all. The camera never travelled above their waists, we never had a hint of the sort of guys they were.

Even in the titles I had noticed that the three girls were named, pseudonymously or not I had no idea. But their partners were billed simply as The Three Cocks.

If that sounds like a variety turn, they were certainly that. Maybe, I thought, the German male is more timid, more solicitous of his privacy than his glorious sisters!

I missed the actual changeover because I had got up to refresh our drinks, but at some point before the quarter-hour sounded, our brunette was joined in her charitable work by one of the two background blondes. The screen now showed all three of the men – or at any rate the nether fifty percent of them – in an upright position. They were standing in a straight line, with military precision, in front of the armchair. Each of them was standing too, in the Victorian sense, so far as his equipment was concerned, and the military theme was continued in that, cockwise, it was tallest on the left, thickest on the right.

Before these splendid examples of masculine rigidity, the two naked girls, the blonde and the brunette, kneeled upright with hands and mouths at the ready. The second lesbian, who was wearing thigh boots and a black leather bra, stood nearby, apparently giving instructions – or maybe even advice – to her fellow females.

If it was advice, it would have to have been the result of sophisticated scientific evaluation and analysis of available data.

For we now had three cockstands but only two girls.

Yet it seemed to me that each of those hard and stiffened

tools received precisely the same amount of nibbling, sucking, licking and manual stimulation, for exactly the same amount of time – and at the same time moreover – as the other two.

I was trying to work out mathematically how two mouths, two tongues, four hands and two pairs of lips were physically able to achieve this desirable result when Diana and I were suddenly provided with visual evidence why the video had been titled *Fountains Of Lust*.

The three Herrs didn't actually come at once, not literally. But the effect was almost as if they had – and they certainly, thanks to the matchless expertise of those girls, came in the same reel.

It's not often that you see male ejaculation in commercial videos – never in English ones – but I had noticed in my limited experience of porn movies and tapes that the manner of this joyful phenomenon was almost as varied as the female pudenda provoking it.

Describe a male orgasm, or read a description of one, and the elements of the narrative, as it were, invariably – and inevitably – have a sameness about them. Heightened tension, an accelerating surge of emotion, a sense of being irresistibly swept onwards or outwards . . . and then release epitomised by the rhythmic jerking of the penis which spurts/shoots/squirts the cargo of semen towards its goal (hopefully a female cell anxious to be impregnated). The image is not unlike a series of slow-motion bullets shot from a gun.

According to the evidence on film and tape, however, this is a ludicrous over-simplification.

I quote film and tape as the only available evidence because, after all, those of us not on the wife-swap roundabout very rarely see – in most cases, I imagine, never see – any ejaculation but their own.

My examples of course are untypical in so far as the act, obviously, has been preceded by a withdrawal or is the result of masturbation, auto or assisted. It is reasonable to suppose, nevertheless, that similar parameters apply when it occurs within the female form.

141

Even the inarticulate cries, or roars of joy, or streams of obscenity which accompany the orgasm can precede it, accompany it, or produce themselves after it. Their intensity and volume vary enormously. By no means all the cocks shoot off in the rigid position and go limp afterwards: in some cases there is an appreciable pause, and when the semen finally appears, rather than being propelled skywards it seems almost to fall out of the cock-head and spill down the sides of the deflating shaft. In others the separate drops, like Westminster Bridge on the third of September in 1802, can be seen all bright and glittering in the smokeless air.

It may have been just the lighting in the room. It could on the other hand have been cunning and deliberate work on the part of the film crew. But in any case the two kneeling girls were literally douched with silver showers as their men (or, at any rate, to keep to the billing, their cocks) erupted one after the other in spasms, jerks, penile contortions and straight shots. Between them, you see, just to make me a liar, they contrived to embrace all of the categories I cite above! Isn't that just like life?

I can't be precise about the vocal performances. This is partly because they were in German, a language with which I am not familiar, partly through poor sound quality, but mainly because of the background music. I haven't mentioned this before, but it was hysterical. The soundtrack, throughout this raunchy, erotic (and/or obscene) group-sex saga was a pretty, tinkly Mozart piano sonata – the one called 'Turkish Patrol' – repeated endlessly, time after time, with no let-up or variation whatsoever. As the video ran for an hour and a half – and the sonata for a minute and a half – the total effect was, shall we say, a trifle repetitive. What started off by being an amusing anachronism, a stupid choice of highly unsuitable music, rapidly became monotonous, hysterical as I said, and finally almost hallucinatory. God knows what prompted the choice. Perhaps they were working on an ultra-tight budget and could only afford one record. At all events it finally got to Diana and I, and started us off giggling. We imagined

142

that there was in fact a live pianist – an elderly Viennese with long white hair – slaving away at an old upright somewhere at the back of the set. And every time, thankfully, he arrived at the last chord, and was reaching exhausted for a foaming tankard of beer, the director got stroppy and signalled: 'Play! Play! For God's sake, we must have music here!' And the poor guy had to start the same bloody piece for the Nth time. Immediately. Time after time. On and on and on . . .

We became helpless with laughter. We could see the ancient musician, probably fished out of a second-rate piano bar or persuaded to leave an impecunious retirement, more clearly than the energetic performers on screen.

We scarcely watched the development of the two-girl-three-cock drama.

It certainly ended with the brunette on her back on the floor. Once again she was supported on her elbows – maybe her knees were getting bruised – and the back of her head resting on the low seat of the armchair.

The knees, of course – it occurred to us in our light-hearted mood – might have become fixed through over-use in the kneeling position, because her legs, spread wide, were still drawn up.

Between them, the sucked man who had originally been in the armchair was alternately shafting her with long, deliberate strokes and then dropping to his own knees to pay tribute (as if she needed it!) to her plundered cunt with his lips and tongue.

The man who had been banging her with such force was now in the chair – kneeling (it was becoming an obsession with this director), with his pelvis pushed forward so that the long, hard, slickly glistening stem of his cock was poised above the brunette's open and eager mouth.

The rhythm was completely different now. It takes, after all, all sorts.

The tempo of the fucking man – when he was fucking – was easy, thoughtful, practically contemplative as he fed in the stiffened length, the entire up-to-the-hilt shaft of his inflamed cock, drew slowly out, out . . . and then, with as measured a stroke, thrust it powerfully in again.

The same near-studious approach characterized his oral attention to the girl's genitals. At times the head would be partly raised, as if ruminating; subsequently it would plunge downward once more, only for the snuffling, tunnelled, squelching progress of lips and tongue to be interrupted a further time for yet more savouring and analysis. In his dreamlike and thoughtful appreciation of the girl's qualities, the fellow reminded me of an expert wine taster, deciding professionally whether this year's vintage was superb enough to qualify for the Gold Medal in the annual oenological fair in Beaune.

The girl's breasts nevertheless – despite this cautious assault and partly because of her own efforts to suck the cock speared down towards her mouth – were still being jolted up and down on her heaving chest. And this made things difficult for the naked blonde, who was (don't tell me!) kneeling beside her companion's prone body, trying to keep at least one of the mobile nipples between her teeth.

The dancer Eartha Kitt, who subsequently gained worldwide fame as a singer of slightly risqué songs, once told a newspaper columnist: 'Of course sex is a joke. It's always a joke except to those actually in bed.'

Chortling at the hard-working performers who made this video, Diana and I were perhaps proving her right. But she had prefaced her remark with the words: 'The so-called civilized, the sophisticates, are rebelling against their instincts all the time.'

So where did that leave us that night, Miss Kitt? We were laughing . . . but we were in bed!

Well . . . it was comfortable; it was friendly. It was only after the two gentlemen had come again that the status quo changed. And we still hadn't seen their faces – only the back of the sucking one's head. The third cock, with its owner, had meanwhile vanished. We hadn't noticed him go – only seen him come, the first time.

Anyway, the blonde girl was to go now, summoned away by her mistress with the leather bra. I was going to

144

switch the set off, but Diana stopped me.

'Oh, leave it, darling,' she said, gesturing towards the screen. 'Do look.'

I looked. The blonde had been followed by the camera and crew. We were now witnessing the start of what was clearly going to be a torrid lesbian scene. The mistress had removed her bra.

I dare not tell you what position the hetero blonde was in . . . but her face was very near the other girl's loins, and her hands were already busy about the sinuously folded outer lips of her prominent cunt, probing, stroking, prying apart to expose the surprisingly red bud of a clitoris.

'I want to watch,' Diana said. 'I always wondered exactly what they did – the dykes, I mean.'

'You watch,' I said. 'I'm going to do.'

Because – don't get me wrong: I'm not saying the video had turned me on, not salacious Silver, the civilized sophisticate. But I was in a sense rebelling against my instincts, Miss Kitt.

It had occurred to me, you see: why waste more time goggling at a crowd of people I didn't know, sucking each other off in two dimensions, when I had a real mouth here, and a real cunt beside me, and I could do it more enjoyably in three? Dimensions, I mean.

And without that *fucking* musical-box soundtrack too!

'Have a good time,' I told Di. 'But if you don't mind . . .'

I fingered the remote control to expel Mozart from my bedroom.

I shifted my body down from the pillows, turned face down, edged sideways, displaced a shapely leg and then eased myself in between two thighs, half propped up on my elbows.

I stared at my wife's pussy, with its geometrically neat vee of thick and astonishingly silky black hair. I stroked the apex, the tip of the vee, where soft flesh parted the bush in a crescent of the palest coral. The hips between which the pussy was slung moved slightly. The mons furred by this glossy thatch – infinitesimally but definitely – canted itself upwards off the mattress. I lowered my head. Still on my elbows, I raised two forefingers to part, very gently, the two tenderly creased lips that together formed that crescent. Then, swift as a lizard's, my tongue flicked out and the tip darted between them.

I heard a tiny start of indrawn breath somewhere above me. The mattress creaked. Diana's hips rose an involuntary couple of inches to meet my invading mouth.

My lips were closed over the outer labia now. My tongue lashed up and down between them, widening, penetrating warm folds of flesh that were now sliding wet under my ravishing entry.

Diana's buttocks clenched. Belly tensed, her pelvis arched up, down, up again.

I shaped her opened cunt between my two cupped hands, forcing the clitoris out of its sheath with my swishing tongue as I sucked and slavered.

'Thank you, darling, I'm having a *wonderful* time!' I heard a voice gasp, although I hadn't in fact said anything.

I placed my hands flat on the base of Diana's belly, pressing upwards to draw the splayed lips – and indeed the entire moist complex of the cunt as a whole – up and further out from between her thighs, lewdly exposed to my raping tongue.

I sucked the clitoris into my mouth, worrying it with lips, grazing it now this way, now that with careful teeth. I thought I heard a repressed squeal, but I couldn't be sure because my ears were closed by the two thighs abruptly clamped to my head. I felt the soft pressure of calves crossing below my shoulder blades. I thought I felt heels drumming on the small of my back, but it could just have been the blood thumping through my veins towards the plank-stiff erection trapped between the mattress and my belly.

The body beneath me was, in small ways but constantly, in continuous motion now. Muscles trembled in back of the thighs. There were quiverings of desire threaded through the diaphragm to the nerves of the hips and arms and lower abdomen. The heart beat wildly, the pulses raced.

I was aware of all this but I made no conscious, physical connection. After all, she was watching television!

My tongue continued its devouring, probing, deeply, darkly penetrating exploration of the hot depths of Diana's secret inner flesh. And, however her eyes were occupied, her organic functions continued to react in their normal way.

I say normal. Much has been written, by women, about the female orgasm. To a male, there is a big difference – that is to say an objective one, noticeable to us – between ours and theirs. With a man, however different in detail they are, however separately they can be described, you know where you are. And you know where they are. They're coming; they arrive, big deal – they're over. End of story.

How much more complex (and more sophisticated, Miss Kitt?) the women's are.

At times they follow a similar pattern to a man's. More often they are totally different. Some ladies hiss like snakes and throw themselves about. With some, it's so down-key that you're not sure they've had an orgasm at all. There are those who seem capable of experiencing what seems to be a continuous performance, with throes and spasms during a whole afternoon. Some come as quickly as jumping out of a window – at times with a similar result; others favour the long, mounting build-up, rising to a crescendo – itself brief or extended – with a similarly drawn-out descent on the far side.

Diana, when she was really into it, had an involuntary system of advance signalling – a certain trembling of nerves, translated into an inner shudder that jerked the knees and sent the hands clawing all over the shop. This was followed, more rapidly now, by the threshing violently up and down of the pelvis, a heaving of the breasts and belly, and a final explosive shout.

It was soon after the drumming of the heels that I heard the shout.

I would have known anyway, since by then I had almost been thrown off the bed.

In her case the recovery was always quick. I knew I

147

didn't have to worry about the cockstand: it would be attended to when she was good and ready.

Telepathically, she picked my thoughts out of the air. 'I promise,' she said softly. 'Just give me a minute.'

I dragged myself up into a sitting position and kissed her. I subsided on the pillows by her side.

On the screen of the silent television, the two blonde lesbians were still lustfully – and purposefully – coupled.

Diana flicked them a glance and then smiled at me. 'Do they do it as well as you do, darling?' she asked.

'You'll have to find that out for yourself,' I said.

Chapter Thirteen

It was about this time that I began to think seriously of Sir
Walter Scott – he of *Ivanhoe* and *Rob Roy* fame. It was
however a quote from a lesser-known work called *Marmion*
that had begun to impress me. You know: 'O what a tangled
web we weave, when first we practise to deceive!'

Begun to, because Smart-Alec Silver had at one time
fancied himself a dab hand at such minor deceptions as
two-timing his employers or being sucked off by a secretary
while his wife thought he was working late. But it became
a different matter – even a moral matter – when the escort
lark required at times a double deception: that of the wife
and of the sexually demanding client. And I found I was
totally out of practice (if I may misuse the master's verb)
when things descended to the third degree of subtlety. I
mean like the *clients* were beginning to deceive *me*!

Here I was accepting money for sexual favours – a thing
I had specifically agreed with Diana that I was on no
account going to do. And now I found, with the affair of
the white glove and Di's furious order to its owner, that I
was faced with a two-can-play-at-that-game situation in my
own home. I had thought I was double-crossing her, only
to find that she was double-crossing me, in some way or
another, even if she didn't know I knew it.

Add to this the extraordinary revelation concerning
the proper Mrs Porter, with her temples, her half-nude
librarians and her employment of Eve Lorrimer to employ
me . . .

Well, you can see that after all this I was in no state to
deal with complaints from one client that I was daring to
escort another – and severe instructions to stop this
forthwith! I was beginning to realize that when it came to

the deeper complexities of deception, I *was* . . . just a beginner.

Before this last complication arrived to plague my life, however, there was a slight alteration to the balance on the positive side in the shape of a second meeting with Muriel the ex-matron.

Not, this time, by way of a telephone call and a booking for a second date.

It was something that happened entirely by chance, what you might call an innocent affair.

Relatively, that is. If – er – adultery can ever be called innocent.

It was a Saturday afternoon. I'd had lunch (no sex) with Geraldo Porrelli and his mistress at the riverside restaurant while he paid my account and we discussed future plans for the further deception of his wife. (I often wondered if he knew that Carol was a raving nympho: surely, I thought, there must have been *some* indication in their own personal relationship?)

Anyway, I was back in the West End. It was a sunny day. People were feeding the pigeons in Trafalgar Square. Nelson was still at attention on top of his column.

I was at a loose end. Hardly surprising, Diana might have said. You're the loosest man I know! But she couldn't have said it that day: she was down in Kent, spending the weekend with her Mum.

So there I was, no client in sight for once, wondering how I could amuse myself for the next forty-eight hours as I ambled past the shop-window Rolls-Royces near Berkely Square.

And suddenly . . . not a nightingale to be seen, but there was indeed a client in sight.

Muriel Savage. Steel-grey hair. A well-cut tweed jacket and skirt. Walking briskly across the square with approving glances through those large round spectacles at the birds – pigeons again – strutting importantly among the flowers massed by gardeners employed by Westminster City Council.

'Muriel! What a surprise – but how nice to see you!'

150

'Wham? Oh! Mr Silver! Well, yes, a surprise indeed. How do you do? Er . . . that is to say, how are you?'

Clearly, apart from the surprise, she was a little embarrassed. After all, the last time we'd met she had been naked in bed!

All at once, I felt a surge of . . . compassion, I suppose. At any rate a wave of sympathy for this really very charming, attractive retired lady up in the Smoke from her neat little house in Croydon. At the same time – and honestly, for once, I didn't feel smugly that I would be doing a favour – it occurred to me how agreeable it might be, how warm and friendly, to spend the rest of the day in her company.

'What brings you here on this sunny afternoon?' I asked.

'Just window-shopping,' she smiled. 'It was a nice day. Since I'd nothing better to do, I thought I might as well come up to town and have a look around.'

'Er . . . me too,' I said. 'Look, if you've nothing better to do . . . why don't we . . . that is to say, could I possibly interest you in – I don't know – maybe a cinema and an early dinner?'

Behind the large round lenses, her eyes blinked at me like birds trying to escape. She cleared her throat. 'It's gallant of you to think of it,' she began, 'but at the moment, I'm afraid that—'

'It's Saturday,' I cut in abruptly. 'I don't work weekends! This is an invitation, not a plug for business. Really . . . it would give me great pleasure . . . I mean I'd be awfully happy if you would permit me to offer you . . . well, anything you'd like to do. As my guest.' I turned on the Richard Gere smile. 'Please.'

Abruptly, her still-pretty face lit up. 'That's terribly kind of you,' she said impulsively. 'And of course I'm flattered—'

'Don't be. You'd be doing me a favour: it would make my day,' I said truthfully. 'Then, if I can persuade you to stay for dinner, I'll run you home afterwards in the car.'

There was a slight pause. Then: 'I think that would be absolutely lovely,' Muriel Savage said.

★ ★ ★

151

As it turned out, we did have a delightful day. I think she enjoyed it. If she did, I hope it gave her as much simple pleasure as it did me.

We found a small cinema off Shaftesbury Avenue that was showing Jacques Tati's comic masterpiece, *Mon Oncle*. We were still falling about at the memory of that when I took her to the Formule Veneto, a small and admirable Italian restaurant in Fulham – yes, with candle-lit tables! – which hadn't yet been discovered by the jet-set or the tourist trade.

The meal was great. We had fun. I really enjoyed myself. It was only in the car, on the way back to Croydon, that reservations elbowed their way in and risked spoiling the evening.

There were several different elements to contend with. Most important, to me at any rate, was the fact that . . . well, to tell you the truth and not to put too fine a point on it . . . I had the hots for her.

On and off, ever since we met in the square, I'd stolen the occasional glance. You know the way one does, visualizing her without the neat jacket, beneath the blouse, inside the uplift bra. And again, skirtless, without panties or tights, the smooth curve of the belly and the wiry pubic thatch – how would she look if she was naked now, here in the candlelight on the other side of the restaurant table? The odd thing was, you see, that we'd had a super fuck . . . but it was all in bed and half covered at that. I'd never actually seen her naked at full length. And wondering what she'd be like was making me horny as hell!

Okay, she was nearly ten years older than me but what the hell did that matter? I liked her laugh, her warmth, her quick intelligence. In a word, I fancied her like crazy.

The thing was – was this mutual? Bearing in mind what she'd told me the first time about her need – and the successful outcome when we made it together – well, that and her attitude this evening would appear to signal the green light glowing. But there could be problems – for both of us. The stupid, idiot behaviour priorities that should never tie our tongues or make us hesitate, but often do.

They arose simply because she had been a client but tonight was on the house. We had fucked together but I had been paid, to put it brutally, to do it. So if I took it for granted that tonight was a return engagement, exploiting – or taking advantage, she might think – of the fact that it would be free . . . well that would put us on the wrong footing at once. If, on the other hand, she handed me the time-honoured come-on when we arrived ('Won't you come in and have a coffee and brandy?'), then she might feel that *Silver* would think he was being conned for a free fuck!

Ridiculous, but it could be embarrassing – and in that case louse up the end of the evening. I mean there are some situations so silly that they are irretrievable, and you just pack it in and go.

In the event it was Silver who was silly and not the situation. I needn't have worried. In her usual sensible, honest and down-to-earth way, Muriel rode straight over the top of the problem – not by assuming it wasn't there but by tackling it head on.

We were held up by traffic lights in some suburban high street when she said suddenly: 'Tom, I don't believe in that old prevarication – we won't attempt to cross that bridge until we come to it. I believe bridges should be crossed, at least mentally, long before they're even in sight.' She paused. The lights changed. I shoved the stick into first. The traffic crawled forward. 'Unless, that is, it's feasible to make a detour around the head of the valley and miss the bridge altogether,' she finished.

'Sounds a reasonable . . . approach,' I said evenly.

We passed under a very wide railway bridge. Clapham Junction perhaps? She looked up at it and grinned. 'That's another option, of course!' she said.

And then, turning towards me as I passed three buses nose to tail with a burst of acceleration: 'I have really enjoyed today. It has been . . . super.'

'Me too.'

'Now we're coming to the end of it – and there's something unsaid in the air between us, isn't there? There must be. After all . . .' She let the sentence die a natural death.

I nodded. There was no need to say anything.

'I think we have to consider ourselves, today, as two different people from the couple . . . that other time. That was a . . .' She cleared her throat. 'A business transaction. A highly . . . successful . . . one, for me at any rate. Today was social and it was fun. And now I'm almost home.'

She turned again and stared ahead through the windscreen. Drops of water speckled the curved glass. It had begun to rain. I switched on the wipers. 'I shouldn't be saying this, I know I shouldn't,' Muriel resumed. 'I know you're married. I know your wife's away, because you told me so. I also know how I feel. But I don't know how you feel. And, Tom, I have to say . . . I have to say it in case you think . . . in case you think anything! But I want you to know that, on this one night, I feel very close to you.' Two fingers rested briefly on my arm, just below the hand on the steering wheel. 'I want you to know that, *should* this feeling in any way be mutual – as I suspect from your eyes over the dinner table that it may be – then nothing whatever should force you to drive all the way back to London in this traffic and this rain.' Another pause. 'But I also want you to know . . . I mean I don't know how fond you are of driving – and there's no obligation *whatsoever* attached to anything I've said.'

'You don't mean you're going to ask me would I care to drop in for a coffee and a brandy?' I said lightly.

She shook her head. 'No, I'm afraid I can't possibly do that.'

The bottom dropped out of my world. I realized suddenly how very much I wanted this woman. Surely there couldn't be someone – a mother? a daughter? – *staying* with her? Not after everything she had just said?

My disappointment was so total, so acute, that I could manage no more than a dismal: 'Oh.'

'I'm afraid there's no brandy in the house,' Muriel said. 'But there's still some of that whisky left.'

My sigh of relief was not only heartfelt. We were at the

154

end of her street. 'I'll drop you at your door and park around the corner,' I said.

'That's very discreet of you. And very thoughtful,' Muriel said.

So there we were. It was all fixed. I was going to stay the night.

No jockeying, no embarrassment, no clumsy or awkward hesitations. Everything had been explained, everything agreed, without a single explicit word spoken!

There's something to be said for people old enough to be sophisticated. And they're not rebelling against their instincts *all* the time, Eartha!

Chapter Fourteen

By the time I ran back through the rain to Muriel's house – the front door had been left ajar – the scene was already set. A gas poker sent flames crackling through a fire laid in the sitting room. Heavy curtains drawn across the window shut out the night and the rain. Beside the bottle of whisky and glasses, coffee dripped through a glass filter on the low table. And this time, after all, she hadn't had the slightest idea that I, or anyone else, would be coming home with her. Our meeting had been entirely by chance.

It must, I reflected, have been a super-efficient hospital that she ran!

There was no sign of the lady herself, but I could hear footsteps crossing the floor of the bedroom above.

She appeared in the doorway exactly as the last few drops of coffee escaped the filter and fell through into the bowl. I wouldn't have expected anything less.

She must have had time to think too, because her make-up had been removed but she was freshly scented (*Jolie Madame*, I thought – a perfect choice), differently dressed and without the spectacles. The garment she had chosen was a floor-length, dark blue housecoat with a wide collar and long sleeves

Admirable, I thought. The plain, sombre, unpatterned material would make a perfect background for a pale nude body if she was wearing nothing underneath it. At the same time the stuff – some kind of jersey, I think – was warm enough not to be silly. And unexpected visitors to South Croydon could hardly expect (shades of Minerva Collett!) sexpot costumes from the Folies Bergère.

'Ah!' Smiling, approving the coffee situation, Muriel nodded, undulated across the small room, kissed me briefly on one cheek in passing – as one old mate to another – and bent over the low table. 'Sugar?' she asked. 'One lump or two?'

She subsided into one of the armchairs and poured from the glass bowl into two demitasses.

I intercepted – and interpreted – the signals at once. This was to be no lustful, God-I-want-you wrestle on the sofa or hectic plunge into bed upstairs. Hell, we *knew* I was staying the night; it was unstated but understood. We knew we were going to fuck. We knew there was no have-to-be-home-before-two hurry. So why not relax and savour every aspect of the situation?

Once more, with her talent for discreet organization, her genius for the implicit rather than the explicit, this oddly straightforward lady had made her wishes known in the simplest – yet subtlest – fashion possible. Without actually turning it into a Derby and Joan situation, she was setting the scene for a companionable fireside evening for two, knowing what we knew – virtually a foretaste of the foreplay – before, when the time was right, we went on upstairs.

In other words, even if it was only for this one night, she wanted a relationship . . . and not just a hasty poke in an unmade bed.

That was fine by me. Knowing that I was going to see it, to enjoy it later, I could let my eyes dwell on the exterior, imagining the nakedness of the body I hadn't really had the chance to appreciate before while we chatted and drank. 'I've enjoyed – I mean really enormously enjoyed – today,' I said.

Muriel nodded. Smiling, she looked down at her coffee cup. 'It has been very . . . special for me,' she agreed.

I knew what she meant. It wasn't the sex – which I knew she wanted and would appreciate – but the being *with* someone, doing ordinary things, walking in the park, eating out – that was almost more important. I was aware of flesh moving, shifting within the loose contours of the housecoat as she leaned forward to pour more whisky. I felt a hardening at the top of my thigh.

How often, I thought, we miss out on the tenderness

and contentment that even the most ordinary encounter, even with the most occasional of partners, can stimulate . . . because we're so damned avid, so damned *rabid*, to have the need expressed by that hardness immediately satisfied.

Muriel switched on the wide-screen television. We watched a documentary on the life of the snow goose. Magnificent. A black girl won a skating championship. The stiffness at my loins was more pronounced. There was a late-night newsflash: British tourists killed in a train smash in Portugal. The Lagavullin bottle was empty. Muriel got up and went to a cupboard to produce a different brand. We were having it with water now.

Bringing my glass, she lowered herself to sit down on my knee in the most natural way in the world. She crooked an arm around my neck. 'Love me,' she whispered, 'a little.'

It was an imperative, a gentle command, but I chose to interpret it as a question. 'More than a little,' I replied. 'I think you're absolutely stunning. If I was twenty years younger I'd say smashing!'

Very slightly, she squirmed her hips, rolling her backside against my lap. Through the stuff of my trousers and the jersey of the housecoat the rigidity of my hard-on was obviously evident. 'Thank goodness for my female pride that you don't even need to put that in words!' she murmured.

I turned my head and kissed her.

Exactly as it had been that first time, the touch of our lips – or more precisely of the tips of our immediately invading tongues – triggered a reaction in her that was as unexpected as it was exciting. And as instant.

In a moment, desire flamed through her, consuming as a forest fire. Her small, voluptuous body, without actually leaving my knees, virtually exploded into action!

The arm around my neck tightened, my head was forced back as her tongue blazed more deeply between my lips and her mouth opened wide. The shifting of her hips against the hardness of my cock became pronounced, demanding. Small shivers tremored through the backs of her thighs, shook her belly and thrilled the pulse beating wildly at the base of her neck.

My right hand, between two buttons, was inside the housecoat – and she *was* wearing nothing underneath it! I could feel the warmth of soft skin, the rapid beating of a heart, the deliciously tempting weight, against my forefinger and thumb, of a full, well-formed breast.

At the touch of my hand, Muriel's breath jetted through her nose to explode against my cheek. Her own cheeks hollowed and her mouth clamped more tightly against mine as the tongue forced itself still further into the burning cavern of my mouth.

She clenched and unclenched the cheeks of her bottom alternately, shifting the stiffened rod of my cock from side to side within the tight confines of my pants.

Hearing my breathing quicken, she lowered both hands, fiercely clenching one on the flesh of my leg just above the knee. The other she forced between her thigh and my belly, searching with her fingertips until they homed in on the hard bulge at the base of my cock.

She gave a final pelvic wriggle, permitting her buttocks to signal the cock-head that it was not forgotten, and freed her mouth suddenly to slide off my lap and squeeze herself beside me between the arms of the wide chair. It was less comfortable than being in the next seat to Fanny Elmore in the back row of a cinema, but considerably more exciting.

Muriel twisted the top half of her body towards me, leaving the one hand still resting on the prick-shape thrusting out the trousers over my crotch. With the other, she fumbled beneath my jacket for my belt, unbuckled that, and then reached for the tag of my zipper.

Turning, she had thrust the breast I was touching hard against my groping hand. I opened the hand and spread the fingers to cradle the whole swell of that taut and luscious weight. My thumb teased a nipple now erect, unusually prominent and undeniably hard. At the same time I felt the base of my belly expand as the zipper gaped and the warmth of the fire caressed the patches of skin not completely covered by shirt-tails or the elasticated waistband of my Y-fronts.

I caught my breath as the two hands wrenched material aside, seized the shaft of my cock, and hauled it out into the open air.

The breast I was cradling was on the side of Muriel furthest from me. My free arm was cramped between us, but I managed to manoeuvre the hand up and over her thigh, searching for the opening of the housecoat – which had, mysteriously, at some time or other become un-buttoned.

My hand crept in through the opening.

The thigh parted slightly from its fellow. The hand sculpted a smooth curve of flesh, knuckles grazing stiff pubic hair. Then the fingers, prompted perhaps by a slight, subtle forward thrust of hips, found tender flesh trembling and burning heat . . . and all at once wet and slippery the yawning entrance to an excited and eager cunt.

We kissed again. Our bodies heaved, creaking the springs of the chair. A hand closed itself fiercely around the base of my cock. Another skimmed the sensitive flesh sheathing the upper end beneath the glans, milking me to a quivering awareness of the lust shaking us within the clasp of the easy chair.

My pulses raced. My left hand burrowed into the hot wet grip of hidden cunt so lewdly tempting my intruding fingertips. Here he goes again! I thought crazily. Tom Silver on the warpath screwing another client, although this time it's for free!

('And this . . . this man, your Lordship – if so I may term him – this gigolo, pimp, *maquerau* fornicator, toy-boy or whatever his disreputable trade calls him, has the audacity to claim that on this second occasion no money changed hands! A likely story, the members of the jury may well think.')

Abruptly, I was in need of freedom. The confines of the armchair were – very literally – cramping my style. And cramping Muriel's too. I was not an employee tonight. I was the man in the act and it was up to me to decide!

I disengaged myself as elegantly – and as swiftly – as I could. I leaped to my feet, shaking off the claustrophobic clasp of the chair. I wanted to feel the whole of that woman's sexy body close to me, against me, visible to me.

I reached out my hands, grabbed her wrists, and hauled her to her feet, Spinning her around, I snatched open the housecoat – soft curves of woman flesh, bulbous and pale against the dark blue as I had thought – and I pulled her ferociously against me. Cool curves of rounded body warm along my whole clothed length, my obscenely exposed cock clamped sideways to the swell of belly above the greying pubic hair. The top of her head was beneath my chin. I leaned down to kiss her again. And once more the contact of lips and tongues generated an electric tension that raced through the two of us and left us clinging together in a trembling ecstasy of desire.

But this wasn't something to be satisfied rapidly, a flaming need to be quenched as quickly as a cold beer slakes a raging thirst on a hot summer's day. Muriel, I was certain, despite the urgency of her own compulsive demon, was one hundred percent in agreement that this was an occasion to be savoured.

I rembered once, when I was a kid, reading one of those books secretly passed around which purported to catalogue different patterns of sexual behaviour around the world. I don't recall the title of the book, but I do remember the chapter on one technique – Turkish, I think they said – which was called the *Carezza*. An obvious enough label if you know about words!

The object of this was to bring each partner, manually, as near as humanly possible to orgasm without actually crossing the threshold . . . and then you pause, drawing back and starting again from the beginning. This, the writer pointed out, was equivalent to climbing a mountain, venturing as far as the very lip of the crest and then returning to base, time after time, without ever crossing over and going down the far side. A single 'encounter', the chapter promised, could thus be made to last an entire night without either of the protagonists – each, I wondered, wearing a red fez with a black tassel? – ever becoming exhausted or losing the desire to continue.

I wasn't too sure about the lack of exhaustion – perhaps all Turkish lovers are young – but, okay, this particular Saturday night, fez or no fez, the South Croydon Carezza was going to be entered in the book of London lovemaking.

Still holding her against me, I slipped the housecoat off Muriel's shoulders and allowed it to slide to the floor. I released her and stepped back for an instant to take her in, as it were.

She stood naked before me, even more than naked because of her nude body's proximity to the coffee table, the cups and saucers, the bookshelves, the marionettes still silently cavorting on the turned-down television screen.

I saw this smallish, shortish woman with her pleasant face and short grey hair – a woman nevertheless whose figure was still as near-perfect as possible, whose shoulders were wide for her height, whose waist was trim and whose legs were elegant. A woman whose small, full breasts were ample for her size – and almost aggressively prominent!

A woman, in short, who looked sexy as hell and whom I wanted like crazy.

I dropped to my knees in front of her. I placed my two hands on her softly padded hips. I drew her gently towards me. Then I buried my face in the smooth, warm, satined curve of her belly and, as tenderly as I knew how, flicked out the tip of my tongue to salute, just once, the double crescent of pink flesh glistening amidst the springy triangle of her pubic hair.

Somewhere above me I heard an inarticulate gasp, something between a choked-off word and a moan of pleasure. Muriel edged herself even closer to me, the cool skin of her belly indented by the impression of my features.

Totally unexpectedly, she raised one leg and draped it over my shoulder. Then, pressing hard against the small of my back with the heel, she managed to lift herself off the floor and drape the other leg over on the other side of my head.

She was sitting astride my shoulders, virtually in the piggy-back position, but facing me from the front and not looking over me from behind!

I tensed my muscles to remain upright and support her in that position.

Muriel tensed. Very slowly, she leaned back, pressing harder still against me now with both heels and calves, lowering herself until, from the clenched buttocks upwards, her small, voluptuous body projected horizontally from my shoulders.

And the moist cunt between her tensed thighs was raised until it was just beneath my chin.

I lowered my head and closed my lips over the warm, wet flesh.

Her head and shoulders grounded on the seat of the armchair she had so recently left. Supported now at both extremities, she released a dreamy, misty smile, and reached out both hands to clasp my head and force it further still into her quivering loins.

I started at once to lap and suck, exploring inner crevices with the tip of my tongue, drawing the tightly folded inner and outer lips into my mouth, grazing a discovered clitoris with my teeth.

She was moaning now with small, continuous cries, squirming her hips in front of my face as I tongued the hot, moistly sliding depths of her eager sex.

For a while, allowing my oral penetration to send shivers of desire racing through her frame, I continued to suck and slave, burrowing deeper still with every lash of my swirling tongue. Then, sensing that the rigors trembling through her belly were accelerating dangerously, I changed gear, as it were, as rapidly as she had.

I leaned back suddenly on my heels, so that her legs automatically began to withdraw over my shoulders and her cunt drew away from my mouth. I reached up both hands and jammed them under her thighs, at the same time pushing her legs up and away from me.

She was lying half on and half off the chair cushion with her legs held high in the air. Between the closed thighs, the compressed lips of her ravaged cunt glistened between fringes of grey hair.

I pushed myself upright. My prick, which had been

rammed against the front of the armchair, sprang free, still stiff as a plank.

Still holding those legs aloft with one spread hand, I lowered myself again and used the other to guide the distended, throbbing head in between those inviting lips.

Muriel uttered a soft squeal as I plunged the hard shaft deeply in once, twice, three times – just enough to show what was there – and then totally withdrew, my wet cock tingling still from the burning clasp of that inner flesh.

I lowered Muriel's legs to the floor after this temporary invasion and stepped away.

It was then that I realized – forgotten in the heat of the thrilling moment – that, by God, apart from the shaft wagging obscenely from the open fly, I was still fully dressed!

I whipped around to the back of the chair as she rearranged herself in it, and tore off my clothes. Too many risks of awkwardness, since she was already naked, if I undressed – or allowed myself to be undressed – openly in front of her. Unlike a woman, a man is not at his sexiest when only half his garments have gone.

Nude myself now, with the fond caress of the fire warm on my skin, I lifted Muriel out of the chair and laid her gently down on a white fur rug spread between the coffee table and the grate.

Catlike, she stretched out with a contented smile, then curled herself around my knees as I knelt beside her. She stretched out a lazy hand to fondle my cock, turning it this way and that, trying a tiny milking run between finger and thumb, wrapping the other hand gently around the balls, staring all the while with an almost bemused expression as if she had never seen it before (and in fact, I reflected, it was quite possible that she never really had).

I transferred my attention – temporarily again – to her breasts. Not for the first time, I had admired them eagerly as their rounded and resilient contours swelled up from her chest when she was projecting horizontally from my shoulders with her legs clenched over my back. Now I was able to offer them, if only briefly, the treatment they richly deserved.

I modelled them with my hands, as if I was sculpting them from clay. I cradled the fleshy weight of them, moving them slightly over the ribcage, thumbs caressing the dark brown, wrinkled areolas to ride over the stiffened buds of taut nipples. I lowered my head once more to lick around the dark flesh, to draw those nipples up into my mouth, to suck them to stiffer erection as my teeth grated tenderly against the swollen skin.

And all the time Muriel's two hands continued their compulsive, monotonous, almost dreamlike but always infinitely exciting, milking massage of my cook and balls.

I raised my head once from her breasts to intercept a warm glance that was both affectionate and thrilled. 'Tonight is my private view of heaven!' she confined with misty eyes. 'I want it to go on for ever.'

'We'll do the very best we can,' I promised, wishing that I had a photocopy of the Carezza chapter on auto-cue in front of me. 'But I have to tell you, my foxy darling, that finally, heaven or no heaven, how ever many times we almost get there and deliberately don't, in the end my sweet I'm going to fuck you to death!'

'That's my boy!' Muriel said.

I don't know how many changes we rang that night – I suspected the Turks would have been obliged to print a supplement – but it seemed to me we explored every possible . . . attitude . . . to sex. I took her from behind when she was facing the fire, on all fours on the white rug. A limited number of strokes again, to whet the appetite but in no way to approach the crest. I had her impaled for a short time on my cock with her legs twined around my waist – and although she twisted and writhed in an attempt to keep it in, bouncing her hips up and down in a burst of lewd energy, I took it away again leaving her wanting more, with the Turkish author in mind. I took her lying on the floor with her ankles crossed behind my neck. I had her on my lap again, skewered from below. I let her suck me almost to the final moment while I was lying in the chair with my feet splayed wide to rest on the arms.

Later we turned the chairs away from the fire, sat

companionably with our backs resting against them and explored manually every ridge and wrinkle and nook and cranny of each other's quivering genitals – always halting the caresses, the probing, pistoned cocktail shaking and the tunnelled interior explorations before the small cries grew too sharp or the breathing too fast.

I took her, for longer this time, astride me, riding up and down my poled cock like a horse-woman without stirrups until I was afraid the glans would catch fire. And after that I took her upstairs.

But that is another story.

Chapter Fifteen

It's a pretty good story, on the other hand – or at least it was for me – so I might as well tell it now.

I said I took Muriel upstairs. That is to say, I literally carried her there. For someone I had originally thought of as a small woman, she was surprisingly heavy. There was a lot of flesh there – but, my God, it was enticingly arranged!

There were twenty-four stairs, with a spare room leading off the mezzanine landing. I had a good chance, perhaps the first chance, objectively to admire my burden as I climbed those two flights . . . even if the objectivity was only from a distance of a couple of feet.

She had one cool arm around my neck. I had one, considerably more heated, around her shoulders. The hottest area, though, was around the lower part of my other arm, which supported the backs of her thighs. She was really burning there. The buttocks, still moist and slippery after our fireside athletics, blazed against my forearm. Wet hairs tickled the base of my thumb and my wrist. Higher up I could feel warm breath fanning across my chest. And between these two extremities my gaze lingered on that delicious swell of belly, on the double contours of breasts pressed sensuously together in my cradled grasp, on the hint of pubic hair almost concealed between those clamped-together thighs.

I could feel her dangling heels against my own rising thighs as I mounted. And somehow she had contrived to insert her free arm between our bodies to clasp the flaming cock bobbing so near her vulnerable backside and cunt.

Pausing to draw breath on the tiny landing, I couldn't resist moving the arm underneath her – just enough to slide my thumb into the scorching, hair-lined crevice separating the cheeks of her arse and tease the sliding depths of the inner maw so eager still for attention.

Muriel smiled up at me, squirming her pelvis slightly to deepen the intrusion. 'What did you say you were going to do to me?' she asked sleepily.

'I said I was going to fuck you to death,' I replied. 'The threat still stands – though I may stop a little before that final conclusion!'

'I can't think of a better way to die,' she said.

I shouldered open the bedroom door and carried her inside. The room was delightfully warm, vibrant with the pulsations of dancing firelight. I could see in the undulant illumination that the covers were once again turned down, with a bottle and glasses winking on the bedside table.

Extraordinary Muriel!

I laid her gently on the exposed part of the sheet, pushed the duvet further back, and kneeled beside her. Still upright, I allowed my eyes to rove along the whole shapely length of her, from trim ankles neatly crossed, to slender calves, plump thighs and the breath-catching swoop of belly to shadowed pubic hair; from that fiery clasp I was now so crazy to invade, past hips and waist to the jutting swell of nippled breasts and a mouth half open in lustful anticipation.

Roved along, I said. And back. And then up again. She really had a beautiful little body.

Muriel was looking at me misty-eyed. As I smiled, she held her arms out towards me with an impulsive gesture. I lowered my hands, leaned down, and began to kiss her all over.

Holding her by the hips, I rocked her naked body gently from side to side, allowing my lips and tongue to hollow out armpits and the space behind each ear, to trace the fleshy swell of each taut breast quivering above her chest, to promenade the delicious valley between them. I covered the whole tremoring curve of her belly with tiny sucking clasps. I licked along the crease at the top of each thigh. I nibbled the thatch of pubic hair, drawing the skin up minimally between my teeth to shake the flesh beneath, veering nearer and nearer – but never actually touching – the widely gaping lips of her cunt as her pelvis jerked involuntarily up towards me.

I brushed, wet-mouthed, the cool slopes along the insides of her thighs. I pushed her legs up one by one and tongued the hollow behind each knee as she started and shuddered with increasing joy. I ran my tongue in lewd arabesques around the tapered swell of her calves and licked the small depressions between heel and ankle. Finally I raised her feet again and sucked all ten of her toes, one by one.

She was quaking all over now, breasts heaved up over her labouring lungs, her entire frame tremored by the nerve thrills racing from skin to nerve to muscle. I remembered a line from the translation of an Asian love poem in which the writer spoke of his darling's skin as 'the whitest, so soft parchment on which my lips have written such excellent stanzas of kisses'.

Hey-ho, Silver, I thought: this is the limit of your own Required Composition for tonight!

I wrenched Muriel's trembling thighs apart, sank down between them, and lowered my mouth to the fiery, throbbing lips of her cunt.

This time, I began to suck her in earnest – not just a tease, a titillation, a trailer advertising the entertainment to come.

She was moaning now in a continual low croon, an exciting sound orchestrated to the threshing of her body on the mattress. The duvet had been flung to the floor. The firelight speared dark shadows across her writhing hips. Her head flailed wildly from side to side on the pillows.

I reached up, high, high beyond her heaving belly to fondle those shivering breasts. My lips and tongue plunged ever more deeply, ever more savagely into the hot, wet secrets of her cunt.

And then, all at once, she was still. Hard fingers clamped to my head raised it up.

'Yes!' Muriel whispered hoarsely. 'Now!'

The words, and the urgency with which they were

171

uttered, triggered a total switch in emphasis for me. Once again my hard, stiff cock was the centre of my being, the point of my existence, the one valid belief at the still centre of the turning world. Those other sexual weapons – the mouth, the lips, the tongue, the hands – so recently all-important, were reduced to lovemaking accessories.

Very slowly, very deliberately, I transferred my hands to the mattress on either side of her hips and dragged the length of my body up from between her legs. When my chest was touching the raised points of her nipples, I transferred my weight to my elbows and allowed my upper half to subside onto her pliant body. Feeling the soft flesh shift beneath me, the gentle upthrust of cool skin against the flat plane of my belly, I craned my head to kiss her – just once, briefly on the lips, not long enough for our tongues to engage. Our entire concentration, the total impact of our twin desires, must be permitted to flower unhindered in its own magical space.

Agonizingly aware that, for her, this was the most important moment of the whole night, a preliminary to the orgasm of orgasms which would remain in her memory and ratify the 'relationship' we had so carefully created, I flexed the muscles of my backside.

The throbbing tip of my cock-head just touched wet hairs, the warm lips of her ready cunt.

Sliding my hands slowly beneath her hips, I raised her pelvis fractionally off the mattress.

Slowly again, Muriel drew up her legs.

I held my breath, hesitated for a small eternity, then lunged.

My cock glided into her as easily, as greasily as a shafting element in a perfectly designed and exquisitely balanced machine. Without any guidance from me, the whole aching length of it was effortlessly swallowed in the hot, moist clasp of her eager, trembling belly.

At that first long, sliding penetration of her vagina, Muriel's breath exploded beside my ear in a deep, ecstatic moan whose long-drawn exhalation carried within it everything of longing and loneliness and loss – and the sudden joy of frantic desire assuaged.

Still buried deep and motionless inside her distended cunt, I kissed her again. 'I'm going to love you,' I whispered.

Two bare arms twined around my neck. Spread fingers cradled the back of my head. I felt a moist cheek against my face, the abrupt pressure of muscled flesh as her legs scissored over my back. 'Please,' she breathed.

Her whole body was clamped tightly against me. Within the restriction of that grasp, I lifted my hips enough to withdraw – perhaps half the burning length of the shaft.

She caught her breath.

I lunged, sliding the shaft fully in once more.

I didn't know, this time, if there were words formed within her exhaled gasp, but there was everything affirmative and accepted and content in its groaning delight.

I withdrew again, more fully this time, and drove my cock forcefully back inside.

Another breath-catching choke . . . and then, as I began the long, slow, pumping in and out that was going to transport us – I was certain – into realms of delight which were impossible to describe, the breathing beneath me relaxed into that heaving but controlled crescendo which charts yet again the climb up the Turks' mountain, but this time permits no drawing back at the edge of the crest, but only the dizzy, delirious drop beyond.

We settled into the compelling rhythm – flesh against excited flesh, pistoned cock convulsively gripped within contracting cunt – that seems to have had no beginning yet foresees no end . . . until the crest is so near that there is nothing to do but go on. And on. And on . . .

With Muriel's small, voluptuous body thrillingly clamped within my embrace, her hot breath panting in my ear and her belly effortlessly raised to meet my every demon plunge, the two of us sailed joyfully, energetically, dramatically out of the everyday and into the infinite.

I've no idea how long we fucked, and I don't recall precisely how; I don't remember whether we drank again or not; the dawn could have come and gone and I wouldn't have noticed. Even the memory of that final, soaring leap over the edge that we took together escapes me. All that remains is the conviction that it was perfect and it was shared.

I know too – though it would be incorrect to say that I *remember* – that the night held other surprises, other joys. I know we made love several times again. And I know it was good. But that first enthralling orgasm we had worked – and played – so hard to perfect, that shared joy which had hurled the two of us so far among the stars, remains indestructibly in my memory as the emblem of that magic night.

It was certainly dawn when I finally awoke. Daylight filtered past the drawn curtains and I could hear the greasy rasp of tyres on the wet street outside as the world went to work. Rain was still pelting against the window and drumming on the roof above.

Muriel slept beside me. She lay on one side, a pink flush suffusing her cheeks and an arm flung across her eyes as if to shut out the arriving day. And too many memories with not enough joy.

I slid out of bed without waking her and crept downstairs to the sitting room to recover my clothes. It was better to leave the whole night with her as a happy memory, a unity complete with no beginning and no end. Goodbyes are distressing at the best of times, and if she saw me dressing, leaving, spoke to me before I went ... well, it seemed to me that it might not only underline the fact that the relationship was ... temporary ... but also possibly risk spoiling her memory of what had gone before.

Better to leave the dream whole and undamaged.

I eased open the front door. 'Sweet lady!' I murmured with an upward glance. The door clicked shut behind me and I walked out into the rain.

Chapter Sixteen

I didn't know quite how to take the next offer from Eve Lorrimer. 'A ball,' she said. 'At Grosvenor House. Ambassadors and things. And Guarnieri is showing his collection – like a preview of the Paris shows.'

I was doing nothing else that evening – it was a Wednesday – so I agreed. But I wondered how much Mrs Porter was paying her this time. Or, much more intriguing, why.

Or had the previous occasion, which I had stumbled on by mistake, been no more than a one-off job, some kind of aberration on Mrs P's part for a reason even more obscure?

If anything a woman who lectured bare-breasted librarians did could be called aberrant.

Since the only way I could find out would be to challenge the lady and ask her personally – probably losing two clients at the same time – I decided to leave the questions on the shelf.

I dusted off the penguin suit and drove into town to collect Eve.

She was looking sensational. A clinging, ankle-length ball gown in vertical strings of some gold, near-metallic fabric sculpted the trim lines of her reined-in figure closely enough to show that she couldn't possibly be wearing anything, except perhaps a G-string, underneath it. The décolletée of the dress, which left her arms, shoulders and neck bare, was astonishing: not only, so far as hips and belly and waist and bottom were concerned, did it look as if it been sprayed on her, but the heart-shaped neckline caressing her splendid breasts almost as far down as the areolas, made the swelling slopes of those delicacies appear part of the same daring designer's dream. She wore a heavy gold bracelet on one wrist, and a gold locket in the form of a camera at her throat. The only other ornament visible was a crimson rose, so dark as to be almost black, braided into her hair above one ear.

I'll leave you to guess the colour of her satined stiletto heels.

Looking the way she did, I understood why she required a male escort in tow: if she had been alone every man's hand in the place would have been against her. I mean like literally.

I wasn't even sure about my own hands when the thought of dancing with her arrived. Fortunately, as the dress was virtually backless, a pair of thin white gloves were stowed in the rear pocket of my tails.

We stopped at the hotel's ballroom entrance, handed the keys of the convertible to the doorman and walked under the glass canopy into a maelstrom of heat and light and noise.

Several hundred people were already there. Formal black and white, splashed with the bright shades of that season's in colours, swirled and eddied between crowded dining tables and around a notice board on which the seating plan was displayed. Somewhere in the background, a band was playing 'Love For Sale'. In front of a gangway evidently ready for the fashion parade, my first glance had already taken in half a dozen older women whose minimal gowns risked making Eve look almost overdressed.

Our table was for twelve people. Two doctors, a military attaché, a vice-consul, an account executive I knew slightly. And our women. Luckily, most of the high-powered advertising brass whose false sympathy I wished to avoid were among the top table heavyweights and the he-shes of the fashion world. One person I did see, however, was Minerva Collett, very pretty and very proper indeed in black velvet with a three-string collar of pearls. ('Why, Mr Silver!' – very coolly – 'How nice to see you! I trust you are keeping well?')

I wondered which of the lantern-jawed, blue-chinned

QCs around her would be tearing off her frequently repaired négligée that night.

The dinner was okay, the conversation general. Thank God, apart from the fashion spiel, there were no speeches. The dress show itself was par for the course – skeletal late teenagers with stringy hair and haughty, dumb expressions flinging their arses from side to side as they sashayed up and down the walkway. The collection, as to be expected, was ludicrous. Clothes 'designed' by a London yobbo with an adopted foreign name – semi-transparent trousers, nipple-revealing tops, haystack hats and metal brassières, destined not to be worn – perish the thought! – but only to make the photo pages of the Sunday supplements.

I remembered my father, who had been fashion editor of a London daily, talking about the top models of the late forties and early fifties, after Dior's New Look had revolutionized a woman's world sick of wartime restrictions. 'There were four of them,' he said, 'each famous worldwide. Barbara Goalen, Shirley Worthington, Pat or Pam someone – three syllables, I think – and Joan North. The clothes they showed, of course, created by people like Fath and Schiaparelli and even Corrèges, were bought by rich women and actually worn, at least once or twice! But the sheer elegance . . . boy, you should have seen them! Goalen was incredible. Every single bloody thing she did – resting her chin on one hand, flinging an arm over a chair back, standing with her weight on one hip, anything – was a photographer's dream, a poem in line. And it wasn't studied: like the others she was just a superbly balanced woman.' All four of them, the old man told me, had continued at the very top of the fashion tree well into their forties.

Maybe, I thought, staring at the sulky children pouting at the flashbulbs that night, the nineties wasn't quite the super-world my ex-profession said it was . . .

Parts of it were okay, though. In particular, that night, the employer I was escorting.

I don't know about poems in line, but what I could see emerging from what there was of Eve's dress was a lot of woman!

There was a time, with everyone milling around at the end of the dress show, when she was absent from the table. But after that, it was clear that whoever she had wanted to chat up had been chatted, for she stuck to me as closely as if we'd been a real couple, out on the town and having a ball.

Since it was a ball, and since there was a ballroom, most of the music was designed for what used to be called ballroom dancing. You know – instead of everyone doing their own thing, the couples remain linked together, touching even, doing whatever the man leading decides.

From time to time, however, the orchestra dived into a rumpty-tumpty version of some quasi-rock number or other, to give the yuppies a thrill.

Here, Eve and I retired into the wings, as it were, to witness one of the more hilarious aspects of contemporary social life in Britain: the cavorting of jet-set youth when anything even resembling jazz or rock, or anything popular from the Rolling Stones to heavy metal, was played.

I don't know what it is that could have influenced the male young of the professional classes in this country to behave in this way. But the behaviour is unmistakable and it can be found nowhere else and among the members of no other class. It manifests itself in a distinctive, gauche, heavy-footed, pump-handling series of leaps and bounds, some yards from the female partner, often accompanied by such archaic expressions as 'Swing it!' and 'Yeah!' A performance, I may add, causing much merriment among musicians, black people and French girls.

The old ballroom stuff, to be honest, isn't my cup either. But once the red-faced brill bounders had flipped the hair out of their eyes and dragged their girls off the floor, we glided out there and pretended we knew about foxtrots and slows. It was nice anyway, holding that superb half-nude body against me, much of it evident even through a stiff shirt, and we swooped and slided and chasséd and turned along with the prancing older folk.

It was during the third or fourth dance – a slow waltz, as I recall – that I was suddenly aware of certain, well . . . very positive signs on Eve's part. She had been very bright and alive and amusing all evening, but the friendliness was distant and reserved, as if she was someone's sister. Now, however, her eyes too were dancing and her smile was warm. Her back leaned hard against my guiding hand and her fingers were wrapped tight around the other. On one of those tight, swirling turns, I could have sworn that her knee was thrust, quite deliberately, between my thighs!

In a *waltz*, for God's sake! Even though I learned later that it was an oldie called *Sympathy*!

My suspicions, agreeable as they were, were confirmed during the next number, a slow slow.

We had stopped trying out the tricky reverses and were eddying quietly in a corner by one of the Ionic columns, allowing the fast traffic to sweep past. The whole of that trim, svelte, rather held-in but definitely fleshy frame was plastered against me. I mean all the way down, including that knee, which was of course about to nudge a very positive reaction from the Silver crotch.

So far as the dance was concerned, we were keeping time with the music but kind of treading water, if you know what I mean. The fingers of the hand that I wasn't holding tightened on my upper arm. A squeeze, my lord; a very palpable squeeze!

I looked down at her. The eyes were brighter, the smile had widened.

She leaned even harder back in my half embrace – enough to bring her splendid shoulders into sight and expose the rounded swells of those breasts so nearly spilling out of the metalled neckline of her dress.

'Tom,' she said in a low but matter-of-fact voice, 'I want to go to bed with you. Now.'

Collapse of stout party! This was just about the most unexpected thing that had ever been said to me. Quite apart from the place, the occasion, the social context and the manner in which the words had been spoken. I mean, hell, okay this was a sexy lady and who wouldn't . . . but, until the past few minutes, there hadn't been the slightest, subtlest hint of anything whatever suggesting . . .

I swallowed. No words had so far emerged from my open mouth.

Seeing my astonishment, my stupefaction even, Eve laughed. 'Oh, I don't mean that I'm going to rip open your fly,' she said, 'or take your cock out. But I see a lot of men. I have to in my job. And it happens there are very few of them who attract me. It happens also that tonight I feel suddenly sexy . . .'

'And I'm the first of the few?' I couldn't resist saying.

She laughed again. 'And the last. Tonight anyway.'

A pause. She oscillated slightly from foot to foot as the number swelled into the last chorus, rotating her hips gently against me. 'Well, good-looking, are you game?'

'Game, set and match!' I gasped, switching authors and metaphors in one fell swoop. My tool was hard against her thigh. 'Good Christ, Eve, of course I would . . . I mean there's nothing I'd like more than to . . . you're absolutely the most . . . the most fabulous . . .' The smart-ass wordsmith was at a loss for words.

Eve's grin was more mischievous than sexy. 'Perhaps we don't need to dance any more?' She suggested.

I gulped. 'I'll go find the doorman and have him fetch the car,' I said.

She shook her head. 'Don't bother. There's no need.'

'No need?'

'I have a room booked here.'

I stared at her.

'Oh, I didn't know I'd be inviting you into it,' she explained. 'I always do when it's one of these late-night shows, hunt balls, midight matinées and stuff.'

'Just in case?'

She nodded. 'Just in case. But not just in case of escorts. I find it a drag if I have to stay out until two or three a.m. – four sometimes if it's a business do – and I'm all dolled up like this. It's usually raining, cabs are impossible, driving's a risk if one's been drinking – and there are always kerb crawlers waiting for an opportunity to open their flies. Much better to have a room waiting, flop into bed, and leave at a decent hour in the morning, dressed in something

180

you brought when you reserved the room. It's one way of getting at least part of a good night's sleep.'

She raised her eyes and favoured me with a level stare. 'Or not,' she said.

We slipped out when the dance floor was juddering to the stamp of elderly feet and the band was making a manful attempt at a Brazilian mambo.

In the foyer of the hotel proper, I said: 'Would you prefer it if I – er – came up separately?'

'Certainly not,' Eve snapped. 'We're not in the nineteenth century! I've paid for a double room: I've the right to do whatever I like with it. We live in a permissive age. Remember?'

I remembered. I wondered if the permissiveness extended to the full use of the room on every occasion. Or whether, again, the double booking was 'just in case'?

In the lift going up to the fifth floor, I pondered once more my father's comments on the model girls of his day. It was certainly true that today's wretched, skinny little females – showing not so much dresses or clothes as 'costumes', and villainously overpaid as they were – had little in common with the women he described. But the fashion business had done a smart about-face since the fifties and sixties. Now it was the people on the production and promotion side who were really glamorous. The women who ran the glossy fashion magazines in London, Paris and Rome – most of whom had been at the Mayfair cocktail party Eve had taken me to – were infinitely more chic and sophicated, in some cases actually gorgeous, than the kids showing the stuff they dealt with. And the same was true of the press relations, advertising and lady spin-doctor types. Media interest again.

Eve herself was a case in point. Apart from the exaggerated dress, which had clearly been chosen for this particular occasion, the person standing close to me as the cage whined upwards was by any standards a beautiful, super woman. An infinitely alluring, desirable example of the species.

And she was not only paying Silver for his time – or at

any rate being employed to pay him; she was actually *inviting* him, of her own free will, to share her bed!

Remembering the clinging resilience of that splendid body when it was even closer to me than it was now, on the ballroom dance floor below, I felt again that anticipatory thrill stiffening my eager cock at the thought of what joys the next few minutes might provide!

I had to wait a little longer than that. Eve took an unconscionably long time to quit the bathroom. Most women do. What the hell – I amused myself opening a bottle of champagne in an ice bucket on one of the bedside tables and pouring myself a glass. With the compliments of the management, a discreet card propped against the bucket said.

Interesting.

When at last Eve emerged, I saw that the wait had been worthwhile. Although, oddly enough, ready for bed and for sex she was wearing considerably more than she had been at the ball!

This time her entire body was covered, from shoulders to wrists, from throat to ankle, by a loose, flowing négligée in smoky organza – and beneath that there was a knee-length, halter-neck nightdress in the same filmy material.

I said her body was covered. But I didn't say it was invisible.

In fact the shadowy veil of the gunmetal-coloured organza showed very much more – or at any rate drew attention to very much more – of the body which had so nearly escaped from the clutch of the gold dress at the ball.

The breasts, for instance. Instead of displaying their fullness and roundness and suggesting their fleshy weight, the négligée and its team-mate obscured them, hinting only at their prominence with its double swathe of diaphanous material, showing only as a promise of things to come the darker circles of nipples and areolas thrusting out the flimsy stuff.

In the same way, half hidden by the dusky swirls, the thrusting movements implicit in the exhibition of hip and belly and bottom, were no more than rumoured by the sight of an opaque triangle of dark pubic hair visible when the garments tightened across her hips.

To complete the low-key atmosphere of an invitation that was as discreet as it was subtle, she had removed the rather garish make-up that went with the cleavage and the gold dress, replacing it with a *maquillage* so unemphatic that it was hard to see whether or not it was there at all.

The black rose, however, remained in her hair and she swept into the room on a cloud of perfume so rare and so expensive that it was virtually unidentifiable.

'I'm glad you helped yourself,' she said. 'Now perhaps you'd fill a glass for me?'

I poured from the bottle I'd deliberately left on ice, handed her the glass. 'Happiness!' I toasted, raising my own. 'Now, if you'd be kind enough to excuse me . . . ?' I whistled into the bathroom.

I was naked when I came out. Eve grinned at me over the rim of her glass. 'Admirable!' she approved, eyeing my rigid tool. 'Sometimes things . . . turn out . . . exactly the way one expects.'

The lighting was dim: two sconces opposite the bed, bracketed low down on the wall. Eve sat near the pillows, allowing warm light diffused through the silk shades to silhouette her behind the organza. There was a slight smile, challenging, twisting her lips and her eyes were half closed.

I knew virtually nothing about this cool, assured young beauty: she was a client; we had been out together a couple of times; our conversation had been general, almost banal. She had made absolutely no advances, ambiguous or direct, in the way that certain others had – Minerva, Mrs Fitz, Muriel, for example – to suggest anything, well, physical. Why would she, looking the way she did?

Until tonight. When, right at the end of the evening, she says without any preamble that she fancies me like crazy. Or words to that effect.

It was this, you see, that left me somewhat at a loss – without any preamble.

Until the dancing, there had been no hint, no veiled suggestion, no lead-up whatsoever. And even the hard leaning and the knee between the thighs could have been no more than the usual friendly no-sex-we're-British physical enthusiasm of the young. There hadn't even been that sudden pressure of the hand that passes for sexual invitation among Englishwomen.

So I was kind of left in the middle of Act Two, without even having read the script of Act One.

I mean, usually, by the time you're naked, beside the bed, you have at least an idea of the *kind* of person you're about to fuck. Do they appreciate verbal appreciation of their astounding allure? Are they foreplayers – and, if so, is the oral acceptable? Do they like to be rogered, as they say, in what could be a fit of sudden passion?

With Eve, I didn't have a clue.

I know the answer, of course. When in doubt, dive in. If you're doing wrong, you'll soon find out! The silence of the turn-off is as eloquent as a snapped Don't-do-that! And I never heard of any sexpot throwing a guy out of her bed or getting up herself and leaving just because he made a clumsy start.

But this was, indeed, her bed. And her invitation. Right from the start. I hadn't made a bloody move! For all she knew, I might think I was doing her a favour. Eve Lorrimer!

She was standing now by the bedside table, sipping champagne. Your move, Silver.

I sat on the bed.

I smiled up at her, the full Richard Gere. 'Here I am, with the most . . . fascinating . . . girl in London,' I said. (I knew at least that words like ravishing, sexy, seductive, even beautiful would be so square in this context as to be o-u-t.) 'Here I am – and at the same time I don't know where the hell I am! You took me so much by surprise that . . . well, to tell you the truth, I don't know where to start!'

Eve laughed aloud. 'Eight out of ten for originality,' she said. 'Tom, I'll tell you something. I like sex. But in my job I can't afford to show it. Not openly anyway. Too many problems.'

She put down her empty glass on the night table and

reached for the bottle. 'I like sex – and I like any sex and every sex, if you know what I mean.'

'You mean you're eclectic? That you have . . . catholic . . . tastes?' I ventured.

'I mean that I'm bisexual – but I'm an enthusiast in both directions,' she said.

I nodded. *Verb. Sap.*, as the Latinists say. A word to the wise.

The indications, the implied directions were clear. Message received and understood, ma'am. If she was bi, evidently she enjoyed making love to ladies. If she loved that kind of love, equally evidently, she must be in favour of the stroke and the caress, of mouths and lips and fingers and tongues. I mean what else was there?

The night, then, was for Silver the smoothie – for subtlety and understanding, the murmured intimacy and rape in whispers. I hoped that the veined and rigid staff speared upright and throbbing from between my thighs would be indication enough of my own tastes, of who and what I myself was in favour of on this night of thrills and surprise.

I had made up my mind. Jokey at first, to get over the hump of an upside-down situation (after all, this particular dance was a Ladies' Choice) – two mates together, old friends enjoying a mutual kiss and cuddle; then, when the steam began to rise, the complicity of untold secrets shared and the delicate friction of two skins.

The hell, I thought, with Mrs Porter and her fucking cheque book. I swung my legs up onto the bed, reclined with my weight on one elbow, and held an arm out towards her. 'The fig leaf has gone,' I said, with the tiniest flick of the eyes towards my stiff tool. 'Adam awaits, madam!'

She replied at once in the same vein. 'Dinner – one apple – is served!' she said.

In a cloud of filmy, billowing material, she sank down next to me on the bed and took my prick in one hand.

For an instant, I took her in visually – not for the first time that night.

Under the smoky veils of that shadowy organza, swathes

of which had settled across my bare legs, her body positively glowed in the discreet lighting. I could see now – the silk shades were behind her and she was once more in silhouette amongst the layers of translucent material – the breasts jutting promiscuously below her shoulders, a buxom curve of hip, the sudden intense dark where her belly sloped softly away towards loins equally compelling for ladies and gents.

Under the organza, one of her knees – it was becoming a habit! – rose between my thighs, nudging the tightened scrotum to veer my cock tighter still into her cool grasp. Feather-light, her fingers began skimming up and down, over and around the skin stretched, distended and gleaming outside the iron-hard shaft. Beyond the shadow of her milking arm, I saw that her nipples, surprisingly long, were taut and erect.

My free hand rested on the firm flesh of her hip, very gently smoothing the layers of sheer material over the satined skin. I lowered my head towards her enticing mouth.

Eve closed her eyes and tilted back her face. The line of her neck rose in alabaster perfection from the halter of her nightdress. Above her determined chin, lips half open in anticipation and invitation widened into a sleepy smile.

Dipped lower still, I allowed my own lips fleetingly to brush them.

Very slightly, the pressure of the fingers stroking my tool increased. The knee below my balls rose higher. I could hear her breath now, feel it warm against my mouth.

We kissed.

No passionate, tongue-wrestling suckery with hollowed cheeks; no close-up of that curious chewing movement so much beloved now of movie and television directors. Just a minuscule peck here . . . the briefest tightening of my two lips over one of hers . . . a swift withdrawal and another dab, dry-mouthed, at the corner of the smile. Tongues, when they emerged, would be all the more exciting.

Before that happened, my head was elsewhere. The lips stroked gently, smoothly over the dun material tightened across one silky shoulder. My hand moved from the curved hip to the hanging breast. I could feel my own pulse accelerate as my palm signalled the warm weight of that rounded shape along my thrilling nerves. In Eve too I was aware of the blood quickening, the heart perhaps starting to hammer behind that cradled swell.

I sat up, releasing my elbow and my other arm.

The hand on the breast stayed there. The freed one took the other breast, held it for a moment, teased the organza covering them both just enough over the nipples to make Eve catch her breath, then snaked down, one on either side, to caress the superb swell and hollow and swell of ribs and waist and hips.

I seized the négligée and nightdress together on either side of those hips, tightening the double thickness of the sheer material over a curve of belly, sawing it gently from side to side to roll the flesh a little this way, a little that.

With my two hands I shaped the tender swell of each hip, smoothing light fingers over the tense muscles, relaxing them, sliding down towards the thighs, sweeping, stroking, venturing in the direction of that fathomless dark that concealed the pubic hairs but never approaching near enough actually to touch them through the garments.

There was a sudden extra stillness, a controlled tension about the lower half of Eve's body now. A sense, as my roving fingers explored, that it was only with a supreme effort that she stopped herself exploding into action.

Her breathing had become very shallow, very quiet.

She looked up at me, sitting above her, with that curiously vacant stare that women have – seeming at first as expressionless as the eyes of a marble statue, but in fact acting only as a fragile palisade behind which a private world of phantasms, sensual as well as sexual, writhe and squirm.

Should I climb over it now – or wait until the maelstrom on the far side seethed into view?

I decided to climb.

A mental choice, metaphoric! In physical fact I lowered myself abruptly.

With a swift and – I hoped – unexpected movement, I transferred myself to the foot of the bed.

I took her two ankles, under the hem of the négligée, and prised them apart – not wide, as though I might be about to make a sudden penetration, just far enough to separate them.

I turned back the organza hem to bare her feet.

Then, all at once aware that the stillness had been replaced by an inner quivering, distant but intense, I slid a palm beneath each heel and raised the feet a few inches off the mattress.

The intensity of that interior tremor increased. Under the diaphanous cloak of the dark material, I could make out the sudden shudder of a muscle on the inside of her right thigh. My cock, snatched out of her grasp when I made my move, throbbed hard between my own thighs.

I bent almost double, lifted the feet a fraction higher, and started to kiss them, one after the other – lips working, tongue licking down each instep, around the ankle bones, into the hollow beneath. When I knew that the entire body above me had stiffened, that Eve was in fact holding her breath, I started to suck her toes up into my mouth, again one by one, first the left foot, then the right (I'd read, or heard, somewhere that this was a move appreciated by some gay girls).

Next best thing to a prick, I suppose, some macho idiot had said coarsely once, in one of those drink-on-the-way-home pub sessions I used to frequent.

Whatever the psychiatric reasons, my informant, visual or verbal, had not been wrong – at least in the specific case of Miss Lorrimer.

Eve's breath was released in an explosive gasp as I tongued the first big toe, the left, inside my mouth.

Her body arched spasmodically up and down on the bed. Before I had arrived at the right foot, she had shot down both hands, grabbed négligée and knee-length nightdress together, and dragged both up to her waist in a single frantic dart.

She lay on her back before me with her thighs trembling

and her loins shamelessly exposed, the two hands clenched on the organza lewdly raising the garments to emphasize the gesture.

Before I finished with the right foot, she had lifted her hips enough to pull up the parts of each that she was lying on. Now she was totally naked from the waist down, darkly tufted pubic hair obscenely prominent against the whiteness of her skin.

During the movement, her legs had parted and her thighs were now spread wide enough to reveal the serpentine creases of labia closed beneath that thatch.

But I didn't shuffle up to that particular buffalo in a brutish stampede.

No way. The invitation, if it was one, related to something far more sensitive and discreet, a technique much subtler and more tender than a cock-in-hand plunge towards waiting cunt.

I continued with the kissing. Back up past the ankles, around each calf, licking behind each knee, swaying my head from side to side, from the left leg to the right leg and back again, as I rose slowly, with an intense, held-in complicity, nearer and nearer to her bared loins.

It had been an invitation all right!

I was at knee height when she half sat up, reached down one hand and grabbed my thigh just below the hip. Once her fingers had clawed into my flesh, she reclined again, flexing the muscles of her arm to exert pressure, to pull, coaxing thigh and hip and pelvis in the direction of her own head and shoulders.

I read her at once. She wanted to play as well as be played with. So much the better!

I rolled over her leg on that side and swung my whole body, from the waist down, through something like a hundred and eighty degrees, so that my feet were now towards the pillows, my loins, hinged slightly, at the level of her shoulders, and my head resting on the thigh of the leg I rolled over. Between my open lips, the wet tongue traced lazy arabesques down the cool flesh of that inner thigh.

But now, immediately, the name of the game was changed.

What had been a restrained – I hope delicate – tribute paid by the squire to the beauty of his receptive lady was now a thrilled and thrilling embrace of mutual stimulation.

Eve's hands snaked out towards my genitals. Those same feathered fingers explored the creases between scrotum and thigh, fondled the balls, traced the contours of the belly through the upper limits of my bush. Wrapped again in that delirious, skimming clasp, my distended cock pulsated with excitement in her pistoned caress.

My head turned slightly. I permitted my tongue now, instead of idly circling, to rove in a definite direction – sometimes left, sometimes right, but always, relentlessly moving higher, nearer the untouched cunt.

In my ear, pressed against the skin of her thigh, I could hear the accelerated, thumping pulse of my own blood pumping through my veins.

A sudden change of tempo above. My balls were released; the hand around my cock tightened, the frequency of those milking strokes increased. Nearer, much nearer to my face, Eve's other hand, palm downwards, slid across the base of her naked belly, over the matted black hair to the pink flesh nestled at the top of her cunt.

With forefinger and middle finger spread, she parted the outer labia, splayed wide the inner, exposing the whorls of the whole dark inner rose to my lustful gaze.

A sudden change of pace should be met by an equally swift response.

Shifting my chest across Eve's thigh, I twisted my head, sank my face rapidly down, and lashed out my tongue to lap the shining crevices of that lasciviously splayed cunt.

The physicists say that action and reaction, in the case of colliding bodies, are equal and opposite. Collision wasn't quite the term I would have used, but the rest of the precept was certainly proved true that night on the fifth floor of the Grosvenor House Hotel in Park Lane in London.

The moment my tongue penetrated the trembling folds

of Eve's inner labia and my mouth closed over the outer, I felt the hot, sucking clasp of lips closing over my cock-head, and the tight grip of imperative fingers pulling me forward, forcing the stiff shaft deeper into her slavering mouth.

We stayed for a short time sucking, while the pulses raced and the electric thrills flared through our tingling, tight-stretched nerves. Then I moved again. My turn! I glided both hands beneath her bottom, clenched hot fingers on each buttock, and lifted her entire pelvis towards my craned face, gobbling wide and wet the soft depths of cunt so invitingly held open for me.

Eve's hand moved, clasped the back of my head, forced my face still more deeply into the flowering flesh. Her other hand pumped the rigid stem of my tool while she tongued and nibbled the distended glans.

Once more I imposed a move. The position was exciting. But it was awkward, it could soon prove fatiguing, and it missed out on the essential togetherness of total intimacy. It was in effect both ends playing against the middle, as the saying goes . . . only in our case the middle wasn't there!

So I withdrew head and shoulders without warning, rolled again over a thigh – but relapsing this time onto my back – and kept both hands firmly clamped to my partner's arse. With a single titanic heave, I raised her hips up again, spun her around until the length of her body was face down, and levered my hands under her hip bones to lower her pelvis gently over my face.

I allowed the weight of her to settle, a thigh on either side of my head, breasts through the gauzy material of the ruched-up négligée squashed against my own hips. Then I wrapped my arms around the cushioned flesh of her pelvis, stretched out my fingers to pry apart the cheeks of her backside, and resumed my slaving worship of her cunt – but from a much better angle.

Pulling her a little towards me, I buried my face between those cheeks, lashed my tongue up into the heated depths of her vaginal cleft until it located her gaping cunt, and closed my mouth once more over the swollen lips.

Throughout this complex manoeuvre Eve had contrived

to keep my cock-head between her lips. Now, resting on her elbows, the stem buried deep in her mouth, hands busy about the balls and the base of the shaft, she lay face down along me, sucking with all her force – and I lay face up beneath her, sucking with all mine. We were locked into the age-old position known to the French as *Soixante-Neuf*, and to the more vulgar of jokey schoolboys as 69.

Forget the labels, though: the important thing was that now the contact was total: we were making love with *the whole* of our bodies, each of us. And this made it, in my book anyway, an experience that much more valid than any awkward manoeuvring, however gymnastically adroit.

For what seemed a long time, we remained locked together like that, mouth to genitals, genitals to mouth, arms wrapped around our straining bodies. Occasionally only, hands strayed away to break our ferocious concentration on the agonizing thrill of lips and tongue against, inside and around quivering flesh. The sounds of traffic in the Park diminished, no music filtered up now from the ballroom five floors below, somewhere in the neighbourhood a church clock chimed the quarters, the hours, as we rocked together in sensual bliss.

At some point, Eve rolled away to strip off négligée and nightie. After that, naked and trembling, she hauled me over on top of her and took my cock back into her mouth. But my weight on her slender frame, together with the deeper, gagging penetration this provoked, soon had her wrestling back on top where she could gauge and manipulate precisely how much of the shaft she could comfortably take and still go on sucking and working her tongue.

Later, much later, for daylight was threatening to enfilade the drawn curtains and I thought I heard the first bus careering southwards down Park Lane, we separated into a mind-blowing variety of different positions, criss-crossed and wrapped over, stretched out or cramped together. But whatever the bodily contortions, however closely we clasped, wherever the wild hands explored and probed, the same butterfly-wing sensitivity, the same delicacy of touch kept the hearts pounding and the thrills searing through our entwined limbs.

So much of that *dizzy* night passed in this continuous dream of tactile ecstasy that I lost count of such details as how and when and how many and even where. Orgasms there were, of course. Eve, after the initial reserves were overcome, seemed tensed on such a high that I could believe she was in the throes of a continuous climax the whole time she was with me. I came too, naturally – several times. But I cannot for the life of me recall exactly how or when. I don't even know for sure that I ever actually fucked her – the full penetration, cock buried in cunt, I mean – but what did it matter if the heart still hammered and the nerves still sang?

Eventually of course we slept. When I awoke, she was no longer there. It was nine o'clock. I slipped into the bathroom, showered, then dressed – feeling a little foolish – in my white tie and tails (fortunately with a short, dark topcoat to hide them). When I came out Eve, wearing a neat two-piece with a sweater and pearls, was packing make-up and what there was of her ball gear into a small valise.

To this day, I don't know why I did it. I was suffering, I guess, from exhaustion. Who wouldn't be? But that was no explanation. There was something at the back of my mind, arising from that fatigue or the cause of it – something within the transports of our night-long sexual delirium – something, in spite of the lustful furies flaming through us, that hadn't been quite *right*.

It was, I thought much later, perhaps that what we had so frenziedly enjoyed together was a relationship simply between *organs* rather than people; with little or nothing of significance – climaxes or no climaxes – happening between Tom and Eve. Something deeper than the difference between love and lust, because we certainly weren't intimate enough, in one sense of that word, to love. But whatever it was, it seemed to have left me on waking in a surly or churlish mood.

Got out of bed on the wrong side, as they used to say.

And a bed of such delights too!

Whatever the reason, I came out with the unforgivable.

Eve hadn't spoken when I emerged, dressed, from the bathroom, just nodded briefly and got on with what she was doing. Maybe it was that slightly dismissive attitude – no Darling-what-a-super-night! – that triggered my sudden fit of pique. At any rate, I said it.

Looking her straight in the eye, I said: 'I trust Madam Porter will settle up with you for the *whole* night?'

Eve rounded on me with her own eyes blazing. She slapped my face, hard. Then, snatching up her case, she flung out of the room without a word and slammed the door behind her.

Driving home, I was in no mood to waste time trying to rationalize either my own rage or Eve's reaction to it. My cheek still stung. And when I got home there was another problem to deal with.

Diana wasn't back yet. Knowing that I was going to be at the ball until the small hours, and that I'd have to take Eve home after that, she'd gone out of town herself and spent the night with the friend who'd lent us the sexy video.

So why, when I unlocked the front door and went in, should the hallway and indeed my study upstairs be tainted – although neither of us smoked – with the unmistakable odour of cigarettes and cigars?

Chapter Seventeen

Sitting in my study with the windows wide open to clear out the smokers' fumes, I was faced that morning with a bewildering list of questions.

Who had been in my house last night while I was at the ball with Eve, and why?

My wife had herself been away. Would she know they were there? This seemed likely: they could hardly have been burglars, because nothing was missing.

Was the visitation connected in any way with the mysterious woman who had left the white glove while I was here in the office sucking Sally? Had the house been lent to her by Diana?

Could she by any chance be the friend – whom I had never met – at whose house Di had spent last night? Could the two of them, for some reason, have swapped houses for one night? Secret lovers maybe? Unlikely again: I had overheard a telephone conversation in which White Gloves had been told sternly that she must never, ever come to the house again.

Back to Eve then. Why was she being sub-contracted by Mrs Porter to hire me as an escort?

Would she tell Mrs P, after my ill-tempered outburst this morning, that I knew about this? And if she did would I be justified in cashing the cheque Eve paid me before we left for the ball? Or should I play outraged, return the cheque, and wash my hands of the whole deal, Mrs P included?

Lastly, still the most puzzling of all, why on earth would the proper Mrs Porter have been hidden in a bedroom at a Mayfair cocktail party, yacking about temples and quorums to a bevy of female librarians with bare tits?

Why, for fuck's sake, I asked myself irritably, should I be lumbered with *any* of this shit?

As our American friends say: go figure!

There must be *some* bloody connection, though. At least between some of those points.

I couldn't for the life of me quarry out any link that would be remotely believable which could be common to all of them. But at least there was somewhere I could start. I went downstairs to find Diana's address book.

On the way down I thought – the hell with it: it was obvious that I was being made use of in some way by the Porter-Lorrimer duo. But even as an escort I was made use of: that was what the clients paid me for. So Eve's case, though I might not know the real reasons for the contract, was theoretically – and morally, as far as I was concerned – no different from the others.

So I would pay the damned cheque in!

In the address book I looked up the name of the friend I didn't know. I picked up the phone and punched out her number.

If Di was still there, I'd make some excuse and relay some message or other. If she had already left . . . well, the friend must be approachable: after all she'd been enthusiastic about the porn video. I'd turn on the Silver charm and try to find out if she wore white gloves!

As it happened, I didn't get the chance.

The phone was answered at once.

A female voice, rather low: 'I'm listening.'

Odd response, I thought. But she sounded agreeable. 'Sorry to trouble you,' I said. 'This is Tom Silver. Diana's husband. I was wondering—'

'Oh, Tom! How are you? We've never met, but of course I know all about you. What can I do for you?'

'It's just that . . . I was wondering if Di had already left. A message from—'

'Already left?'

'Why, yes. She said she was spending the night with a friend, and—'

'Not with me, Tom. I haven't seen Di for over a week.

196

Must be some other friend. Sorry.'

'My mistake,' I said. And then again: 'Sorry to trouble you.'

But the mistake, of course, was Diana's, not mine. She'd neglected to tip off her mate that she was supposed to be staying the night there, to ask her to stall if anyone checked.

Okay, she'd played hostess to the smokers, whoever they were. Why in secret, I wondered?

Should I tax her with it, straight out, the moment she came back from wherever she was? Ask her what was so special about these people – and what they did – that they had to be asked on an evening when hubby was known to be absent until the small hours? Ask why she herself must pretend to be away while they were in the house (which at least seemed to rule out the obvious theory of a secret lover). Ask again about the white glove?

On reflection, I decided no. Clearly this was complicated. I had a clue – two in effect – so I would box crafty. I would play the waiting game, all eyes open, picking up what I could until I could piece together something that would make at least some kind of sense. A direct confrontation, I was pretty sure, would at this time bring me no more than a packet of more lies.

And you, Silver, in your case for sexual reasons, haven't you lied often enough about your extra-marital activity?

Guilty, m'Lord.

I went back to my study. Maybe I should snatch a couple of hours' sleep?

The phone rang.

Wearily, I picked up the handset. It was Carol. I was supposed to take her to lunch, again to a restaurant where we were likely to be seen by Geraldo Porrelli's wife. She was calling to cancel the date. And this time, I have to say, that was a relief!

'And, darling,' she added, 'I'm afraid ... I'm awfully sorry, but I'm afraid I have to announce the sudden death of Roland Harris.'

'Roland who? Oh ... you mean my alter ego, your phantom lover? What happened?'

'The play is over; the curtain has fallen,' Carol said. 'It's too bad, but Gerry's not going to shell out any more.'

'That's too bad, love, as you say. I shall miss you! But what happened? What did I do?'

'Sweetie, it's nothing *you* did: it's Signora Porrelli.'

'The Putney hostess, the lady wife? But what could she—?'

'She's flown the coop,' Carol said. 'Run off with Gerry's chef and fled to France!'

'She *left* him?' I'm afraid I laughed. 'After all that! We spend weeks building an elaborate scenario to hide the fact that – excuse me – he's cheating on her. And all the time the bitch has been cheating on him!'

'Ain't it the truth,' Carol said.

She paused, and then said carefully: 'I've really enjoyed our . . . relationship, Tom. It's been fun.'

'Me too.'

'And, although professionally it's over, I'd like you know that my place, as the brewers and wine merchants say, is by way of being a free house. So if at any time you're free and lonesome during restaurant hours . . . well, remember the offer.'

'I'll do that,' I said. 'I might well take advantage of it. And of you.'

Carol giggled. 'Be my guest,' she said.

Well, that was one good client gone. Three maybe, with Mrs P and Eve. I still had Mrs Fitz, Fanny Elmore, the point-to-point horsewoman, the surgeon's widow and a dozen or so other occasionals. Clearly I could never accept money from Muriel again. But there was always the possibility of a return bout with Minerva. Or even Beryl if I was really skint.

I sat down at the desk and started gnawing away at those mystery problems again.

But the more I thought of them, the more I thought of Eve. And as soon as Eve came into my mind, the only thing I could concentrate on was her actual body.

A French photographer, a couple of years ago, enjoyed a *succès de scandale* with an exhibition in Paris which consisted of nothing but close-ups of naked female genitalia. I'd seen illustrations of the exhibition in a magazine – more than two hundred framed cunts, double or treble life-size, plastering the walls of one small gallery!

And I'll tell you something: I reckoned I was smart with my division of ladies' pudenda into four main categories. But in all that delirious photo collection, there wasn't one cunt that could have been mistaken for any other!

Not if you were taking into account the whole shoot, the *ganz*, including the pubic hair.

Because it was here, in those photos, that the differences were more pronounced.

Think of pubic hair, and think therefore of cunts – what man doesn't? – and the average bloke pictures a neat triangle of springy curls, rather like a Van Dyck beard, punctuated along the median line by the aperture, the labia. But it ain't, as the song says, necessarily so. By no bloody means!

Nor does the bush always, as we tend to think, swoop down from the belly to surround the cunt and then fur what we call the vaginal furrow, disappearing between the legs.

In the simplest design, to me personally the least fascinating, the hair hardly notices the actual cunt, fringing it on either side with with a sparse ration, then continuing the line of the opening up towards the navel – a thin scimitar of hair bisecting the curve of the belly but never wide enough to come anywhere near those creases that separate the thighs from the pelvis. At the other end of the scale, usually worn by ladies with a faint moustache hinted on the upper lip, there is the bush that has spread so far out of hand that it's almost as though its owner has a rug across her knees.

But at least that's predictable – and usually symmetrical. Some bushes on the other hand are all over the shop, sometimes having virtually no apparent relation with the cunt at all!

Eve's was a case in point here, which is probably why I was still thinking about it.

So far as shape was concerned, her bush was a mess. If somebody had chucked a dark snowball at her and hit her squarely on the mons, that's the kind of pattern it made. But the fascinating thing was that this splodge of hairs had damn all to do with the cunt. Instead of nestling within the sexual thatch, whatever its shape, the labia were definitely below it, almost like two separate elements. And it was the cunt thus exposed which had really turned me on.

It was of course, in the Silver Collection, what I would have listed under Number Four: The Gash. That is to say the opening was long and the outer labia full and very visible. But it was the structure of these cushioned lips that astonished, almost as though the labia themselves had labia!

I can't say that I have exactly the camera eye. I mean all the pictures in the exhibition were posed (if that is the word for genitals) stills, whereas I was regarding a moveable feast. The labia in front of me – or above, or at one side, or underneath – were for the most part in motion. Or their owner was. Or I was. So my global view of The Gash, the equivalent of one of those photos, was in fact (you should excuse the word) a montage, assembled from dozens of different snapshots, each only fleetingly registered at the time.

The pieced-together whole, nevertheless, was sufficiently original to count as a one-off.

What could be seen of the vertical opening, in a non-excited state, was not a straight line but a series of wavy curves – left, right, left, right, closely folded, almost interlocked, with a small gap at the very top that could have been left deliberately to give access to the clitoris!

The flesh compressed in this way was not what I call inner flesh: it was a similar colour and texture to the meat forming belly and thighs, equally dry but of course looser because of the expansion required in sexual, and normal clinical use. It was only when the mental stimulation telegraphed to the vaginal nerves took effect – when she was getting turned on, if you like – that this outer barrier pouted enough to reveal the darker flesh, the wrinkled creases of the real outer labia.

And when these, moistened by the formation of female juices, dilated outwards to expose the inner, these again were complex enough to intrigue the exploring fingers or tongue.

Visually, the opening in its entirety was extraordinarily long. In the initial stages of excitement the lower half, the part nearest the anal region, remained firmly closed while the upper gaped wetly to welcome any intrusion. It was as if the full penetration, the entrance to the vagina itself was more strongly guarded than the entry to the clitoris and the manual-oral zones.

(I had wondered at the time if this was in her case a matter of usage. As she was bisexual, her lesbian half would presumably have less need for the tunnel than a hetero girl – I wasn't certain myself that we had actually fucked – and at the same time hands and mouths and masturbatory massages might automatically have increased the accessibility of the non-reproductive areas.)

Anyway, it was only when she was turned fully on and horny as hell that the entire cuntal organization was in full view – a splayed maw, redly gaping, quivering with lust, flowering open (I have to use the image again) like a tea rose in the sun.

A citadel, just the same, secure behind three rows of fortifications rather than the usual two!

Reflecting on the infinite diversity of this private organ, I remembered a dreadful story current when I was at school concerning a cunt, a teenage boy and an older woman.

The mature lady was trying to tempt the kid into her bed. But try as she would, although she had already wanked his cock stiff as a plank, she couldn't persuade him to put it in her.

'No, no,' he groaned. 'Not in there; I'm not having any of that.'

'But why not?'

'I know about those.' He indicated the wet lips of her excited cunt. 'I've read the shrink books. I know about emasculation, the female castration complex. You'll bite it off!'

'Baby, what *are* you talking about?'

'You've got teeth in there!' he cries. 'I know you have. You'll bite it off.'

'Don't be so silly,' she scolds. 'You've misunderstood technical jargon. Of *course* there are no teeth in there. I promise.'

'You're sure?'

'I promise.'

So at last she gains his confidence, persuades him again ... and helps him to stuff it in. They fuck. After a few energetic minutes he comes.

After he withdraws, zipping up his pants, he looks down at her cunt and says: 'If that's the state of your gums, I'm not surprised you have no teeth.'

The phone was ringing.

I scooped up the receiver. It was Sally Beaton.

Oh, my God! I thought in a panic. Not *again*!

But she was doing me a favour, not a moral injury. Her new job was in the morgue – the reference library – of a mass-circulation daily newspaper. I had asked her to check something out for me and she thought she had found the answer. Or at least an answer. Would I come over?

'Sure,' I said. 'Be glad to – and thanks, Sally. I'll be right there.'

'Leave it until a little later,' she said. 'I'm not really supposed to have outsiders in – only people from the non-editorial departments. But there should be no one around during the lunch hour. Tell the doorman you have a message for me and come on over then.'

I went on over then.

Chapter Eighteen

Sally, apparently alone as advertised, was sitting behind a
desk in a huge room completely filled with banks of chest-
high filing cabinets. They were arranged in parallel rows,
the aisles between them just wide enough to allow the deep
drawers to be pulled open without bothering anyone busy
at a drawer in the opposite row. Some of the cabinets were
wood, and clearly quite old; most were green or grey steel,
the type supplied to every office in Europe since World War
II. The room, Sally told me, was an annexe to the main
morgue, which housed hundreds of thousands of press-
cutting files, under hundreds of different headings, concerning current news over the past ten years. 'Here,' she
said, 'we're mainly background. Feature material, biogs,
critical stuff, armaments details, what the Home Secretary
said ten years ago and now denies. That kind of thing.'

'And you managed to dig out something on my monogram, or acronym, or whatever it is, bless you?'

'I certainly did!' Sally laughed. She shut a drawer and
came out from behind the desk. Scarlet leather miniskirt,
tight black rollneck with no bra, red tights and ankle boots.
Very sexy, very nice.

To be avoided at all costs, except for business reasons!

'You may find the results of the dig a bit surprising,' Sally
said. 'I did myself, but probably not for the same reasons. I
happened to be hacking into the News data bank, running
a cross check' – she gestured towards a computer screen –
'and I discovered that your query tied in with a scandal
exposé the paper's planning to run this Sunday!'

'No kidding!' I said 'Tell. Omit no detail, however slight.'

The monogram was a twist of four capital letters I'd
noticed by chance when I was prying into Mrs Porter's

cheque book. It was embossed, quite small, on the handle of a rubber stamp which stood on its ink pad beside the desk phone. So far as I could make out, the heavily entwined letters were L and T and G and S. They meant nothing to me, and I could find no repetition of the monogram during a rapid shufti around desk and bookshelves. I'd asked Sally to check because, in the circumstances, *anything* concerning the Porter woman might possibly be of interest.

But I'd certainly no idea that here I was going to strike pay dirt.

'Does it mean anything to you – LTGS?' Sally asked.

I shook my head. 'Nothing . . . unless it's, let's see, Lewd Trips for Girl Secretaries?' I gazed meaningfully at her leathered crotch.

That was a mistake, but I'll come to that later.

Sally said: 'I'm not surprised it meant nothing. You got the letters right – but you had them in the wrong order. It took me half a day to work it out. The monogram is actually GTSL.'

'Sounds like the chromed model type on the rear of a sports car,' I said. 'Okay, pour it on.'

'The letters stand for Golden Temple of the Sisters of Lesbos.'

'Good God!' I exclaimed. '*Lesbos*? And you did say *Temple*?'

She nodded. 'That took another couple of hours. It's very hush-hush. But finally I found out – not much I'm afraid – but it seems this is a secret society; not a cult and not a sect, but a circle of very rich—'

'Christ, do you mean to say—'

She held up her hand. 'Let me finish, Tom. A circle or club of very rich women who practise – and are no doubt very good at! – lesbian activities in secret.'

'Why secret? I mean it's not exactly illegal! Think of—'

'Secret because most of them are married, and if they are it's to very prominent men. Secret because it has to be – because of possible blackmail, public scandals, "revelations" by papers like ours. You know.'

I knew. But my mind was reeling at the thought of the austere, remote Mrs Porter actually being a *dyke*! Reaction totally illogical, I know. Why shouldn't she be gay? Lots of people were. They didn't always have neon lights on their shirt-fronts saying so.

At least it explained – partly anyway – the bedroom scene and the ladies I'd chosen to call librarians. 'About this golden temple part,' I began. 'Do you have any—?'

'Like I said, it's not a sect, not in any way religious – unless you make sex a religion – but they do have rules; they do have rituals.'

Like baring their chests when they meet? I thought. To accentuate their femininity?

'The so-called temple,' Sally said, 'is simply a place where they have weekly meetings. Orgies, our investigating team would like to think. Or where individual couples can go if they want to be alone. But the team could find no proof of orgies, no evidence of group sex, not even an approximate address for the temple. The flow of information simply dried up.'

I nodded. 'Sewn up very tight. If they're rich ladies, doubtless they pay well.'

'Until this week,' Sally said.

'Ah. Your exposé? Can you tell me about that?'

'Officially, no way. But come over here.' She went to the computer and started fingering keys. The screen blinked to life. Charts and diagrams and chunks of text unscrolled, flashed past.

'You know *Wicked* and *Whisper*, of course?' Sally said. 'If anyone does, you do!'

Men-only magazines run in tandem by their competitors. *Whisper* was a girlie glossy, more daring than the Hefner or Guccioni monthlies, full of sex scandals and beaver shots taken by photographers apparently lying on the floor between their models' heels. Top-shelf material. The sister mag pretended to be a glossy *News of the World*, saying isn't such and such a thing awful and then gloating over every prurient element of whatever the thing was. Its main reason for existence was to dig up dirt on characters featured against their will in *Whisper*, then threaten to print it to prevent them suing. Of course I knew them. What lecher didn't?

'Do you know Olaf Krassner?' Sally asked.

I knew of him. His name was Jack Briggs and he came from Huddersfield. Under the more exotic byline, he became a Central European professor-psychiatrist writing a regular column for *Wicked* revealing, and commenting at length upon, the more extreme sexual peccadilloes of his fellow men and women.

'We're going to fuck Herr Krassner over, this weekend,' Sally said. 'The own-medicine touch. Just take a look at this.' She nodded towards the computer.

The display had steadied. The screen showed a blow-up of one page of a handwritten letter – curly, discursive script below an apparently embossed north of England letterhead.

'We're chasing him as Kassner,' Sally said, 'first exposing his own deviation, then showing him up as a fake with the revelation that he's Briggs. The letter's in his handwriting; the address is his own; but he's writing as Krassner.'

I bent down to peer at the screen. 'Who's the letter to?'

'An old perv who lives in Eastbourne. Retired music teacher, regular client of the more . . . devious . . . London call girls. Must have written to ask advice. We only have this one page. But read it, Tom.'

Dear Mack – Forgive me ending my last letter so suddenly. Hildegarde, my lovely German wife (and, I am happy to say, cruel Mistress) summoned me unexpectedly to perform those personal hygiene duties which she craves – and for which, if insufficiently well carried out, I risk being so severely beaten.

Before these very particular tasks, I am dressed in a skintight latex catsuit and a rubber helmet leaving the mouth free, then forced into heavy bondage, totally immobilized in an excruciating leather harness (specially made for her in Hamburg). This leaves no part of me active but my mouth (I enclose a rough sketch).

*You ask how I came to be initiated into 'our club'. I was
lucky. Some years ago I chanced to meet the High Priestess
of the Golden Temple of the Sisters of Lesbos, a being
known only by the initial P. And for one delirious week,
after a ritual whipping by the Duty Slave, I was forced to
act as Altar Boy at the meetings of this shrine dedicated to
female superiority and—*

The page ended there, leaving one to guess . . . and what?
I looked at Sally, the eyebrows raised.

She shrugged. 'Very Freudian. It's total wish-fulfilment
of course. His secret life as Olaf K, with the domineering
German wife – the whole boots and whips and chains
scenario – exists only in his mind. His wife's name is Lucy,
and she comes from Blackpool. We suspect half the 'cases'
he quotes in his column are imaginary too.'

'But the references to the Temple, the GTSL stuff . . . ?'

'The organization exists all right. We know that. Whether
they have "altar boys" or not is another matter. Like us, he
probably heard about the cult – then imagined himself into
it!'

I was wondering if the letter P stood simply for priestess
– or could it possibly be Porter? I said: 'And you're going
to front page an exposure of this poor fantasy-deprived sex
maniac?'

'As an example of the degradation of modern life,' Sally
said. 'A man who invents a series of sexual perversions and
deviations – and then makes a living by giving himself a
fake psychology doctorate and analyzing them!'

'There's something more, isn't there?'

Sally grinned. 'The exposure is really only a lever – if we
use any of it at all. We're really after everything – or anything
– he knows about the genuine Temple people. Clearly it's
more than we know. If we hold the story over his head,
there's a good chance Mr Briggs will sing.'

'Well, darling, it's good to know that the integrity of the
press is still alive and kicking,' I said.

'Kicking anyway,' Sally said.

* * *

If my invesigation of the problems puzzling me had been part of a Hitchcock movie, there would doubtless have been two sinister individuals with hidden cameras following my every movement and noting times and places minute by minute. Had there been such sleuths on my trail that day, they would have observed with surprise that although Sally had told me all she could by one-ten p.m., it was not until one-fifty – forty minutes later – that I actually left the press building. This was because (a) Sally was Sally, and (b) Sally and I were in a sense trapped.

It had started when she switched off the computer and went down to the far end of the huge annexe. 'Come here a moment, Tom,' she called. 'I want to show you some-thing.'

She was behind the furthest bank of filing cabinets, a row of wooden elements at right angles to all the other rows. Thinking that she might have found some other ref-erence to my queries (silly me!), I hurried down the nearest aisle to join her.

But this time it was her own problem, not one of mine, that occupied her.

Sally's problem, as you might have gathered, was that she was never really happy unless she was engaged in some sexual activity or other, preferably of a forbidden or at least daring nature.

One of mine was that – God knows why – I never seemed able to resist her promiscuous advances: mentally biting every single nail with fear at the risk of discovery, I allowed myself time and time again to be coaxed, persuaded, blackmailed or just dragged into the most wildly compromising scenes.

The excuse this time – in a newspaper reference library, can you imagine! – was to show me an acquisition to what I called her sex wardrobe: a new pair of panties she termed revolutionary.

Behind a chest-high barrage of filing cabinets blocking off more than half the width of the room, she simply hoicked her miniskirt up, inside-out, over her slender hips, leaving the waistband still in place.

Her choice of time, place and risk of discovery were something else.

I think it was Robert Browning who wrote, 'Never the time and the place and the loved one all together!' If Sally had a family motto, it should have been that legend simply with the first word removed and the word 'Always' put in its place.

The panties were less skimpy than I expected. Scarlet like the leather mini, frilled of course, but covering more of Sally-below-the-waist than was usual. She was wearing them, oddly, under the red tights, which she rolled down to her knees. What was revolutionary about them, she explained, was not just that they 'gave access' as most men's underwear did, but that this was via nothing so banal and vulgar as a split crotch: the opening, closed with a nylon zip, was at the back *and it was horizontal!*

She reached behind her and drew the zipper. This freed a six-inch panel of the gauzy material, open at each side, to fall down below the buttocks, from where it could be drawn forward between the legs. And of course it freed the entire vaginal furrow, from clitoris to anus, to those with an interest therein.

At one-fifteen that afternoon, Sally had that interest.

I did not share it. Not then. 'What do you think?' she asked excitedly.

I was crouched down behind her, the better to see. I cleared my throat. 'Very . . . neat,' I said. 'Very ingenious. But in fact it's the same technique as the opening in front of a sailor's bell-bottoms – except that this is, quite literally, arse about face.' I stood up swiftly.

She had folded her arms and was leaning forward to rest them on top of the filing cabinets. 'I think they're dreamy,' she said. 'Tom, I want you to . . . to christen them.'

'Christen them?' I repeated huskily.

'Here, Now. For me. I want you to be the first!'

'*Sally!* You must be mad; you're out of your pretty skull. We can't *possibly*—'

'Oh, Tom – come on! We're safe for half an hour, I promise . . .'

'But not *here*!' I almost screamed.

I was standing close behind her. Suddenly she reached down an arm and seized my cock and balls through the trousering at my crotch, opening and closing her hand over the mass of . . . Well, you know the effect that kind of treatment has on the male member. Fear or no fear, I was hard in a moment. 'Come on,' she crooned again. 'Put it in. Stuff it up me. Just for a minute, darling, a tiny minute. Please!'

Christ! She already had my cock out; she was wanking it hard with four fingers and a thumb.

I gulped. 'Sally,' I said for the last time. Then, in my turn: 'Please! Look, we really mustn't—'

But we did.

Forcefully, she dragged my genitals towards her bared rump. I suppose, in that wild moment, I must have thought: the quicker you do it, the quicker you come, the faster it'll be over and the danger will be past. Or something like that. Plus, of course . . . well, by then I did have the urge.

Opening her legs as wide as the peeled-down tights would allow, she eased herself slightly towards me, leaning her top half further over the cabinets. Keeping a tight hold on my stiff cock, she brought back her other hand, grabbed one of mine, and shoved it into the welcoming heat between her thighs. She was as wet as a rock pool at low tide.

For an instant I fondled her cunt, curled fingers moistened as they explored the fleshy depths. What else could I have done? What would you have done?

Sally lifted her hips a little, canting the cleft a fraction higher towards me. An expert touch guided my cock-head until I could flex my own hips and plunge the velvet tip into the tunnel all at once easily, deliciously into the hot clasp of her lustful pussy.

I leaned against her as she sprawled forward over the cabinets. Feeling a little like a randy dog homing in suddenly on a bitch in heat, I began humping her power-fully from behind.

At that moment Sally smelled like a bitch in heat. She

rolled her hips, squirming firm buttocks back against my pounding loins. 'Ooooooh!' she gasped. 'Oh, God, that so gooood!'

And then, a few pumping strokes later, when my inflated glans rammed the neck of her womb: 'Aaah! Oh, Tom, you dear man, do it, do it! Stuff it into me, shove it up as far as you can!'

I was breathing pretty hard myself by then, although I couldn't say how much my blood pressure was due to fear of being caught literally in flagrante.

My lungs were groaning, the pace accelerating, the thrusts seeming to penetrate ever more deeply into Sally's eager belly . . . when abruptly her whole body stiffened. She heaved herself almost upright, spilling my skewering cock out of her with an audible squelch. 'Christ!' she hissed. 'There's someone coming!'

' "I know, said the plumber: it's me!" ' I quoted from the old limerick.

'I'm serious,' Sally whispered fiercely. 'I can hear footsteps on the stairs. For God's sake drop down out of sight!'

I dropped.

I could hear footsteps myself now. Heavy ones. They approached. 'The bloody Diplomatic Correspondent,' Sally murmured. 'Oh, *dear*!'

I was crouched down on my heels with my wet cock out, shivering suddenly, expecting at any minute to see beyond Sally's naked loins a head peering over the rampart of wooden cabinets.

She had folded her arms again and leaned forward as they rested on the scarred wood. 'Why, Herr Golding,' she said aloud in a forced voice, 'whatever brings you here in the lunch hour?'

'A rush job for the edition, my dear.' A deep voice, male, with a heavy European accent. 'I am wanting the quick check. Something Beria is saying in a speech to the Party Conference a year before he dies – which is being quoted to the Presidium last night by Boris Yeltsin. Only I think he is misquoting. Deliberately. But I must know before I comment.'

'And you want to check the files on policy speeches? Well, I think you'll find—'

'*Ja, ja.* The dossier, I think, on Soviet policies will be in the old files where you are standing.' The footsteps grew louder.

'No, no! Not here!' Sally's voice had risen a full octave. She was striving now, with one secret hand, to push the miniskirt back over her hips. 'I don't think . . . I'm sure you'd find it much easier to find . . . much, much quicker . . . if you tried the Personalities section, over near the entrance.'

'Ach, so? I was sure the files in those old dossiers—'

'They're out of order,' Sally said desperately. 'All these old cabinets . . . we're reorganizing this whole bank. The librarian is working on a more modern filing . . . a system with easier reference . . .' she let the sentence fade away as the footsteps, accompanied by a muttered grumbling, receded. 'For the moment you'll find it much simpler . . . Yes! There. Right over there beyond my desk. I'm sorry I can't help you right now, Herr Golding, but I have a rush job on myself, even if it is still my lunch hour.' She pulled open a drawer beside her and pretended to rifle through the files hanging inside.

I released my breath. I could hear steel drawers sliding out on rollers at the far end of the room. I could hear the man muttering crossly to himself. All right, you little bitch, I thought angrily. You talked me into this, you forced me into this trap. Now you can bloody well take it yourself. See how much you enjoy the own-medicine game from the other side of the net!

I'd put away my rampant cock and zipped up without making any noise. Now I shuffled warily closer to Sally's doubled up figure to position myself on my knees immediately behind her calves. I jerked the tights abruptly down to her ankles, reached up both hands and prised her thighs as far apart as I could. Then I flattened my hands on the cheeks of her backside and splayed them apart.

For an instant I gazed at the lewdly sodden hairs matting the valley between them, at the labia glistening obscenely

212

below the puckered ring of her anus, at the yawning gap gaping within, which had so recently been distended by my cock.

I ducked my head forward, clamped my mouth to those quivering lips, and shot my tongue deep into the dark of her inner cunt.

Sally had caught her breath as I savaged her tights, trying ineffectually to brush my hands away with a flapping hand. Now she stifled a sudden small cry as I sucked hard on the folds of swollen pussy flesh and lashed the tip of my tongue up, down and around her trembling clitoris.

'You have say something, my dear?' the old man asked from the far end of the room.

'No, no, Herr Golding. Excuse me.' She had taken a file from the drawer and was making like she was scanning two or three sheets she had taken from it. 'It's just that . . . I was searching for something difficult to locate . . . something unclassifiable – and I think I find it – er – found it.'

'If I should be so lucky to find my speech so quick!' the newspaperman said.

There was nothing Sally could do. My hands were clenched firmly on the resilient meat of her backside, my mouth filled with the salty folds of her cunt. No matter how much she writhed and rotated her hips, how ferociously she tried to heave herself away from my grasp, she remained at the mercy of my relentless hands and slavering tongue. She couldn't come out from behind the row of filing cabinets until I let her go and she could 'adjust her dress' as they say. Or until Golding found what he wanted and left the annexe.

It took him more than twenty minutes, during which he kept up a desultory – but agonizing – conversation with my prisoner and slave.

I went on sucking, relishing both the self-imposed task and Sally's discomfiture.

The insides of her thighs began faintly to shudder. Small tremors ran up and down the spinal column ridged above my busy mouth. I knew that she was building up to a climax

213

– partly because of my remorseless lingual massage of her inflamed clitoris, partly because of the nerve-stopping excitement that was so much part of her scene – when she was doing it to someone else.

I refused to release her. I sucked harder.

Her legs stiffened. The centre of her body convulsed. A whole series of small, rapid contractions spasmed her belly. She was holding herself back with a titanic effort, keeping her natural ebullience under control in a way I could only admire. But when the peak of the orgasm shook her frame she was unable totally to suppress a low moan of delight – almost a growl – bubbling at the back of her throat. Once more I awarded her full marks for the expert way in which she turned this into a sort of minor humming tune – a researcher delighted with the success of her labours.

Herr Golding was less delighted. He found the Beria speech – and it had not been misquoted! But at last he went away, leaving us less than ten minutes to calm down, dress and make ourselves fit to face the staff due back from lunch at any minute.

Sally wriggled free of my pelvic embrace the instant Golding's footsteps died away. Brushing away my hands, which I had slid up in the last moments to fondle the breasts naked beneath her tight black sweater, she turned on me, scarlet-faced. 'You bastard!' she choked. 'Tom, you utter, bloody *bastard*!' But she was laughing. The choking was due to the merriment shaking her whole body.

And it burst out into loud shrieks of mirth when she saw the stain on the front of my trousers. For me too the thrill of forbidden sex in this fraught situation had triggered an explosive release and my aching cock had without warning shot its load.

I left the building, hoping to find a quick taxi, before work on the afternoon shift began.

As I passed the doorman on my way out, Sally came to the top of the stairs. 'Goodbye, Mr Silver,' she called after me in a demure voice. 'And thank you again. It was *so* nice of you to come.'

214

PART FOUR

His, Hers . . . or Theirs?

Chapter Nineteen

What it came down to, finally, was a single question. When I had the answer to that, I was certain – don't ask me why – that all the problems puzzling me would fall into place and all the questions would as it were answer themselves.

The single question? Was there or was there not a connection between what I called the domestic mystery (Diana's absence, the use of the house, the white glove, the friend who wasn't) and the riddle involving Mrs Porter, Eve, the librarians and the supposed Sisters of Lesbos temple?

Thinking of Olaf Krassner, I decided to do a little inventing myself. If anyone could dredge up a believable response to the question it had to be me.

And the way to do it, I was convinced, was to keep watch as far as possible on the characters with rôles in these two scenarios. I would myself take the part of the Hitchcock villains I had imagined after my session with Sally in the newspaper morgue.

For this, evidently, I needed time. Happily, it was available. We had enough in the bank now for the escort racket to have become humdrum, so it was easy enough to account for my absences from home by inventing a few extra jobs with regular clients. A lunch here, a theatre or conference there, a cocktail party with the surgeon's widow or a visit to Mrs Fitz in Brighton – none of these would occasion comment or even particular interest at home, even though the clients themselves were unaware of these imaginary outings.

I went to the extent of hiring a car as unlike my own as possible (a Mini instead of a Volkswagen convertible). With this as cover, I followed my wife on several occasions and spent a number of uncomfortable – and unfruitful – hours parked outside hairdressers, the public library, a cinema and a lot of shops.

I looked up the address of the friend with the video, a Victorian detached house in the outer London suburb of Stanmore. I drove north and eased the Mini into a space between the cars parked on either side of the quiet residential street.

I spent the whole day there. I couldn't get near enough to garage myself immediately opposite the house, with its square portico and its deep windows, but I could keep an eye on those who came and went.

I was surprised at how many there were. Four men in the morning, five in the afternoon. Most of them stayed in the house at least an hour. There were a couple of overlaps. The only woman – a tall, slender redhead wearing a black leather coat – came at midday and left at two.

Nobody came out of the house that I hadn't seen going in. So the owner remained indoors.

Well, it doesn't take an Einstein . . . So it was that I used my favourite phrase. 'Oho!' I murmured to myself.

The men were all well – indeed soberly – dressed. Some arrived on foot, presumably having parked in another street. Others cruised up and down as I had, looking for a space. All the cars I saw were fairly new, fairly expensive: a BMW, a Renault Safrane, a Porsche, one of the big Fords.

By lunch time, cramped in the Mini, I was ravenously hungry. To hell with James Bond: I had to find something to eat. But there was nothing in the shape of a pub within a radius of a quarter of a mile in these shady streets of clipped lawns and blossoming roses. The only place I could find at all was a corner newsagents from which I was able to carry away nothing more than a single doughnut and a tin of lukewarm Coke!

There was however a phone box outside. I called Diana's friend's number. I got the same deep, rather pleasant voice, with the same unusual opening line.

'I'm listening.'

'Linda?' I said, relying on the hope that, after one short call, she wouldn't recognize the voice.

'Who's asking?'

'Roland Harris,' I said, remembering the defunct sup-posed boyfriend of Carol Dagois. And then, in a burst of improvisation: 'A friend of Roger's.'

The gamble paid off. 'Roger who? Roger Maltby or——?'

'That's right. Maltby. We were at school together.'

She laughed. 'Well, if your tastes are as simple as his . . . ! What can I do for you, my friend?'

I nodded to myself. I was right: the street was shadier than it looked! 'Something perhaps a little more . . . special?' I hedged.

'Whatever you want,' Linda said. 'I have a lot of equipment.'

'Would you care to quote a figure?'

'The straight century. But if you want heavy bondage, laced-up thigh boots, that sort of thing – in other words if you're going to be here more than a couple of hours – I might have to add an extra pony.'

'That seems just right,' I said.

'But, darling, I'm afraid I'm completely booked up today. And tomorrow's Sports Day at my little boy's school, so it'll have to be Wednesday.'

'Wednesday would be just great,' I said.

'Come at eleven,' she said. 'Then we can talk and get to know each other, and I can find out what you like before anyone else arrives. Okay?'

'I can't wait,' I said.

'One thing before you go, sweetie: how did you get my number?'

'Roger gave it to me,' I said. 'But I had to twist his arm.'

I went back to the Mini, ate my doughnut, and drank some Coke. So Diana's friend was a pro, and a specialized one at that, heavily into the Krassner scene. She was also, clearly, a high-class operative, working only by personal re-commendation. None of your stickers on newsagents' win-dows or sexy messages scrawled, with telephone numbers, on call box walls.

Interesting.

The question that obviously followed: was she in any way connected with Krassner himself?

If the answer was yes, that made a very definite connection, even if it was indirect, between my wife and the Porter complex.

So all I had to do was wait, and all the problems would fall into place?

Well, not exactly. I didn't know yet whether or not the answer *was* affirmative.

A little more fieldwork, Silver, if you please.

I waited in the car. Maybe seeing the girl would help. If she left the house.

She did. At five-forty-two, a quarter of an hour after the last man departed. She was a tall, willowy girl, about thirty, with dark shoulder-length hair and very discreet make-up. She wore a short, flared camel coat over a pleated, cinnamon-coloured, knee-length skirt. Her shoes were low-heeled brogues and her tights or stockings dark. Evidently not the kind of hooker who looked for trade on the sidewalk.

I decided to follow her. She had a splendid carriage – a firm, decisive, rather springy walk, with a straight, straight back and hardly any movement of the hips.

Visually, she didn't know me from Adam, so I chose to tail her on foot. A slow-moving car in these deserted streets would attract attention at once, and the last thing I wanted was for her to take me for a kerb crawler.

Visually again, to follow this brunette was a pleasure. She walked briskly to a nursery school, half a dozen blocks during which I had time to regret that my Wednesday date would not be kept. From the school she collected a small boy of about six. She took him around the corner to another line of parked cars, put him into a very shiny Mercedes 190, and drove him away.

'You're earlier than I expected,' Diana said when I got home. 'How was your point-to-pointer?'

'She was suffering from saddle sores,' I said.

So much, I thought, for the home team. Phase Two, surely, should be directed towards the Porter organization. But where to start? I hadn't heard a word from the lady – or from Eve – since I let fall the minor bombshell that I was onto their mysterious private arrangement to handle me – and I guess this was hardly surprising. People hate being found out. Me too, if it comes to that.

But their reasons for the deception remained shrouded in mystery. What, if anything, could it have to do with their gay circle?

This, frankly, was the question I'd be happiest to see answered first. But where to start?

Start at the beginning, the Red Queen said.

Yes, Your Majesty. Go on until I reach the end, then stop. I know. But the beginning, in this case, was the Porter apartment. Maybe I should go there again? Just on the off chance?

I got no reply from the Queen. Okay, I thought, I'll go there anyway.

It was a big block. The doormen knew me. They were not going to know, if I arrived openly, that I didn't have an appointment with Mrs Porter as usual.

I strode in past the porters' glassed-in office, glanced aside, said a brisk, 'Good morning.'

The uniformed man on duty looked up from a newspaper spread across his desk. He nodded, said an agreeably deferential, 'Good morning to you, sir!' and resumed his study of the racing tipster's forecast for Newmarket.

I took the lift to Mrs Porter's floor.

Her flat was at the end of a long corridor. Thirty feet beyond the front door, the passageway ended in a heavy barred door which led to the fire escape. The door could be opened, during daylight hours, from the inside but not the outside. Beyond it, the iron stairway zigzagged up to the roof and down to a courtyard flanked by lock-up garages.

And at each side of it there was a stone ledge – a string course, the architects called it – leading left and right along the facade of the building. The ledge projected four or five inches from the brickwork. And from a position only ten feet away on the left-hand side, a man of my height could easily reach up and grasp the stone balustrade surrounding Mrs Porter's balcony . . .

I was lucky that day, twice. I don't know what I intended to do when I reached the balcony. Deal with that later. But I don't suffer from vertigo and I reached it without too much trouble. Cue for lucky dip Number One: the noise of rolling shutters below; Mrs P's chauffeur was backing her Daimler out of a garage. A moment later she appeared and got into it. They drove away.

I was left looking over the balcony with a jaw definitely dropped. The lady – Evelyn proper Porter, if you please! – was dressed in riding breeches, a tweed hacking jacket, and tall boots more highly polished than her chauffeur's.

Only two explanations for this phenomenon suggested themselves to me: either she was going riding (at her age? never having given a sign of horsiness?) or the fancy dress was part of her rôle in the Sisters act. If she was in fact the Priestess – or Chief Dyke, I couldn't resist thinking – that could figure. The figure of authority, the riding mistress, gave the orders; the acolytes, bare-breasted to underline their subservience, obeyed.

I wished I could have been in a position to follow her. Another time, perhaps?

As it was, I was in an excellent position to do what I had hoped to do, waiting in the wings for the cue which could lead me to the second lucky dip.

I didn't need a cue: the prompter was being driven away in a Daimler. And the luck I'd hoped for was ready and waiting, on a plate. I'd noticed on several visits that Mrs P tended to leave the French windows leading to the balcony ajar, if it was sunny; latched, but not locked, if it wasn't.

Today was sunny. The geraniums glowed brightly in their urns; the trees in the gardens below tossed silvered leaves in a breeze blowing from the west.

The windows hadn't been left ajar, but they were not locked. I unlatched them and went in.

I won't bother you with details of the search, but it took me almost two hours to find the book. It was lying quite openly in the drawer of a bedside table. Not the one by Mrs Porter's own bed, but in one of the three spare rooms. Not a bad choice, considering the whole apartment was awash with bookshelves, glassed-in cabinets, period escritoires and desks with filing drawers.

Only half of my attention was concentrated on the search; the rest was confined to my ears. The front door was at the far end of the apartment. I'd sussed the terrain out, and I reckoned that if I heard a key in the lock, I could be out on the balcony, over the balustrade, and onto the string course before whoever it was walked down the corridor into the study. After that it was only ten feet to the fire escape and safety. It would mean leaving the French windows open if I was going to make it – but I hoped that could be put down to the breeze stirring those garden trees.

The book, about half an inch thick, was bound in olive green leather and the GTSL logo was embossed, discreetly, in a circle only half an inch across, in the top right-hand corner of the cover. The pages inside, half the size of a sheet of A-4 typing paper, were lined. Fifteen or twenty had been covered with Mrs Porter's neat handwriting.

I sat on the bed, opened the book on the bedside table, and started to read.

It was pay dirt all right. There were three different kinds of entry: chunks of close-written text, lists of addresses and telephone numbers, and what seemed to be timetables – a series of dates reaching back several months and ending in ten days' time.

It took me a while, sorting it all out. The text looked like the minutes of a succession of meetings over the same period, each keyed in to a particular date. I couldn't make much sense of them, partly because they were written in a personal code, partly because the individuals mentioned were referred to only by numbers. But the numbers themselves also appeared against the addresses, none of which had a name attached. But if the address was familiar, then the number . . . ?

I started leafing through the addresses. One of the first I came to was my own. This was hardly surprising: Mrs P was, after all, a client. But it was odd, just the same, to find it linked to a book devoted to a group of lesbians. The figure against it was a four.

Another surprise. Amongst twenty or thirty other addresses, I found that of the high-class hooker, Linda. And she did have a link with my address: she was a friend of my wife's. The only other one I could identify was the address of an actress we knew – and knew to be gay – a highly sexy redhead called Zelda Cornwell.

In my head, the machinery was beginning to turn. I had a sudden hunch. The number against my address was four. My wife's name was Diana. D, her initial, was the fourth letter of the alphabet.

Since I was familiar with a second address, I could cross-check. I turned back to the address I knew to be Linda's ... and, right enough, there was the number twelve, L being the twelfth letter of the alphabet! As a final confirmation, I saw that the figure identifying Z for Zelda was twenty-six.

Message received and understood. But if four was Diana – hastily I returned to the texts – she must according to the minutes have attended at least half a dozen meetings in the past two months.

So *Diana* was part of this set-up? My Diana, my wife?

The hunch was widening its terms of reference. I returned to the timetables. Each date had a number in brackets against it. Only one, a short time previously, had the number four bracketed.

The date was that of a Wednesday. The day of the Grosvenor House Ball.

The coin dropped. No change was given. Mrs Porter had paid Eve Lorrimer to hire me, specifically to keep me away from home all evening, all night, because my house was to be the site of a meeting – a ritual? an orgy? – involving members of her gay circle!

I looked up from the book. I was aware of my pulse beating rather fast. The hell with it: I went back to the study and poured myself a stiff whisky. Back in the spare room I returned to the dates.

I found one with the figure twelve, Linda's number, against it. I checked the date against my own engagement diary. Yes – the weekend Diana had 'spent with her mother', the second time I had been to South Croydon.

Was Muriel, then, part of this conspiracy?

No way. She hadn't known I was to meet her, to invite her. In any case, if the meeting was in suburban Stanmore, there was no need to keep me away from home.

At least *something* was a coincidence and not part of a scheme!

I looked up a date with twenty-six against it. There were several, the last of which – so the minutes told me – had indeed been attended by Number Four.

Back to my diary. Yes, a weekend. Di was playing Happy Families with Mum again.

Well, Tom, you did want those questions answered.

It was after I had escaped from the apartment, washed the whisky glass, closed the French windows and left via the fire escape (the porter, I hoped, would assume I'd gone in the Daimler) that I pieced together what I thought must be the circle's modus operandi.

I was sitting in a pub in Gloucester Road, munching a late sandwich and sipping my third large Johnnie Walker.

I was remembering Mrs Porter's words to the librarians at the Mayfair cocktail party. *For the moment, the temple will remain available to members on weekdays, but it will be closed on Saturdays and Sundays. Quorum sessions will continue . . .*

With what I had found out, this now made sense. Or some sense anyway.

The way I read it, the Temple didn't exist at all, as a specific *place*, a particular building. It was an abstract, an idea. It was wherever the twenty-six members of the group – for I could find no number higher than that – chose to meet, or were directed by Mrs Porter to meet, for their ritual sex parties. Or where individual members chose to meet for less numerous sessions. From what the book told me, I guessed that the full meetings – the quorums the boss lady referred to – were held from time to time, in no particular order, at the homes of those women able to make them available. But no longer at weekends.

And, of course, there was nothing to stop individual

couples – or trios or quartets – getting together, via Mrs P, whenever they felt horny enough or there was space available at some home or other, free of the unwelcome presence of husbands.

Mrs Porter's book was no more than a handy method, lightly coded, of keeping a record of all these complicated arrangements.

I guessed, too, that there was a touch of Sally in all this: the thrill of cheating on Jack, of belonging to a secret society, with rituals and passwords and clandestine sex, and doing this – naughtiest of all – with other *women*! Not the thing to attract normal gays who had come out ages ago and were perfectly open about it, or feminist activists, or SM/Dykes and Feminists Against Censorship! But sweet music to ladies who still wished to say no to Mummy and Daddy, and were heavily into kicking against the pricks (as you might say).

I wondered if the 'priestess' of this quasi-religious sex cult kept other records – in which, for instance, her members were referred to as A and B and C.

And I wondered too – I hadn't thought of checking – whether the address of Eve Lorrimer was among the twenty-six? Or whether Mrs P simply happened to have met her because she was bisexual and decided to row her in to help on this one occasion (I found out much later that it wasn't and she had).

Right now however, weaving my way to the Gloucester Road bar to order my fourth whisky, I was more concerned with a new problem of my own.

Okay, I had discovered that my two main mysteries were indeed connected, you might say intimately; I knew about the lesbians, the quorum, the use of my house and the employment of Eve; I was aware of the involvement of my own wife.

So what was I going to do about it then?

Chapter Twenty

You might as well start at home, I told myself. Charity, they say, starts there too. Maybe I could find it in me to be charitable about certain deceptions if I tackled Diana head-on before deciding on a general plan of action?

The difficulty, you see, was that apart from the fact that I was naturally smarting because I'd been taken for a sucker, I found the whole idea of the temple thing something of a turn-on.

Like all men, I was at the mercy of my own automatic reflexes; like a lot of them, I discovered that I found the concept of lesbianism sexually exciting. Like all small boys, I was burned up by the thought that something thrilling was going on – and I was excluded, I wasn't a part of it.

All those breasts and bottoms and heaving cunts; all those red-nailed fingers probing and caressing; the lipsticked mouths opening and the wet tongues flicking out – such images unfailingly provoked a distant roaring in the ears, a high tide in the adrenaline sea. Don't ask me why: ask Dr Freud and Professor Jung.

Or perhaps, snide thought, you could write to *Wicked* and ask the Herr Doktor Olaf Krassner!

Here I was, anyway, with all this secret knowledge, all these provocative fantasies of female excess . . . and I was stuck because I wanted to get my own back, but at the same time I dearly wished that, some way or other, I could be rowed in, made a part of the sexual scene.

Diana, of course, was the obvious port of entry. But how to handle it without pushing her off into the deep end – with the risk of blowing the whole Porter scenario wide open and cutting myself off from any rôle, even a small one, in future productions (you want mixed metaphors, we stock them in all sizes)?

And so far as future productions went (here was my third-time-lucky: never two without a third, as the French say) I was fortunate enough to have noticed that the next 'temple' was going to receive its faithful on Thursday of the following week – and that the number against it, on the last page of Mrs Porter's timetable, was twelve.

So the girls were going to meet at Linda's place. And I knew the address. So far, very good.

Another point: I actually had a date with Linda myself, which I'd had no intention of keeping when I made it. But now I was having second thoughts. She was after all a professional: maybe I could make use of her services – but not exactly in the way her other clients did!

But first, Diana.

I was going to let her know that I knew something, but not that I knew it all. After that I'd see what happened, playing Act Two by ear. Act Three, though, was what I hoped to be in on.

I was handed the opening over Sunday lunch. 'Are you busy next week, darling?' Diana asked.

'Not especially. I've Mrs Fitz on Tuesday, a conference at Oxford with the surgeon's widow on Friday, somebody new on Saturday. Why do you ask?'

'I thought . . . I just thought I might pop over to see Linda again one day,' she said carelessly. 'Probably Thursday.'

'Fine,' I said. She didn't need to use Mum as a cover this time: she really would be going to Linda's. 'Will the other girls be there?'

'The . . . other girls?'

'The ones who were here when I was at the ball. Tell me, which one smokes the cigars? Zelda, I'll bet. Do let me know in advance next time, and I'll get in a couple of ashtrays.'

She stared at me. She had gone very still. 'You know, don't you?' she said at last.

'I should have thought that was obvious,' I said. 'When

you see Linda, do thank her again for so kindly lending us a piece of her professional equipment.'

Suddenly there were pink spots on Di's cheeks. 'Just what do you mean by that?' she flared.

'Well, she's a whore, isn't she? Porn videos must be part of the, shall I say, stock in trade?'

'Don't use that word,' Diana shouted. 'I won't have it. She's a sweet person, she's had a tough life. She has a child to bring up. If she has . . . certain tastes . . . and certain of her friends who share them are prepared to . . . contribute . . . Anyway, she's never looked for trade on the street in her life.'

'All right, then: a call girl,' I soothed. 'Nothing against that. Lots of people's daughters are. No reason why your mother's daughter shouldn't be one of them. You too could be the life of the party, especially if you're so heavily into cunt. Maybe you could pick up a few tips from your friend.'

She glared at me.

'You had the brass to ask *me* how the dykes did it when we watched that video,' I raged. 'Well you know fucking well now, don't you? Why not put that fieldwork to good use? You could start another kind of escort agency – techniques courtesy of my kinky friend.'

'You're a shit, Tom,' Diana said between clenched teeth. 'Sometimes I think you're quite unspeakable.'

'I love you too,' I said.

Wednesday at eleven, little more than twenty-four hours before the Golden Temple of the Sisters of Lesbos opened its great bronze doors – that was the time of my date with Linda. I arrived at one minute past, thanks to my own car this time.

'I'm listening,' the answerphone beside the front door told me.

'Roland Harris,' I said. 'We have an appointment at—'

'Come up. First floor.'

The lock of the door clicked. I pushed it open and went in.

She met me at the head of the stairs, dressed a little

229

differently from the proud mother I had followed to the infant school. Today she was wearing a very tight, wasp-waist, black leather corset with shiny black high-heeled boots laced up to the mid-thigh. Below the corset, a scarlet vinyl G-string hugged her mons; above it a bra of the same material cupped generous breasts. Her hair was caught back by a black Alice band and she was heavily made-up.

She sat me down on a knole settee in a pleasantly furnished sitting room overlooking the street and offered me a whisky and soda. I accepted.

As soon as I was sipping, she lowered herself into a chair opposite me and pulled a small riding crop – leather-covered of course – from a bracket projecting from her right boot. Teasing this through the fingers of her free hand, she fixed me with a level stare. 'And so, "Mister Roland Harris",' she said, between obvious inverted commas, 'just exactly who are you? You fell neatly into my customary trap for anonymous punters. I don't know any Rogers, Maltby or otherwise.' The head of the thonged crop thwacked gently against her open palm. 'The workshop is on the floor above. But before I even consider taking you up to it, I want to know the truth – so you'd better come clean.'

Caught out, I felt that my frank smile was a little weak. But in fact she'd saved the most awkward part of my prepared spiel: she already knew that, as a client, I was a fake.

I told her who I was. She laughed – a good, deep, genuine laugh with a lot of warmth in it. Evidently she was amused. That, I thought, wasn't a bad start.

So, truthfully, I told her the whole story. I went into it all, from the Porter librarians at the cocktail party, through my discovery that Eve was being paid to hire me and the night with her after the ball, to the suspicions raised by the smell of cigarette smoke in my house. I explained that what I knew of the Temple, and Diana's connection with it, derived from research in the reference library. The only thing I left out – apart from the fact that I'd fucked the librarian – was the burglarious entry to Mrs P's apartment.

'Well, bravo for you!' Linda said when I'd finished. 'So

now you're Mister Know-all. But tell me, having gone this far, why have you come to me? I gather you're not into this kind of thing?' She raised the riding crop, then tapped it agaist her boot.

I shook my head. 'Unfortunately not. But if anyone could persuade me' – smile – 'you could!'

'I don't think so,' Linda said – and I must say that, if I could have seen her without the gear, at that moment I would have given a great deal to get to close quarters! But, alas, what I had to offer, today at any rate, was for quite another purpose.

'I see enough gentlemen,' she went on, 'for business. I don't want any in private, however charming' – her turn to smile – 'they may be. That's probably why, like so many business girls, I prefer to have ladies for my kicks. But you haven't answered my question.'

I cleared my throat. 'This may insult you,' I said. 'And I'd understand if you threw me out. But I'm speaking to you as a professional. I'm asking you to provide a service – not perhaps the one you customarily provide, but one for which I'm prepared to pay any reasonable sum you quote.'

'Interesting,' she said. 'Perhaps you'd better tell me what it is.'

I told her what it was.

She refused. I coaxed, I persuaded, I explained. She hesitated. I made points, moral, social and logical. I was very careful indeed not to make the slightest, faintest hint that, because of what I knew about her, I could cause trouble with the law. I wanted her to agree because of the force of my arguments, not through any threats of moral blackmail, implicit or explicit. And at last – it was almost midday and I was on my third whisky – she came around to my way of thinking.

'I can't see that it would cause any damage,' she laughed. 'After all, it's kind of in our direction. It's certainly kinky – and I have to admit, although with me it's business too, that for a perv like me, anything *really* way out in the kinky line is a must. So let's say, Tom, that you've got yourself a deal!'

'See you tomorrow then . . . partner,' I said.

Thursday was wet. The rain pelted down from dawn to dusk. It really was a black mackintosh day – even if you weren't driving out to a party at the Linda Gosforth residence in Stanmore.

I parked three blocks away and raced my umbrella to the house half an hour before the Sisters were due to arrive. Linda, back in her discreet suburban mother rôle, fed me a drink and then installed me on the upper floor in what she called the workshop. The business of the Temple was to be transacted in the first-floor sitting room that I knew and two large bedrooms behind it.

I settled down amongst whipping stools and pillories and hanging chains and what looked like a vaulting horse equipped with leather wrist and ankle cuffs. Built-in cupboards with mirrored doors filled one wall of the spacious room. Canes, crops, knouts, switches and a collection of handcuffs and leg-irons hung from battens neatly arranged along another. Above the sloping ceiling, the downpour drummed relentlessly on the tiles of the roof.

They arrived in ones and twos, only about a dozen, over twenty-five minutes or so. Linda was serving drinks, and soon the house was filled with the pleasant sounds of female chatter and laughter. Mrs Porter, as might be expected, was the last of all.

Linda, for obvious security reasons, had installed a slanting mirror above the stairhead in which, without being reflected herself, she could see anyone climbing the two flights of stairs or crossing the landing on the floor below. I settled myself in the dungeon – the most comfortable thing I could find was an old-fashioned dentist's chair – and fixed my eyes on this.

Zelda Cornwell – tightly belted white vinyl mackintosh à la Dietrich – arrived with a young blonde whose straight hair hung in a glossy curtain down the whole of her back. I could smell the actress's cigar from where I sat.

A woman I recognized as the wife of a cabinet minister, mink coat spiked with rain, arrived just after her. I saw

Diana with two well-dressed women I didn't know and – rather to my surprise, because although she was bisexual she wasn't in Mrs Porter's book – Eve Lorrimer. Of the three or four others, only one had a face that was familiar, but at first I couldn't put a name to it.

Mrs P herself, rather as I expected, was again in her breeches, boots and tweed ensemble.

Despite this authoritarian costume, nevertheless – Linda had assured me – none of the Sisters were remotely into her own sado-maso professional scene. I would be a hundred percent safe from discovery up here.

Until the time came . . .

But more of that later. It seemed clear from the drinks-in-hand to and fro I could observe below that the arrival of the 'priestess' was the automatic signal for the ritual baring of breasts that I had witnessed at the cocktail party. For now all the females circulating were nude from the waist up.

I saw the delicate – and familiar – pair of Eve's above a pencil-slim, white leather skirt; my wife's double handful with black jeans I hadn't seen before; great rolling knockers over the thick waist of the minister's wife; insolently pointed tits bouncing in front of Zelda's blonde. The breasts of the hostess, as I had gathered when I saw her 'in uniform' the previous day, were superb: taut, resilient, full and perfectly shaped. She had teamed them with a modest, floor-length skirt in jade-green chiffon and silver slippers.

Fascinating, all of it.

A meeting of this particular circle was scarcely the place for it, but I confess that all this coming and going of jiggling, naked tops above proper, soberly clothed bottoms, all these nippled mounds of swelling female flesh so lewdly exposed, were making Silver horny as hell. Gay though their owners might be, the sight of them swiftly stiffened the staff of this spying hetero!

There was a buffet in one of the bedrooms. The ladies began to appear on the landing with forks poised, mouths full and plates in one hand. Although I was licking my own lips, I was still concentrating on all those tits.

A moveable feast indeed!

Some time after this, when the landing was deserted, Mrs Porter – who had remained fully dressed – strode alone into the sitting room. It was time, I knew from what Linda had told me, for her homily, speech, address – or whatever it was that I'd heard part of at the cocktail do. The Sisters, I knew too, would be undressing in the bedrooms, for total nudity was the rule in the later part of the meetings. Indeed, I could hear giggles and scuffles and the occasional outright laugh filtering up from the rooms at the rear of the house below. Soon, the whole crowd of them, crammed together, flooded across the hallway and into the front room.

Risking a direct view, I abandoned the mirror, extricated myself from the chair and went to the stairhead. Below the now familiar backs, I saw a scramble of bare hips and bums.

For the seconds it took them to cross the landing, I saw over the bannisters the rear view of big hips, slender hips, meaty hips and muscled hips, Diana's 'hinge' and Zelda's bony swell, and bobbing behind them this collection of bottoms and backsides and buttocks and bums – everything from a clenched American ass to a red-cheeked English arse!

Eve was hand in hand with the woman whose face was familiar, and it was then that I remembered: I had seen her at the cocktail party, again with Eve. And she had in fact been our hostess, but I didn't find that out until later.

The hallway was deserted once more. From inside the sitting room I heard Mrs Porter's voice.

'You will all, of course, by now have met our friend Eve Lorrimer. I co-opted Eve for this evening because, as some of you know, she was a great help to us . . . preparing the ground . . . for one of our more recent meetings. I am hoping, as Number Twenty-One will be leaving us to go to America, that a full quorum may be convened so that Eve can be elected a full member in her place. Now, so far as this meeting's official business is concerned . . .'

Someone closed the sitting-room door and I heard no more.

I felt my throat tighten a little. It was time now for me to start the preparations for the little charade I had worked out with Linda – which, fortunately, the rules of the circle permitted us to stage. And of course, now the time had actually arrived, I was suddenly nervous. And shy as hell!

On a rack at the far end of the dungeon, a few items from Linda's wardrobe were laid out. They had been chosen from one of the built-in cupboards – from a tightly packed row of catsuits and combinations, strait-jackets and sweatsuits, drawers and dresses and drag outfits in black latex, leather and brightly coloured plastics. The articles selected were a high-necked, long-sleeved shirt in blue vinyl ('Blue for a boy!' Linda had chuckled), a black leather helmet and boots. And I was to put on these things – and nothing else! – before the curtain went up.

Originally, I'd had some vague idea of playing the voyeur . . . perhaps, if an opportunity presented itself, to make some kind of interruption with the idea of embarrassing Diana. And, if things worked out all right, Eve and Mrs Porter.

Linda's own idea, which was much more specific, was also much better.

At any given 'temple', she told me, the hostess had the right, if she so wished, to introduce a male of her choice.

'You mean introduce like "How d'you do and Meet Jack Spratt" '? I asked.

'No, no. That would never do. Introduce him *into* the evening. Anonymously, with a special task to perform, at a particular time.'

'The gentleman wouldn't by any chance be known as an "altar boy", would he?'

'Why, yes,' Linda said, surprised. 'As a matter of fact he would. How did you know that?'

'Just a thought,' I said.

Just as the Sisters were bare-breasted at the beginning of the evening to underline the fact that they were female, Linda said, so the 'altar boy' must be tightly covered above the waist to show that he wasn't – and bare from the waist down to show that he *was* a despised male.

235

'Don't the girls resent the appearance of a man, even if it's in a somewhat humiliating rôle?'

'You don't understand,' Linda said. 'The members of the circle are not ordinary gays – girls who prefer other girls and have come out openly and said so, living an overt lesbian life. The point of the society is that it's *secret* – that it has to be, because if the members are not bi, at least they're married, and must on no account be known to be gay.'

'And that's why the numbers are limited? So what about Zelda?'

'Zelda's an actress. Everybody knows actors and actresses are crazy! It's expected of them.'

'Why does your "priestess" remain fully dressed? Is that part of the ritual?'

Linda shook her head. 'It's become so. But P is sensitive about her body – two large operation scars and her age shows. The truth is, she's a gay voyeur: she loves to watch girls together.'

'But . . . you're telling me that gays who have come out would never tolerate a man in a situation like this – but your members do, in certain circumstances, because in their day to day life they're *used to* having a male around? Is that what you're saying?'

'Something like that,' Linda had said.

Undressing in her S/M dungeon, I felt peculiarly vulnerable, like a snail without its shell – a condition I hadn't been in, just because I was naked, since my teens. I got into the vinyl shirt. It was cold against the skin until the material took the body heat. I closed the press-studs at the wrists and neck and the fastening that cinched it in at the waist. The boots were thick-soled, low-heeled, zipping to just above the ankle – to underline the cloddishness of man, I supposed. I put them on.

The helmet was a bit like a mediaeval executioner's mask, only more complicated. It was in velvety, very soft leather, with a zip up the back. There were large eyeholes and the mouth was free. Otherwise the whole head was encased. I found it was surprisingly comfortable.

Despite the gear I felt more naked than I ever had in my life.

With the air cool against my nude belly and my genitals flapping, I stole downstairs.

The *Concise Oxford* states that a jeroboam is 'a wine bottle 4–12 times the normal size'. The one I had to deal with at Linda's felt as though it contained the full dozen – of champagne of course.

Part of the ritual was that, at midnight, the hostess – or altar boy if there was one – served the guests with bubbly. It was in fact the signal that the talking was over and action could commence. As everyone but Mrs P was already naked, the transition was not too difficult to effect.

Herr Krassner's letter wasn't all wishful thinking either. He was right about the altar boy ... and he wasn't wrong about the whipping by the 'duty slave' (normally the hostess, as it turned out). 'Do you really have to?' I asked uneasily. 'I mean, couldn't we just—?'

'Imperative,' Linda said. 'The ritual putting of Monsieur in his place. But it's not done in front of everybody.'

I cleared my throat. 'Even so ... ?' The girl was after all a professional beater!

'They have to hear the strokes before the boy brings in the champagne,' Linda said.

'Couldn't you – er – whack a cushion or something?'

'It has to be six strokes, not more not less. I could perhaps for four – but I'll have to give you a couple: you have to back in and show the marks, you see.'

'Oh, Christ,' I said.

She laughed. 'Some guys pay me, you know! You're getting about forty quids' worth for free!'

She found a suitable cushion and we went into the kitchen. Silence from the front room. Linda opened the door wide, then went into the hallway to open the sitting-room door. She mouthed some kind of mumbo-jumbo concerning discipline and order and rules, then assaulted the cushion with a springy ashplant cane.

After the fourth measured stroke, she nodded towards

the kitchen table. Back at school again at the age of forty-one ('Please, sir, it wasn't me, sir. Don't hit me too hard, sir') I bent over and stuck my head under the edge of it.

The two cuts she gave me were ... well, highly professional. And a damned sight harder than anything I ever suffered at school. Maybe the acoustics of the house were poor; perhaps she was just having fun. Whatever, it was all I could do not to yelp.

She'd placed them very cleverly, so that the weals could have been the result of several over-lapping strokes very accurately placed.

'You will now,' she said in a loud, severe voice, 'enter the room with the wine and pay your respect to the Sisters.'

I obediently backed in to the sitting room, holding the giant bottle cradled at arm's length. It took all my strength to totter in without cannoning off the doorpost.

There was a murmur of female voices as I appeared, a lot of whispering, a stifled laugh.

I felt of course absolutely silly – anonymously masked, thrutched up in blue plastic, wearing those heavy boots with my cock and balls dangling between my legs.

I lurched between all these fleshy nude bodies to unload the jeroboam on a rubber-tyred tea trolley loaded with champagne glasses and a cradle geared to tilt the bottle.

I walked to the centre of the room and stood there. That was the bad news; now the good!

Mrs Porter, incongruous as myself in her riding boots, breeches and hacking jacket, went to the trolley, exploded the cork of the jeroboam, and actuated the mechanism allowing her to pour out individual glasses of champagne. One by one, the Sisters approached and were given a glass. At the same time the boss lady indicated one of them with a riding crop and nodded towards my masked head.

This was my signal. 'Paying respect' – as you might suppose – was an obeisance, a tribute to that part of the feminists present which I could never hope to rival.

'You circulate,' Linda had told me rather less elegantly, 'and suck each cunt in the order P will indicate.'

I did just that, starting with one of the heavily-built

women I didn't know. Each tribute lasted until a touch of the crop on my savaged backside told me to move on to the next one chosen. They sat, squatted or stood around, guzzling the drink, while I went down on my knees in front of each chair, settee, table or whatnot and shoved my face into a series of pussies, working lips and tongue into a collection of cunts as varied as anything the French photographer had shot for his exhibition.

The time spent on each 'tribute' varied considerably – presumably as the result of eye contact between the suckee and Mrs P.

The ritual was not, of course, carried out in respectful silence. The champagne was loosening tongues other than mine, and there was a good deal of chatter as well as a certain amount of giggling. This was because, despite my reservations and my initial timidity, the moment I actually started on those pussies, sex reared its ugly head . . . and with it the head of my stiffening cock!

'Just look at his thing!' I heard someone say. 'And that's what they all make such a song and dance about? Not really aesthetic, if you ask me!'

I wasn't asking. Like P.G. Wodehouse's Jeeves, I was endeavouring to give satisfaction.

I think I didn't make out too badly. There were only two complete misses. One was Diana. I was deliberately clumsy and inexpert, and she said crossly: 'That's enough! I get better service than that from a male of my own at home.' The other zero was Zelda's young blonde, who squealed the moment my tongue parted her labia and giggled: 'Stop it – you're tickling!'

The longest session was with the big woman I'd seen hand in hand with Eve, our hostess at the cocktail party (the English wife, I heard later, of a French motor car manufacturer, and very, very rich). Forget the librarian frame: this lady – she must have been pushing fifty – had the most delicious cunt. She was a pouter, the lips plushy, tender as warm velvet, the inner flesh – when at last you got to it – succulent and almost incandescent with moist heat. I must have been slaving away there for all of ten minutes before I heard her say in a ruminative voice: 'You know – you could interest me.'

But it was then that I felt the tap on the rump that meant I had to drag myself away, the big cock empurpled and aching between my naked thighs.

It was after the final tribute that things livened up.

The party, I had been warned, would then be freed of any restrictions and the Sisters left to improvise in any sexual way they wanted – provided they changed partners, like kids in a game of musical chairs, each time Mrs P chose to tinkle a small handbell. I think the original pair bonding was determined by her, drawing names out of a hat. After that there were no rules; the girls could operate in couples – or trios or quartets – wherever they wanted, in the sitting room, on beds in the two back rooms, in the kitchen or on the stairs if that took their fancy.

Linda had given me strict instructions about this section of the soirée.

I was to remain in the sitting room, standing to attention facing the curtained window, no watching unless one or more of the performers specifically asked for it.

'But it sometimes happens,' Linda said, 'that one or other of the girls gets horny for hetero – in association with whatever partner she has, of course. Several of them, remember, are bi. Most have men, welcome or unwelcome, somewhere in their lives.'

'What happens then?' I asked.

'Whoever it is will ask P to fetch you, or contact you herself. After that you're on your own. Be guided by them ... but do what comes naturally. You're no longer a slave but just another guest. One rule remains though: you must *on no account* say a single word. Okay?'

'I can't wait,' I said.

As it happens, I didn't have to. Or not for long. As soon as the first bell tinkled, and the apartment was filled with subdued laughter and the hurried scuffling of nude bodies, I felt a hard hand on my shoulder, spinning me around. It was Eve's friend, the big lady who had declared an interest.

I was a bit leery of Eve, as I had been of the silky pubis

of my bisexual wife; after all, we had spent a whole hectic night together and it was reasonable to suppose she *might* have recalled something about me. Enough for recognition anyway. But she had kept me at her cunt for a very short while this time, talking throughout my efforts to the blonde. And the big lady must have been with her before the first bell, for when I was beckoned into one of the back rooms, the partner waiting for us on the king-size bed was the cabinet minister's wife.

She looked much smaller – and much drier – without the mink. She was sharp-featured and beautifully made-up, with dark cropped hair, unremarkable breasts, slightly dropped, and hands with long, red-nailed pianist's fingers.

There were other sex devotees already in the room. Zelda sprawled in an armchair, smoking her eternal cigar, with one bare leg hooked over an arm of the chair. She was teasing one of her pointed nipples with her free hand. From there, down as far as the knee of the grounded leg, she was completely shrouded by a moving curtain of pale and glossy hair as the blonde girl knelt on the floor before her and sucked.

The lighting was very low-key, but I could also make out a heaving parcel of buttocks and backs and bulging breasts as the two largest Sisters entwined themselves somewhere below us in the position known as sixty-nine. Further back in the shadows, perched on an upright chair, one on the knees of the other, two unidentifiable nudes kissed passionately in a tangle of arms and breasts and jerking hips.

I was flat on my back on the bed, the cock, which had deflated when I was facing the curtains, now rigid as a maypole again and feeling as tall as Nelson's Column. 'Your performance in the other room was admirable,' my captor observed. 'I can think of no better way to end the evening than to command a repeat performance.' She knelt on the bed with a doubled-up leg pressed into the mattress on either side of my helmeted head, facing her partner who was squatting just below my hips with her lean buttocks resting on my thighs.

The big lady lowered her meaty hips, the heavy belly

and the thick hair matted between them to my face. I thrust my chin upwards, nose buried in the tangled thatch. My mouth searched for, and found again, that gorgeous, dreamy cunt. 'Now get to work,' she said roughly.

And then, to the minister's wife: 'Now's your chance, Mavis! He's got a pretty good one, well-formed and beautifully hard. Have fun – do everything Charles forbids!'

My tongue speared up through the velvet ramparts once so closely folded, now quivering so wide in welcome, to lose itself in the hot wet dark of inner flesh. My loins jerked as cool, sharp-nailed fingers wrapped themselves tightly around the distended shaft of my inflamed prick. I caught my breath in the salty tang of wet hairs rasping and the sliding clasp of moistened skin. Big hips gyrated above and around me, muscles tensed as my tongue wallowed and lapped. The hand gripping my tool had begun lazily to milk the tremoring shaft.

'That's right,' the voice above me urged in a hoarse whisper. 'Slowly at first, then faster, faster. Try it with four fingers underneath and the thumb on top . . . press harder, more quickly still: skim the outside up and down the core! Tease that sensitive strip just below the head with your nails; press down on the velvet flesh to widen the opening . . . Use your mouth as soon as he's wet . . .'

This litany of instructions and advice was punctuated by low moans and grunts of pleasure as my tongue slavered around a hardened clitoris or tunnelled up into the heaving belly above. I was uttering too, deep in my throat and chest, each time Mavis's pumping grasp tightened or slid, with each fondling cradle and tug at the wrinkled pouch sheathing my balls.

Each of the two women was leaning forward: I could hear them kiss and murmur above my prone body, feeling the mattress shake as they squirmed and heaved on my shoulders and thighs.

Abruptly they broke apart. The big lady, who had raised her pelvis slightly to reach forward, leaving my tongue lapping only the entrance to her quivering pussy, now settled back over my face so that it could again pentrate the full, burning depths of her love canal. Heat too swamped my cock as a mouth closed wetly over the tip and slid tantalizingly down towards the base.

The whole area of my loins spasmed in ecstasy and my hips arched fiercely up off the bed as she sucked and tongued my rigid prick. If oral sex was forbidden at the ministerial residence, I thought dazedly, gay Mavis was certainly a good pupil, ready and eager to learn about men.

I was aware, all at once, of a rapid change, a switch to a more intense mode. The entire heavy body imprisoning my head stiffened; muscles shuddered along the insides of the thighs, the belly outside and the vagina inside trembled and tensed. I heard a strangled cry, hastily choked off. Not with a man! I could hear a resentful chorus rebuke. Surely not with a *man*!

But the lady was coming. There was no doubt about it. Somewhere deep inside, a series of faint spasms manifested itself, accelerated, gained in intensity, grew stronger, ferociously strong, until the entire frame was shaking, breasts bouncing, hips threshing, and she collapsed across me with a subdued moan of relief.

At the same time, her pupil, breath hissing like a snake, jolted upright and shuddered into a private climax of her own. And my cock, released suddenly from the sucking cavern of her mouth jerked frenziedly into its own orgasm, spewing a shower of white-hot sperm over her trembling breasts.

The bell was ringing.

The big lady disengaged herself from me and levered her body slowly off the bed. 'That means curtains for you, lad!' she said. 'Listen – my name is Chabry. Hortense Chabry. My husband's in the automobile business. Banking too, if it comes to that. But I have a business mind of my own.' She paused, lancing a level stare through the eyeholes of my mask. 'I know you're not permitted to speak here,' she said, 'but you can nod or shake. Tell me – does Linda know your name, address and telephone number?'

I nodded.

'Excellent. Then you'll be hearing from me, young man,' Mrs Chabry promised.

Epilogue

Two for the Road

I did hear from her too. I sneaked out of the 'temple' after that one altar boy session and drove home through the rain, fully dressed again and in (at least part of) my right mind.

Mrs Chabry called me at ten o'clock the next morning. We met for lunch in the Savoy Grill at one. By two-thirty I was back in the Strand with a contract – and a large cheque – in my pocket.

The lady wished to invest some of her money in England. She wished to make a profit, and she wanted the investment to be in a new business angled socially towards the removal of barriers between the two sexes – or three, as the case might be. 'Five, really,' my hostess said after a moment's reflection, 'if you count male gays, bisexuals and our lot as separate categories.'

In a word, she had heard of my escort activities and thought it might be a good idea to develop it, broaden the scope, and row in everybody. She was prepared to stake the cash for a ritzy setup – plush. West End office, secretaries, business manager, accountant, and all that – and she offered me the job of agency boss, no need to continue the actual escorting myself, at a very generous percentage of the take.

And all I had to do in return, apart from running the business, was visit her once a month in her Savoy suite for what she called 'a private conference'.

'A real pleasure,' I told her truthfully, remembering the velvet texture of her labia the previous night. I took the gold Cartier pen she handed me, and signed.

I learned a couple of interesting things during that luncheon too. You may remember, when I was out of work, that it was Diana who really suggested – and subsequently promoted – the idea that turned into my small-ad adventure. Well, it seemed that she had done this very deliberately, egged on by Mrs Porter, precisely because it would conveniently remove me from home at a time when she was beginning to find herself heavily involved with the Sisters and their cult!

Another surprise took me back to her cocktail party. The man I had taken for a surgeon – in fact Mrs Porter's ex-husband and indeed a famous consultant – was in the process of forming a similar circle for gay men whose positions make it inconvenient to admit the fact. The group – I had seen the nucleus of it at the party – had a monogrammed logo similar to the Sisters': SIGN, the four letters standing for Special Interests for Gay Newcomers.

Each of these two circles, Mrs Chabry thought, might be able to direct clients of the more specialized type to the agency's discreet Mayfair consulting rooms.

All of this, of course, was some time ago. Today life has settled into the pleasantest of routines. The Silver Collection – as the agency is called – has turned out to be a big success. Beautiful women, attractive men, career girls or poetic academics – you name the type, we can supply it. No screwing of course – or if there is, we don't want to know about it. But one of the services for which we are justly famed is the provision of, well ... specialized ... escorts for foreign visitors – business folks on short visits who find it agreeable to have a companion with similar tastes in whom they can safely confide.

The Eve Lorrimer group handles our (very discreet) publicity; legal business, if any, is directed to the chambers of Minerva Collett, QC; my three professional interviewers, Andy Tarrant, Sally, and (for visitors from the Orient or the Middle-East) Beryl are widely regarded as the most sympathetic in the escort business.

Life is less hectic on the personal side too. I still live

with Diana, though I never revealed that I was the altar boy on that memorable evening in Stanmore. She does her thing, I do mine, and we have developed the greatest brother-and-sister act since Paolo and Francesca.

Apart from my monthly summons to the Savoy, I spend such free time as I have with my mistress – an older woman – a real sweetie who lives in a small terrace house in South Croydon.

Headline Delta Erotic Survey

In order to provide the kind of books you like to read – and to qualify for a free erotic novel of the Editor's choice – we would appreciate it if you would complete the following survey and send your answers, together with any further comments, to:

> Headline Book Publishing
> FREEPOST (WD 4984)
> London
> NW1 0YR

1. Are you male or female?
2. Age? Under 20 / 20 to 30 / 30 to 40 / 40 to 50 / 50 to 60 / 60 to 70 / over
3. At what age did you leave full-time education?
4. Where do you live? (Main geographical area)
5. Are you a regular erotic book buyer / a regular book buyer in general / both?
6. How much approximately do you spend a year on erotic books / on books in general?
7. How did you come by this book?
7a. If you bought it, did you purchase from: a national bookchain / a high street store / a newsagent / a motorway station / an airport / a railway station / other . . .
8. Do you find erotic books easy / hard to come by?
8a. Do you find Headline Delta erotic books easy / hard to come by?
9. Which are the best / worst erotic books you have ever read?
9a. Which are the best / worst Headline Delta erotic books you have ever read?
10. Within the erotic genre there are many periods, subjects and literary styles. Which of the following do you prefer:
10a. (period) historical / Victorian / C20th / contemporary / future?
10b. (subject) nuns / whores & whorehouses / Continental frolics / s&m / vampires / modern realism / escapist fantasy / science fiction?